a39098 004407093b

BEST
SCIENCE FICTION STORIES
OF THE YEAR
Sixth Annual Collection

BEST
SCIENCE FICTION
STORIES
OF THE YEAR
Sixth Annual Collection

Edited by
GARDNER DOZOIS

E. P. Dutton | New York

Library of Congress Catalog Number: 77-190700

ISBN: 0-525-06495-8

Published simultaneously in Canada
by Clarke, Irwin & Company
Limited, Toronto and Vancouver

10   9   8   7   6   5   4   3   2   1

First Edition

For
Jack Dann

Contents

Acknowledgments

The editor would like to thank the following people for their help and support:

Isaac Asimov, Jack Dann, Virginia Kidd, Kirby McCauley, David G. Hartwell, Susan Casper, Christopher Casper, Janet and Riki Kagen, Tom Purdom, Michael Swanwick, George H. Scithers, C. L. Grant, Ben Bova, Victoria Schochet, Howard Waldrop, Geo. Proctor, Steve Utley, Terry Carr, M.S. Wyeth, Jr., Lynne McNabb, Ted White, Sharon Jarvis, Ellen Asher, James Baen, Fred Fisher and Judith Weiss of the Hourglass SF bookstore in Philadelphia, Tom Whitehead and his staff from the Special Collections Department of the Paley Library at Temple University, the authors whose works appear in this book for their cooperation in supplying biographical information, and special thanks to my own editor, Jo Alford.

FOREWORD
Summation: 1976

Science fiction is a literature concerned with change, and change is a medium that surrounds us so pervasively that, like a fish in water, we may not even be aware that we do indeed swim through it. The world only seems static to us because we are too short-lived to see it change. If we could speed up time, condense eons into seconds, we would see mountains flow like water and fish learn to walk. SF is a lens that helps us to see in this special fashion, an eye that looks at change—and for SF itself, 1976 was a year of changes.

Change has come to this series, Dutton's *Best Science Fiction Stories of the Year.* After five distinguished years of service, Lester del Rey has stepped down as series editor and has been replaced (in case you don't read book jackets) by me, Gardner Dozois. It is useless to pretend that my book will be the same as Lester's—it will not be. My taste is my own, and I have no doubt that I have selected quite a different collection of stories than Lester would have had he compiled this year's anthology; indeed, I have no doubt that every SF writer or reader alive would, if asked, come up with his own list of the year's best SF, and that no two of these lists would agree to any significant degree. In this respect, the title "Best Science Fiction Stories of the Year" is a misnomer. Taste and subjectivism are always implied (and, I hope, understood) in the title of a series such as this; such anthologies should really be called "Gardner Dozois Picks the Stories He Liked Best This Year" or "Terry Carr Really Enjoyed These Stories," or some such. But such quibbling, hair-splitting titles sell no books, unfortunately, and so on we march under the banner *Best Science Fiction Stories of the Year.*

I can't promise to have picked the same stories Lester would have picked, but I can promise that I have adhered to the same uncompromising set of standards in their selection: (1) to attempt to read every SF story published in the English language during the year and (2) to select only those stories that honestly and forcibly struck me as being the best published during that year, with no consideration for log-rolling, friendship, fashion, politics, or any other kind of outside influence.

Of course, there are problems involved. The SF market continues to expand enormously. This year there were at least twelve magazines (some of which were actually only fanzines, in spite of their pretensions) that claimed to publish SF, most of which published at least four issues apiece (some published twelve). As for books, there were seven regular anthology series and at least ten other original anthologies, including an anthology of Cthulhu Mythos stories, an anthology of stories derived from popular DAW novel series, and an anthology of SF stories by Texans. This is to say nothing of SF published in the men's magazines, in the slicks, in "little" literary magazines, in magazines and anthologies from England and Australia, and so forth. One of the better stories this year—Howard Waldrop's poignant and funny fantasy "Save a Place in the Lifeboat for Me"—was published in a fanzine, Tom Reamy's *Nickelodeon*. It is probably impossible right now to even find, let alone read, every SF story published in the English language alone. All I can do is try to keep up with the flood, and pray that my eyes hold out.

Another problem is space. As has been true for the last few years, much of the best work in SF this year was done at the novelette and novella length, with a number of especially fine novellas being turned out. Unfortunately, a book such as this can only be so long. I selected the novella I felt was the year's best, Michael Bishop's "The Samurai and the Willows," but if I had included all of the other deserving novellas that I would have liked to include—Gene Wolfe's brilliant "The Eyeflash Miracles," James Tiptree, Jr.,'s "Houston, Houston, Do You Read?," Gregory Benford's and Gordon Eklund's "The Anvil of Jove," Vonda N. McIntyre's "Screwtop," Richard Cowper's "Piper at the Gates of Dawn"—I would have ended up with a book twice as long as the present volume and no room for novelettes or short stories at all.

SF was definitely an "in" thing this year, and magazines as

diverse as *Newsweek*, *Viva*, *Publishers Weekly*, *Writer's Digest*, and *The New Republic* all carried lengthy articles on the genre. Worst of these articles was undoubtedly the *Newsweek* piece by Peter S. Prescott, which managed to be patronizing, insulting, and grossly misinformed, all at once. Best was probably the *Publishers Weekly* coverage, which also included a valuable address list of SF specialty bookstores.

A relatively new phenomenon, bookstores exclusively dedicated to SF continue to mushroom across the country—there are now at least twenty-five such stores that I know of, and more of them are coming into existence all the time.

This was also the year of the SF spoken-word record. Alternate World Recordings, Inc., now offers more than a dozen LPs of authors reading their own works, including Harlan Ellison, Fritz Leiber, Ursula K. Le Guin, Theodore Sturgeon, Ray Bradbury, Brian W. Aldiss, Robert Bloch, and Joanna Russ. *Harlan! Harlan Ellison Reads Harlan Ellison* seems to be the most popular release to date and made it onto this year's Nebula Final Ballot in the Dramatic Presentation category. Another line of spoken-word records, mostly of or by J.R.R. Tolkien and Ray Bradbury, was available from Caedmon, and *Analog* is also preparing to get into the act with a recording of Isaac Asimov's "Nightfall."

SF- and fantasy-oriented games, posters, and calendars also multiplied rapidly this year; items of particular interest included a Starship Troopers boardgame from Avalon Hill, and Lankhmar, a boardgame based on Fritz Leiber's Gray Mouser sword-and-sorcery series, from TSR Games.

Of particular interest to would-be SF writers were the several critical books published this year: *Writing and Selling Science Fiction* (Writer's Digest Press) with noteworthy articles by Wilhelm, Grant, Martin, and Purdom; *Notes to a Science Fiction Writer* (Condé Nast Books), by Ben Bova, the editor of *Analog*; *The Science Fiction Handbook, Revised* (Owlswick Press) by L. Sprague and Catherine Crook De Camp, especially valuable for the section on SF as business; *The Craft of Science Fiction* (Harper & Row) edited by Reginald Brentnor, with noteworthy articles by Niven on semantics, Pohl on professionalism, and Ellison on screenwriting; and *Hell's Cartographers* (Harper & Row) edited by Brian W. Aldiss and Harry Harrison, a collection of six autobiographies by famous SF writers—the Damon Knight piece in particular standing out as most witty, incisive, and insightful. Also valuable is *The S.F.W.A Handbook* edited by Mildred Downey Broxon, a house publication of the Science Fiction Writers of America.

Hollywood continues to produce big-budget SF films, most of which are very poor. One of the biggest celluloid turkeys of the year was *The Man Who Fell to Earth*, an asinine, pretentious, boring, and fundamentally incoherent film. *Logan's Run* managed to be less actively offensive, without attaining to any real merit. It's an earnest, silly, and hackneyed movie with lots of extras in the background, and it conforms to the seemingly universal Hollywood assumption that the future is going to look just like a shopping center in Dallas.

In 1976 it would have been very nearly possible to attend an SF convention somewhere in the mainland U.S.A. every weekend of the year, had anyone desired to do so. Generally speaking, the trend is still to larger and larger conventions, although the ill-fated SF Expo, self-billed as "the greatest science fiction event ever," collapsed under its own weight, as did several Star Trek conventions. MidAmeriCon, the 34th World Science Fiction Convention, held in Kansas City, Missouri over the Labor Day weekend, may or may not have reversed the trend to gigantism observed in recent world conventions. It was a good deal smaller than expected—only 2,614 attendees, compared to Discon's estimated 3,500 in 1974—but that may have been at least partly the result of the loud, lengthy, and bitter prior squabbles over the stringent security precautions that were being planned to prevent gate-crashing, a controversy that may have caused some people to stay home in protest. Suncon, next year's world convention, to be held in Miami, will be the real test case; if the trend to gigantism hasn't really been reversed after all, then Suncon could become simply enormous.

The 1975 Hugo Awards, presented at MidAmeriCon, were: Best Novel—*The Forever War*, by Joe Haldeman; Best Novella—"Home Is the Hangman," by Roger Zelazny; Best Novelette—"The Borderland of Sol," by Larry Niven; Best Short Story—"Catch That Zeppelin," by Fritz Leiber; Best Editor—Ben Bova; Best Professional Artist—Frank Kelly Freas; Best Dramatic Presentation—*A Boy and His Dog*; Best Fan Artist—Tim Kirk; Best

Fan Writer—Richard Geis; Best Fanzine—*Locus*; plus the John W. Campbell, Jr., Award to Tom Reamy, and a special Grandmaster of Fantasy Award to L. Sprague De Camp.

The 1975 Nebula Awards, given out five months earlier at Los Angeles were: Best Novel—*The Forever War*, by Joe Haldeman; Best Novella—"Home Is the Hangman," by Roger Zelazny; Best Novelette—"San Diego Lightfoot Sue," by Tom Reamy; Best Short Story—"Catch That Zeppelin," by Fritz Leiber; Best Dramatic Presentation—*Young Frankenstein*; plus a special Grandmaster Award to Jack Williamson.

The Second Annual World Fantasy Awards given out at the World Fantasy Convention in New York City on Halloween weekend were: Best Novel—*Bid Time Return*, by Richard Matheson; Best Collection—*The Enquiries of Dr. Eszterhazy*, by Avram Davidson; Best Short Fiction—"Belsen Express," by Fritz Leiber; Best Artist—Frank Frazetta; Special Award (nonprofessional)—Carcosa Publishers; Special Award (professional)—Donald M. Grant; plus a Life Achievement Award to Fritz Leiber.

Just before press time—as I was typing a clean copy of this Summation, in fact—I was given a list of finalists for the 1976 Nebula Awards and was pleased to see that several of my selections for this year's anthology had made the final ballot: "The Samurai and the Willows," in the Novella category; "Custer's Last Jump" and "The Diary of the Rose" in the Novellette category; and "Back to the Stone Age" and "Mary Margaret Road-Grader" in the Short Story category.

1976 also saw the economic picture in the SF field changing, slowly and slightly, for the better. In the fall, the forthcoming new SF magazine *Cosmos* announced that it would be paying six cents a word as its top fiction rate; *Analog* and the new *Isaac Asimov's Science Fiction Magazine* subsequently followed suit. This rate is still low compared to the better mainstream markets, but it is at least a step in the right direction. Although most SF book advances remained around the $2,000 level, certain SF authors were beginning to rise to the big-money levels usually reserved for mainstream heavies. For instance, the following unusually high advances reputedly were paid this year: George R.R. Martin,

$30,000 for his first novel, *After The Festival*; Ursula K. Le Guin, $30,000 for paperback rights to *The Wind's Twelve Quarters*; Frederik Pohl, $50,000 for paperback rights to *Man Plus*; and Joe Haldeman, $100,000 for paperback rights to *Mindbridge*, alleged to be one of the largest advances ever paid for a single SF novel. Several books this year sold very well indeed in paperback, Joe Haldeman's *The Forever War* and Arthur C. Clarke's *Imperial Earth* among them. And Frank Herbert's *Children of Dune* was reported to have sold close to 80,000 copies in hardcover.

Ace Books was purchased by Grosset & Dunlap and shows signs of again becoming a strong and viable line. Their cover art and packaging, in particular, have improved tremendously and are now among the best in the field. Ballantine announced the start of a new imprint, Del Rey Books, which, after an initial twelve-title promotion in March, will be bringing out a remarkable six SF/fantasy titles a month. Harper & Row showed signs of rivaling Doubleday as the major publisher of SF hardcover books. Avon, Bantam, Pocket Books, Gold Medal, and Dell all had strong lists this year, and there are indications that Pocket Books may become a leader in the field. David G. Hartwell continued to do a fine job of revitalizing the Berkley/Putnam line, although their covers are still among the dingiest on the racks.

On the downhill side, Laser Books reportedly has died, although backlog titles will continue to appear throughout the coming year. Presided over by Roger Elwood, this attempt to adapt to SF the mass-market techniques Harlequin had used to turn out an endless stream of nurse novels was not popular within the field and, to put it mildly, not generally successful (although one or two decent novels did appear). Sadly, Avon has also decided to drop their valuable Avon Equinox line of classic reprints, due to poor sales.

The magazine market continued to deteriorate throughout most of the year. *Amazing* and *Fantastic* have gone quarterly in response to steadily dropping sales and rising costs. It is now all but impossible to find copies of either of these magazines on newsstands, even in central Manhattan. Also, the Science Fiction Writers of America has taken strong sanctions against both magazines for alleged violations of copyright agreements and alleged mistreatment of authors. In spite of these troubles some good stories by Davidson, Leiber, Dann, Thurston, Davis, and others did appear in *Amazing* and *Fantastic* this year.

Galaxy began to skip issues early in the year, and gave other strong indications of being a magazine in serious trouble. It has now seemingly steadied down to a monthly schedule again, but rumors were rife last summer that it was teetering on the brink of financial disaster. *Galaxy* was also harried by a number of allegations of professional misconduct, but SFWA has as yet taken no action against them. The magazine was kept on the map this year primarily by a number of outstanding stories by John Varley and serials by Niven, Pohl, Russ, and Zelazny.

Analog remained the healthiest SF magazine of them all in terms of high circulation and financial security, sailing serenely above the quagmires that are foundering other publications. The quality of the short fiction in *Analog* seemed to be down a little in 1976 as compared to 1975, which had been a bumper year for the magazine; good short material by Haldeman, Plauger, Bear, Vinge, Robinson, and Cochrane did appear but the emphasis seemed to be on novels. Almost all of the January issue, for instance, was taken up by an installment of Herbert's massive *Children of Dune*, which ran for three more issues, followed by another hefty serial, Robert Silverberg's *Shadrach in the Furnace* in three parts.

The magazine that was the most consistently superior this year in the quality of its short fiction was undoubtedly *The Magazine of Fantasy and Science Fiction*, which published excellent material by Knight, Bishop, Varley, Benford, Eklund, Russ, Cowper, Lanier, Bourne, and others, in addition to serializing Pohl's *Man Plus* and Budrys's *Michaelmas*.

Interestingly, as most of these magazines struggled to stay alive (*If* and *Vertex* both folded within the past couple of years), three or four new SF magazines were in the planning stage.

First out, and first to fail, was *Odyssey*, edited by Roger Elwood, which lasted for two quarterly issues consisting mainly of second- or third-rate work by first-rate authors. It was also an ugly, shoddy-looking magazine, printed on cheap paper and jam-packed with offensive pulp ads of the "Men, Throw Away That Truss!" variety. Poor distribution and limited newsstand display were other nails in *Odyssey*'s coffin.

Another new magazine, and another bitter disappointment, was *Galileo*, a subscription-only quarterly edited by Charles C. Ryan. *Galileo* was somewhat more handsome than *Odyssey*, but if anything the quality of its fiction was even lower. The magazine will have to improve enormously with subsequent issues if it is to have any chance of establishing itself.

Of all the year's new magazines, the only other one that need be taken seriously, and the *only* one to achieve any real measure of success, was *Isaac Asimov's Science Fiction Magazine*, edited by George H. Scithers. The first quarterly issue appeared late in the year.

You may, if you like, dismiss my opinion in this case as prejudiced; I am associate editor of *IASF*. And, of course, I'm not even going to try to pretend that the first issue of *IASF* was flawless: the magazine is gray and dingy, and, like all issues of all magazines, it contains some mediocre fiction. Nevertheless, it also contains a high percentage of first-rate stories and is at least as good as most good issues of *Analog* or *F&SF*. *IASF* deserves to survive, and I have hopes that it may, if the luck is with it.

I also have hopes for *Cosmos*, projected as a slick, large-format magazine featuring full-color covers and interior illustrations and due to start publication in 1977. My hopes are based almost entirely on the fact that *Cosmos*'s editor will be David G. Hartwell, SF editor for Berkley/Putnam and one of the most astute professionals in the field. Tempering all these hopes is the uneasy knowledge that there has not been a successful SF magazine founded since the creation of *Galaxy* in 1950.

In recent years a number of original anthology series have succeeded in taking up some of the slack left by the dwindling magazine market. This year there were more such series than ever.

Of the established series, Damon Knight's *Orbit 18* (Harper & Row), was up considerably in quality from the dreary slump of *Orbit*s 16 and 17, and in fact was the best *Orbit* volume in years, containing good to excellent material by Wilhelm, Waldrop, Scholz, Varley, Gotschalk, Robinson, Cohn, and others. Robert Silverberg's *New Dimensions 6* (Harper & Row) was not quite up to the standards set by *ND 1* and *ND 3*; some good stuff here by Tiptree, Reamy, Effinger, Gotschalk, Malzberg, and Girard, but for the first time there was also too large a percentage of failed experimentation, enough of it to give *Orbit 18* the edge. Much the same can be said about Terry Carr's *Universe 6* (Doubleday), although it did contain one clearly superior story by Utley and Waldrop, as well as good material by Haas, Ellison, and Aldiss.

Stellar 2 (Ballantine), edited by Judy-Lynn del Rey, was noteworthy for getting some good material out of people like James White, Hal Clement, and Isaac Asimov who don't usually write for original anthologies. The best story here, unquestionably, was Asimov's fine novella "The Bicentennial Man."

Three new original series made their debuts this year: *Science Fiction Discoveries* (Bantam) edited by Carol and Frederik Pohl; *Analog Annual* (Pyramid) edited by Ben Bova and billed as a thirteenth issue of *Analog* in book form; and *Andromeda* (Futura Publications) edited by Peter Weston, an English anthology that has not yet been published in the United States. None of these books is up to the level of overall quality of the established series, but all published some worthwhile material.

Sleeper of the year in the nonseries original anthology category was *Lone Star Universe* (Heidelberg Publishers, Inc.), an anthology of SF stories by Texans. *Lone Star Universe*, unfortunately, besides being the most expensive anthology of the year, is also likely to be a difficult book to find. There's some very good material here by Saunders, Utley, Tuttle, Sterling, Waldrop, and a few others, but there's some appalling crud here as well, making for an amazingly uneven book.

On the other hand, in *Faster Than Light* (Harper & Row) edited by Jack Dann and George Zebrowski almost every story is of exactly the same quality: good, solid, competent stuff that would be snapped up instantly and gratefully by any SF magazine to be used as second-string backup material behind the lead novelette. With one possible exception (Harlan Ellison's original script for "The Starlost," a superior example of its kind), nothing in *Faster Than Light* is really outstanding, and the book is doomed to the gray fate of sitting squarely in the middle of the scale.

In my personal opinion, the best nonseries original anthology of the year was *Future Power* (Random House), edited by Jack Dann and myself.

Also of interest were *Frights* (St. Martin's Press) edited by Kirby

McCauley, *Aurora: Beyond Equality* (Fawcett Gold Medal) edited by Vonda N. McIntyre and Susan Janice Anderson, and *The Crystal Ship* (Thomas Nelson) edited by Robert Silverberg.

Good short story collections appeared in large numbers this year, too many to list *in toto*. Among the best were: *The Best of Damon Knight* (Pocket Books); *The Best of Jack Vance* (Pocket Books); *Orsinian Tales* by Ursula K. Le Guin (Harper & Row); *The Best of Robert Silverberg* (Pocket Books); *Getting into Death* by Thomas M. Disch (Knopf; forthcoming from Pocket Books); *The Worlds of Fritz Leiber* (Ace); *The Best of Poul Anderson* (Pocket Books); *The Enquiries of Dr. Eszterhazy* (Warner) by Avram Davidson; and *Cinnabar* by Edward Bryant (Macmillan).

The novels most talked about this year included *Man Plus* (Random House) by Frederik Pohl, which is my guess for next year's Nebula winner; *Where Late The Sweet Birds Sang* (Harper & Row) by Kate Wilhelm; *Triton* (Bantam) by Samuel R. Delany; *Shadrach in the Furnace* (Bobbs-Merrill) by Robert Silverberg; *Imperial Earth* (Ballantine) by Arthur C. Clarke; *A World out of Time* (Holt, Rinehart and Winston) by Larry Niven; *Children of Dune* (Putnam) by Frank Herbert; *Mindbridge* (St. Martin's Press) by Joe Haldeman; *The Clewiston Test* (Farrar, Straus Giroux) by Kate Wilhelm; *Cloned Lives* (Fawcett Gold Medal) by Pamela Sargent; *And Strange At Ecbatan The Trees* (Harper & Row) by Michael Bishop; *Islands* (Pyramid) by Marta Randall; *Beasts* (Doubleday) by John Crowley; and *The Devil in a Forest* (Follett) by Gene Wolfe.

Promising debuts were made this year by Sally A. Sellers, Carter Scholz, Kim Stanley Robinson, Bruce Sterling, Charlie Haas, Gary Cohn, Cherry Wilder, and James P. Girard, among others I have doubtless overlooked.

Death struck the SF field heavily again in 1976, as it had in 1975. Edgar Pangborn died at age 66, on February 1, 1976. Edgar Pangborn was one of that select crew of overlooked and underrated writers—one thinks of Philip K. Dick, Cordwainer Smith, Jack Vance, Richard McKenna—who have had an enormous underground effect on the field simply by impressing the hell out of other writers and numerous authors-in-the-egg. Pangborn's masterpiece, *Davy* (now in print again from Ballantine), is on my personal list of the ten best SF novels ever written, and his International Fantasy Award-winner *A Mirror for Observers* (also in print again, from Avon Equinox) is almost as good; surely Pangborn is due for a major critical reevaluation somewhere down the road, for to date he has been shamefully ignored. Pangborn had a depth and breadth of humanity that has rarely been matched inside the field or out and a gentle insight that can only be called wisdom, for lack of a better word. He has been accused of naïveté and cock-eyed optimism, but I don't think the charge is true, or rather, it is not all of the truth. Pangborn knew perfectly well the kind of deviltry that we are all capable of—he just refused to conclude that that's *all* we are capable of. SF is smaller and meaner because it no longer contains him.

Another gentle fantasist died in 1976, novelist Thomas Burnett Swann. Swann's fiction was sometimes too saccharine for my taste, but if this series had been in existence in 1966 and if I had been editing it, I would certainly have reprinted his masterpiece, the superb novella "The Manor of Roses." His books included *The Day of the Minotaur* (Ace) and *The Dolphin and the Deep* (Ace).

We also lost Daniel F. Galouye this year, author of *Dark Universe* and *Lords of the Psychon*.

This too, unfortunately, is change.

Next year there will be new faces, and other voices.

Gardner Dozois

BEST
SCIENCE FICTION STORIES
OF THE YEAR
Sixth Annual Collection

Ursula K. Le Guin is one of science fiction's most remarkable success stories. Perhaps the most widely popular author in SF, Le Guin has won four Hugo Awards, three Nebula Awards, a Jupiter Award, and the National Book Award for Children's Literature. And with the possible exception of Isaac Asimov, she is certainly the SF writer most accepted as a major literary talent by the literary establishment. If Le Guin's work does not convince your disdainful friends that SF can be worthy of serious artistic consideration, give up on them; they're dead and just haven't noticed it yet.

Here is Le Guin at the very top of her own high standard with a finalist for the 1976 Nebula Award—the chilling story of a gray and pious world in which the individual is only a soft machine to be rewired and repaired.

URSULA K. LE GUIN
The Diary of the Rose

30 August. Dr. Nades recommends that I keep a diary of my work. She says that if you keep it carefully, when you reread it you can remind yourself of observations you made, notice errors and learn from them, and observe progress in or deviations from positive thinking, and so keep correcting the course of your work by a feedback process.

I promise to write in this notebook every night, and reread it at the end of each week.

I wish I had done it while I was an assistant, but it is even more important now that I have patients of my own.

As of yesterday I have six patients, a full load for a scopist, but four of them are the autistic children I have been working with all year for Dr. Nades's study for the Nat'l Psych. Bureau (my notes on them are in the cli psy files). The other two are new admissions:

Ana Jest, forty-six, bakery packager, md., no children, diag. depression, referral from city police (suicide attempt).

Flores Sorde, thirty-six, engineer, unmd., no diag., referral from TRTU (psychopathic behavior—Violent).

Dr. Nades says it is important that I write things down each night just as they occured to me at work: it is the spontaneity that is most informative in self-examination (just as in autopychoscopy). She says it is better to write it, not dictate onto tape, and keep it quite private, so that I won't be self-conscious. It is hard. I never wrote anything that was private before. I keep feeling as if I was really writing it for Dr. Nades! Perhaps if the diary is useful I can show her some of it, later, and get her advice.

My guess is that Ana Jest is in menopausal depression and hormone therapy will be sufficient. There! Now let's see how bad a prognostician I am.

Will work with both patients under scope tomorrow. It is exciting to have my own patients; I am impatient to begin. Though of course teamwork was very educational.

31 August. Half-hour scope session with Ana J. at 8:00. Analyzed scope material, 11:00 to 17:00. N.B.: Adjust right-brain pickup next session! Weak visual Concrete. Very little aural, weak sensory, erratic body image. Will get lab analyses tomorrow of hormone balance.

It is amazing how banal most people's minds are. Of course the poor woman is in severe depression. Input in the Con dimension was foggy and incoherent, and the Uncon dimension was deeply open, but obscure. But the things that came out of the obscurity were so trivial! A pair of old shoes, and the word "geography!" And the shoes were dim, a mere schema of a pair-of-shoes— maybe a man's maybe a woman's; maybe dark blue, maybe brown. Although definitely a visual type, she does not see anything clearly. Not many people do. It is depressing. When I was a student in first year I used to think how wonderful other people's minds would be, how wonderful it was going to be to share in all the different world, the different colors of their passions and ideas. How naïve I was!

I realized this first in Dr. Ramia's class when we studied a tape from a very famous, successful person, and I noticed that the subject had never looked at a tree, never touched one, did not know any difference between an oak and a poplar, or even between a daisy and a rose. They were all just "trees" or "flowers" to him, apprehended schematically. It was the same with people's faces, though he had tricks for telling them apart: mostly he saw the name, like a label, not the face. That was an Abstract mind, of course, but it can be even worse with the Concretes, whose perceptions come in a kind of undifferentiated sludge—bean soup with a pair of shoes in it.

But aren't I "going native"? I've been studying a depressive's thoughts all day and have got depressed. Look, I wrote up there, "It is depressing." I see the value of this diary already. I know I am over-impressionable.

Of course, that is why I am a good psychoscopist. But it is dangerous.

No session with F. Sorde today, since sedation had not worn off. TRTU referrals are often so drugged that they cannot be scoped for days.

REM scoping session with Ana J. at 4:00 tomorrow. Better go to bed!

1 September. Dr. Nades says the kind of thing I wrote yesterday is pretty much what she had in mind and invited me to show her this diary again whenever I am in doubt. Spontaneous thoughts—not the technical data, which are recorded in the files anyhow. Cross nothing out. Candor all-important.

Ana's dream was interesting but pathetic. The wolf who turned into a pancake! Such a disgusting, dim, hairy pancake, too. Her visuality is clearer in dream, but the feeling tone remains low (but remember: *you* contribute the affect—don't read it in). Started her on hormone therapy today.

F. Sorde awake, but too confused to take to scope room for session. Frightened. Refused to eat. Complained of pain in side. I thought he was unclear what kind of hospital this is, and told him there was nothing wrong with him physically. He said, "How the hell do you know?" which was fair enough, since he was in strait jacket, due to the V notation on his chart. I examined and found bruising and contusion, and ordered an X-ray, which showed two ribs cracked. Explained to patient that he had been in a condition where forcible restraint had been necessary to prevent self-injury. He said, "Every time one of them asked a question, the other one kicked me." He repeated this several times, with anger and confusion. Paranoid delusional system? If it does not weaken as the drugs wear off, I will proceed on that assumption. He responds fairly well to me, asked my name when I went to see him with the

X-ray plate, and agreed to eat. I was forced to apologize to him, not a good beginning with a paranoid. The rib damage should have been marked on his chart by the referring agency or by the medic who admitted him. This kind of carelessness is distressing.

But there's good news too. Rina (Autism Study Subject 4) saw a first-person sentence today. Saw it: in heavy black primer print, all at once in the high Con foreground: *I want to sleep in the big room.* (She sleeps alone because of the feces problem.) The sentence stayed clear for over five seconds. She was reading it in her mind just as I was reading it on the holoscreen. There was weak subverbalization, but not subvocalization, nothing on the audio. She has not yet spoken, even to herself, in the first person. I told Tio about it at once and he asked her after the session, "Rina, where do you want to sleep?" "Rina sleep in the big room." No pronoun, no conative. But one of these days she will say *I want*—aloud. And on that build a personality, maybe, at last: on that foundation. I want, therefore I am.

There is so much fear. Why is there so much fear?

4 September. Went to town for my two-day holiday. Stayed with B. in her new flat on the north bank. Three rooms to herself!!! But I don't really like those old buildings, there are rats and roaches, and it feels so old and strange, as if somehow the famine years were still there, waiting. Was glad to get back to my little room here, all to myself but with others close by on the same floor, friends and colleagues. Anyway I missed writing in this book. I form habits very fast. Compulsive tendency.

Ana much improved: dressed, hair combed, was knitting. But session was dull. Asked her to think about pancakes, and there it came filling up the whole Uncon dimension, the hairy, dreary, flat-wolf-pancake, while in the Con she was obediently trying to visualize a nice cheese blintz. Not too badly: colors and outlines already stronger. I am still willing to count on simple hormone treatment. Of course they will suggest ECT, and a co-analysis of the scope material would be perfectly possible, we'd start with the wolf-pancake, etc. But is there any real point to it? She has been a bakery packager for twenty-four years and her physical health is poor. She cannot change her life situation. At least with good hormone balance she may be able to endure it.

F. Sorde: rested but still suspicious. Extreme fear reaction when I said it was time for his first session. To allay this I sat down and talked about the nature and operation of the psychoscope. He listened intently and finally said, "Are you going to use only the psychoscope?"

I said yes.

He said, "Not electroshock?"

I said no.

He said, "Will you promise me that?"

I explained that I am a psychoscopist and never operate the electroconvulsive therapy equipment, that is an entirely different department. I said my work with him at present would be diagnostic, not therapeutic. He listened carefully. He is an educated person and understands distinctions such as "diagnostic" and "therapeutic." It is interesting that he asked me to *promise*. That does not fit a paranoid pattern, you don't ask for promises from those you can't trust. He came with me docilely, but when we entered the scope room he stopped and turned white at sight of the apparatus. I made Dr. Aven's little joke about the dentist's chair, which she always used with nervous patients. F.S. said, "So long as it's not an electric chair!"

I believe that with intelligent subjects it is much better not to make mysteries and so impose a false authority and a feeling of helplessness on the subject (see T.R. Olma, *Psychoscopy Technique*). So I showed him the chair and electrode crown and explained its operation. He has a layman's hearsay knowledge of the psychoscope and his questions also reflected his engineering education. He sat down in the chair when I asked him. While I fitted the crown and clasps he was sweating profusely from fear, and this evidently embarrassed him, the smell. If he knew how Rina smells after she's been doing shit-paintings. He shut his eyes and gripped the chair arms so that his hands went white to the wrist. The screens were almost white too. After a while I said in a joking tone, "It doesn't really hurt, does it?"

"I don't know."

"Well, does it?"

"You mean it's on?"

"It's been on for ninety seconds."

He opened his eyes then and looked around, as well as he could for the head clamps. He asked, "Where's the screen?"

I explained that a subject never watches the screen live, because the objectification can be severely disturbing, and he said, "Like feedback from a microphone?" That is exactly the simile Dr. Aven used to use. F.S. is certainly an intelligent person. N.B.: Intelligent paranoids are dangerous!

He asked, "What do you see?" and I said, "Do be quiet, I don't want to see what you're saying, I want to see what you're thinking," and he said, "But that's none of your business, you know," quite gently, like a joke. Meanwhile the fear-white had gone into dark, intense, volitional convolutions, and then, a few seconds after he stopped speaking, a rose appeared on the whole Con dimension: a full-blown pink rose, beautifully sensed and visualized, clear and steady, whole.

He said presently, "What am I thinking about, Dr. Sobel?" and I said, "Bears in the zoo." I wonder now why I said that. Self-defense? Against what? He gave a laugh and the Uncon went crystal-dark, relief, and the rose darkened and wavered. I said, "I was joking. Can you bring the rose back?" That brought back the fear-white. I said, "Listen, it's really very bad for us to talk like this during a first session, you have to learn a great deal before you can co-analyze, and I have a great deal to learn about you, so no more jokes, please? Just relax physically, and think about anything you please."

There was flurry and subverbalization on the Con dimension, and the Uncon faded into gray, suppression. The rose came back weakly a few times. He was trying to concentrate on it, but couldn't. I saw several quick visuals: myself, my uniform, TRTU uniforms, a gray car, a kitchen, the violent ward (strong aural images—screaming), a desk, the papers on the desk. He stuck to those. They were the plans for a machine. He began going through them. It was a deliberate effort at suppression, and quite effective. Finally I said, "What kind of machine is that?" and he began to answer aloud but stopped and let me get the answer subvocally in the earphone: "Plans for a rotary engine assembly for traction," or something like that—of course the exact words are on the tape. I repeated it aloud and said, "They aren't classified plans, are they?" He said, "No," aloud, and added, "I don't know any secrets." His reaction to a question is intense and complex; each sentence is like a shower of pebbles thrown into a pool, the interlocking rings spread out quick and wide over the Con and into the Uncon, responses rising on all levels. Within a few seconds all that was hidden by a big signboard that appeared in the high Con foreground, deliberately visualized like the rose and the plans, with auditory reinforcement as he read it over and over: KEEP OUT! KEEP OUT! KEEP OUT!

It began to blur and flicker, and somatic signals took over, and soon he said aloud, "I'm tired," and I closed the session (12.5 min.).

After I took off the crown and clamps I brought him a cup of tea from the staff stand in the hall. When I offered it to him, he looked startled and then tears came into his eyes. His hands were so cramped from gripping the armrests that he had trouble taking hold of the cup. I told him he must not be so tense and afraid, we are trying to help him not to hurt him.

He looked up at me. Eyes are like the scope screen and yet you can't read them. I wished the crown was still on him, but it seems you never catch the moments you most want on the scope. He said, "Doctor, why am I in this hospital?"

I said, "For diagnosis and therapy."

He said, "Diagnosis and therapy of *what?*"

I said he perhaps could not now recall the episode, but he had behaved strangely. He asked how and when, and I said that it would all come clear to him as therapy took effect. Even if I had known what his psychotic episode was, I would have said the same. It was correct procedure. But I felt in a false position. If the TRTU report was not classified, I would be speaking from knowledge and the facts. Then I could make a better response to what he said next: "I was waked up at two in the morning, jailed, interrogated, beaten up, and drugged. I suppose I did behave a little oddly during that. Wouldn't you?"

"Sometimes a person under stress misinterprets other people's actions," I said. "Drink up your tea and I'll take you back to the ward. You're running a temperature."

"The ward," he said, with a kind of shrinking movement, and then he said almost desperately, "Can you really not know why I'm here?"

That was strange, as if he has included me in his delusional system, on *"his side."* Check this possibility in Rheingeld. I should think it would involve some transference and there has not been time for that.

Spent pm analyzing Jest and Sorde holos. I have never seen any psychoscopic realization, not even a drug-induced hallicination, so fine and vivid as that rose. The shadows of one petal on another, the velvety damp texture of the petals, the pink color full of sunlight, the yellow central crown—I am sure the scent was there if the apparatus had olfactory pickup—it wasn't like a mentifact but a real thing rooted in the earth, alive and growing, the strong, thorny stem beneath it.

Very tired, must go to bed.

Just reread this entry. Am I keeping this diary right? All I have written is what happened and what was said. Is that spontaneous? But it was *important* to me.

5 September. Discussed the problem of conscious resistance with Dr. Nades at lunch today. Explained that I have worked with unconscious blocks (the children and depressives such as Ana J.) and have some skill at reading through, but have not before met a conscious block such as F.S.'s KEEP OUT sign, or the device he used today, which was effective for a full twenty-minute session: a concentration on his breathing, bodily rhythms, pain in ribs, and visual input from the scope room. She suggested that I use a blindfold for the latter trick, and keep my attention on the Uncon dimension, as he cannot prevent material from appearing there. It is surprising, though, how large the interplay area of his Con and Uncon fields is, and how much one resonates into the other. I believe his concentration on his breathing rhythm allowed him to achieve something like "trance" condition. Though of course most so-called trance is mere occultist fakirism, a primitive trait without interest for behavioral science.

Ana thought through "a day in my life" for me today. All so gray and dull, poor soul! She never thought even of food with pleasure, though she lives on minimum ration. The single thing that came bright for a moment was a child's face, clear dark eyes, a pink knitted cap, round cheeks. She told me in post-session discussion that she always walks by a school playground on the way to work because "she likes to see the little ones running and yelling." Her husband appears on the screen as a big bulky suit of work clothes and a peevish, threatening mumble. I wonder if she knows that she hasn't seen his face or heard a word he says for years? But no use telling her that. It may be just as well she doesn't.

The knitting she is doing, I noticed today, is a pink cap.

Reading De Cams's *Disaffection: A Study*, on Dr. Nades's recommendation.

6 September. In the middle of session (breathing again), I said loudly: "Flores!"

Both psy dimensions whited out but the soma realization hardly changed. After four seconds he responded aloud, drowsily. It is not "trance," but autohypnosis.

I said, "Your breathing's monitored by the apparatus. I don't need to know that you're still breathing. It's boring."

He said, "I like to do my own monitoring, Doctor."

I came around and took the blindfold off him and looked at him. He has a pleasant face, the kind of man you often see running machinery, sensitive but patient, like a donkey. That is stupid. I will not cross it out. I am supposed to be spontaneous in this diary. Donkeys do have beautiful faces. They are supposed to be stupid and balky, but they look wise and calm, as if they had endured a lot but held no grudges, as if they knew some reason why one should not hold grudges. And the white ring around their eyes makes them look defenseless.

"But the more you breathe," I said, "the less you think. I need your cooperation. I'm trying to find out what it is you're afraid of."

"But I know what I'm afraid of," he said.

"Why won't you tell me?"

"You never asked me."

"That's most unreasonable," I said, which is funny, now that I think about it, being indignant with a mental patient because he's unreasonable. "Well, then, now I'm asking you."

He said, "I'm afraid of electroshock. Of having my mind destroyed. Being kept here. Or only being let out when I can't remember anything." He gasped while he was speaking.

I said, "All right, why won't you think about that while I'm watching the screens?"

"Why should I?"

"Why not? You've said it to me, why can't you think about it? I want to see the color of your thoughts!"

"It's none of your business, the color of my thoughts," he said angrily, but I was around to the screen while he spoke, and saw the unguarded activity. Of course it was being taped while we spoke, too, and I have studied it all afternoon. It is fascinating.

There are two subverbal levels running aside from the spoken words. All sensory-emotive reactions and distortions are vigoroi and complex. He "sees" me, for instance, in at least three different ways, probably more—analysis is impossibly difficult! And the Con-uncon correspondences are so complicated, and the memory traces and current impressions interweave so rapidly, and yet the whole is unified in its complexity. It is like that machine he was studying, very intricate but all one thing in a mathematical harmony. Like the petals of the rose.

When he realized I was observing he shouted out, "Voyeur! Damned voyeur! Let me alone! Get out!" and he broke down and cried. There was a clear fantasy on the screen for several seconds of himself breaking the arm and head clamps and kicking the apparatus to pieces and rushing out of the building, and there, outside, there was a wide hilltop, covered with short dry grass, under the evening sky, and he stood there all alone. While he sat clamped in the chair sobbing.

I broke session and took off the crown, and asked him if he wanted some tea, but he refused to answer. So I freed his arms, and brought him a cup. There was sugar today, a whole box full. I told him that and told him I'd put in two lumps.

After he had drunk some tea he said, with an elaborate ironical tone, because he was ashamed of crying, "You know I like sugar? I suppose your psychoscope told you I liked sugar?"

"Don't be silly," I said, "everybody likes sugar if they can get it."

He said, "No, little doctor, they don't." He asked in the same tone how old I was and if I was married. He was spiteful. He said, "Don't want to marry? Wedded to your work? Helping the mentally unsound back to a constructive life of service to the nation?"

"I like my work," I said, "because it's difficult and interesting. Like yours. You like your work, don't you?"

"I did," he said. "Goodbye to all that."

"Why?"

He tapped his head and said, "Zzzzzt!—All gone. Right?"

"Why are you so convinced you're going to be prescribed electroshock? I haven't even diagnosed you yet."

"Diagnosed me?" he said. "Look, stop the play-acting, please. My diagnosis was made. By the learned doctors of the TRTU. Severe case of disaffection. Prognosis: Evil! Therapy: Lock him up with a roomful of screaming thrashing wrecks, and then go through his mind the same way you went through his papers, and then burn it . . . burn it out. Right, Doctor? Why do you have to go through all this posing, diagnosis, cups of tea? Can't you just get on with it? Do you have to paw through everything I am before you burn it?"

"Flores," I said very patiently, *"you're* saying 'Destroy me'— don't you hear yourself? The psychoscope destroys nothing. And I'm not using it to get evidence, either. This isn't a court, you're not on trial. And I'm not a judge. I'm a doctor."

He interrupted. "If you're a doctor, can't you see that I'm not sick?"

"How can I see anything so long as you block me out with your stupid KEEP OUT signs?" I shouted. I did shout. My patience *was* a pose and it just fell to pieces. But I saw that I had reached him, so I went right on. "You look sick, you act sick—two cracked ribs, a temperature, no appetite, crying fits—is that good health? If you're not sick, then prove it to me! Let me see how you are inside, inside all that!"

He looked down into his cup and gave a kind of laugh and shrugged. "I can't win," he said. "Why do I talk to you? You *look* so honest, damn you!"

I walked away. It is shocking how a patient can hurt one. The trouble is, I am used to the children, whose rejection is absolute, like animals that freeze or cower or bite in their terror. But with this man, intelligent and older than I am, first there is communication and trust and then the blow. It hurts more.

It is painful writing all this down. It hurts again. But it is useful. I do understand some things he said much better now. I think I will not show it to Dr. Nades until I have completed diagnosis. If there is any truth to what he said about being arrested on suspicion of disaffection (and he is certainly careless in the way he talks), Dr. Nades might feel that she should take over the case, due to my inexperience. I should regret that. I need the experience.

7 September. Stupid! That's why she gave you De Cam's book. Of course she knows. As Head of the Section she has access to the TRTU dossier on F.S. She gave me this case deliberately.

It is certainly educational.

Today's session: F.S. still angry and sulky. Intentionally fantasized a sex scene. It was memory, but when she was heaving around underneath him he suddenly stuck a caricature of my face on her. It was effective. I doubt a woman could have done it; women's recall of having sex is usually darker and grander and they and the other do not become meat-puppets like that, with switchable heads. After a while he got bored with the performance (for all its vividness there was little somatic participation, not even an erection) and his mind began to wander. For the first time. One of the drawings on the desk came back. He must be a designer, because he changed it, with a pencil. At the same time there was a tune going on the audio, in mental pure-tone; and in the Uncon lapping over into the interplay area, a large, dark room seen from a child's height, the window sills very high, evening outside the windows, tree branches darkening, and inside the room a woman's voice, soft, maybe reading aloud, sometimes joining with the tune. Meanwhile the whore on the bed kept coming and going in volitional bursts, falling apart a little more each time, till there was nothing left but one nipple. This much I analyzed out this afternoon, the first sequence of over ten sec. that I have analyzed clear and entire.

When I broke session, he said, "What did you learn?" in the satirical voice.

I whistled a bit of the tune.

He looked scared.

"It's a lovely tune," I said. "I never heard it before. If it's yours, I won't whistle it anywhere else."

"It's from some quartet," he said, with his "donkey" face back, defenseless and patient. "I like classical music. Didn't you—"

"I saw the girl," I said. "And my face on her. Do you know what I'd like to see?"

He shook his head. Sulky, hangdog.

"Your childhood."

That surprised him. After a while he said, "All right. You can have my childhood. Why not? You're going to get all the rest anyhow. Listen. You tape it all, don't you? Could I see a playback? I want to see what you see."

"Sure," I said. "But it won't mean as much to you as you think it will. It took me eight years to learn to observe. You start with your own tapes. I watched mine for months before I recognized anything much."

I took him to my seat, put on the earphone, and ran him thirty sec. of the last sequence.

He was quite thoughtful and respectful after it. He asked, "What was all that running-up-and-down-scales motion in the, the background I guess you'd call it?"

"Visual scan—your eyes were closed—and subliminal proprioceptive input. The Unconscious dimension and the Body dimension overlap to a great extent all the time. We bring the three dimensions in separately, because they seldom coincide entirely anyway, except in babies. The bright triangular motion at the left of the holo was probably the pain in your ribs."

"I don't see it that way!"

"You don't see it; you weren't consciously feeling it, even, then. But we can't translate a pain in the rib onto a holoscreen, so we give it a visual symbol. The same with all sensations, affects, emotions."

"You watch all that at once?"

"I told you it took eight years. And you do realize that that's only a fragment? Nobody could put a whole psyche onto a four-foot screen. Nobody knows if there are any limits to the psyche. Except the limits of the universe."

He said after a while, "Maybe you aren't a fool, Doctor. Maybe you're just very absorbed in your work. That can be dangerous, you know, to be so absorbed in your work."

"I love my work, and I hope that it is of positive service," I said. I was alert for symptoms of disaffection. He smiled a little and said, "Prig," in a sad voice.

Ana is coming along. Still some trouble eating. Entered her in George's mutual-therapy group. What she needs, at least one thing she needs, is companionship. After all, why should she eat? Who needs her to be alive? What we call psychosis is sometimes simply realism. But human beings can't live on realism alone.

F.S.'s patterns do not fit any of the classic paranoid psychoscopic patterns in Rheingeld.

The De Cams book is hard for me to understand. The terminology of politics is so different from that of psychology. Everything seems backwards. I must be genuinely attentive at P.T. sessions Sunday nights from now on. I have been lazy-minded. Or, no, but as F.S. said, too absorbed in my work—and so inattentive to its context, he meant. Not thinking about what one is working *for*.

10 September. Have been so tired the last two nights I skipped writing this journal. All the data are on tape and in my analysis notes, of course. Have been working really hard on the F.S. analysis. It is very exciting. It is a truly unusual mind. Not brilliant, his intelligence tests are good average, he is not original or an artist, there are no schizophrenic insights, I can't say what it is, I feel honored to have shared in the childhood he remembered for me. I can't say what it is. There was pain and fear of course, his father's death from cancer, months and months of misery while F.S. was twelve, that was terrible, but it does not come out pain in the end, he has not forgotten or repressed it but it is all changed, by his love for his parents and his sister and for music and for the shape and weight and fit of things and his memory of the lights and weathers of days long past and his mind always working quietly, reaching out, reaching out to be whole.

There is no question yet of formal co-analysis, it is far too early, but he cooperates so intelligently that today I asked him if he was aware consciously of the Dark Brother figure that accompanied several Con memories in the Uncon dimension. When I described it as having a matted shock of hair, he looked startled and said, "Dokkay, you mean?"

That word had been on the subverbal audio, though I hadn't connected it with the figure.

He explained that when he was five or six, Dokkay had been his name for a "bear" he often dreamed or daydreamed about. He said, "I rode him. He was big, I was small. He smashed down walls, and destroyed things, bad things, you know, bullies, spies, people who scared my mother, prisons, dark alleys I was afraid to cross, policemen with guns, the pawnbroker. Just knocked them over. And then he walked over all the rubble on up to the hilltop. With me riding on his back. It was quiet up there. It was always evening, just before the stars come out. It's strange to remember it. Thirty years ago! Later on he turned into a kind of friend, a boy or man, with hair like a bear. He still smashed things, and I went with him. It was good fun."

I write this down from memory as it was not taped; session was interrupted by power outage. It is exasperating that the hospital comes so low on the list of Government priorities.

Attended the Pos. Thinking session tonight and took notes. Dr. K. spoke on the dangers and falsehoods of liberalism.

11 September. F.S. tried to show me Dokkay this morning but failed. He laughed and said aloud, "I can't see him any more. I think at some point I turned into him."

"Show me when that happened," I said, and he said, "All right," and began at once to recall an episode from his early adolescence. It had nothing to do with Dokkay. He saw an arrest. He was told that the man had been passing out illegal printed matter. Later on he saw one of these pamphlets, the title was in his visual bank, "Is There Equal Justice?" He read it, but did not recall the text or managed to censor it from me. The arrest was terribly vivid. Details like the young man's blue shirt and the coughing noise he made and the sound of the hitting, the TRTU agents' uniforms, and the car driving away, a big gray car with blood on the door. It came back over and over, the car driving away down the street, driving away down the street. It was a traumatic incident for F.S. and may explain the exaggerated fear of the violence of national justice justified by national security which may have led him to behave irrationally when investigated and so appeared as a tendency to disaffection—falsely, I believe.

I will show why I believe this. When the episode was done I said, "Flores, think about democracy for me, will you?"

He said, "Little doctor, you don't catch old dogs quite that easily."

"I am not catching you. Can you think about democracy or can't you?"

"I think about it a good deal," he said. And he shifted to right-brain activity, music. It was the chorus of the last part of the Ninth Symphony by Beethoven, I recognized it from the Arts term in high school. We sang it to some patriotic words. I yelled, "Don't censor!" and he said, "Don't shout, I can hear you." Of course the room was perfectly silent, but the pickup on the audio was tremendous, like thousands of people singing together. He went on aloud, "I'm not censoring. I'm thinking about democracy. That is democracy. Hope, brotherhood, no walls. All the walls unbuilt. You, we, I make the universe! Can't you hear it?" And it was the hilltop again, the short grass and the sense of being up high, and the wind, and the whole sky. The music was the sky.

When it was done and I released him from the crown I said, "Thank you."

I do not see why the doctor cannot thank the patient for a revelation of beauty and meaning. Of course the doctor's authority is important, but it need not be domineering. I realize that in politics the authorities must lead and be followed, but in psychological medicine it is a little different, a doctor cannot "cure" the patient, the patient "cures" himself with our help, this is not contradictory to Positive Thinking.

14 September. I am upset after the long conversation with F.S. today and will try to clarify my thinking.

Because the rib injury prevents him from attending work therapy he is restless. The Violent ward disturbed him deeply, so I used my authority to have the V removed from his chart and have him moved into Men's Ward B, three days ago. His bed is next to old Arca's, and when I came to get him for session they were talking, sitting on Arca's bed. F.S. said, "Dr. Sobel, do you know my neighbor, Professor Arca of the Faculty of Arts and Letters of the University?" Of course I know the old man—he has been here for years, far longer than I—but F.S. spoke so courteously and gravely that I said, "Yes, how do you do, Professor Arca?" and shook the old man's hand. He greeted me politely as a stranger—he often does not know people from one day to the next.

As we went to the scope room F.S. said, "Do you know how many electroshock treatments he had?" and when I said no he said, "Sixty. He tells me that every day. With pride." Then he said, "Did you know that he was an internationally famous scholar? He wrote a book, *The Idea of Liberty,* about twentieth-century ideas of freedom in politics and the arts and sciences. I read it when I was in engineering school. It existed then. On bookshelves. It doesn't exist any more. Anywhere. Ask Dr. Arca. He never heard of it."

"There is almost always some memory loss after electroconvulsive therapy," I said, "but the material lost can be relearned, and is often spontaneously regained."

"After sixty sessions?" he said.

F.S. is a tall man, rather stooped, even in the hospital pajamas he is an impressive figure. But I am also tall, and it is not because I am shorter than he that he calls me "little doctor." He did it first when he was angry at me and so now he says it when he is bitter but does not want what he says to hurt me, the me he knows. He said, "Little doctor, quit faking. You know the man's mind was deliberately destroyed."

Now I will try to write down exactly what I said, because it is important. "I do not approve of the use of electroconvulsive therapy as a general instrument. I would not recommend its use on my patients except perhaps in certain specific cases of senile melancholia. I went into psychoscopy because it is an integrative rather than a destructive instrument."

That is all true, and yet I never said or consciously thought it before.

"What will you recommend for me?" he said.

I explained that once my diagnosis is complete, my recommendation will be subject to the approval of the Head and Assistant Head of the Section. I said that so far nothing in his history or personality structure warranted the use of ECT, but that after all we had not got very far yet.

"Let's take a long time about it," he said, shuffling along beside me with his shoulders hunched.

"Why? Do you like it?"

"No. Though I like you. But I'd like to delay the inevitable end."

"Why do you insist that it's inevitable, Flores? Can't you see that your thinking on that one point is quite irrational?"

"Rosa," he said—he has never used my first name before—"Rosa, you can't be reasonable about pure evil. There are faces reason cannot see. Of course I'm irrational, faced with the imminent destruction of my memory—my self. But I'm not inaccurate. You know they're not going to let me out of here un—" He hesistated a long time and finally said, "unchanged."

"One psychotic episode—"

"I had no psychotic episode. You must know that by now."

"Then why were you sent here?"

"I have some colleagues who prefer to consider themselves rivals, competitors. I gather they informed the TRTU that I was a subversive liberal."

"What was their evidence?"

"Evidence?" We were in the scope room by now. He put his hands over his face for a moment and laughed in a bewildered way. "Evidence? Well, once at a meeting of my section I talked a long time with a visiting foreigner, a fellow in my field, a designer. And I have friends, you know, unproductive people, bohemians. And this summer I showed our section head why a design he'd got approved by the Government wouldn't work. That was stupid. Maybe I'm here for—for imbecility. And I read. I've read Professor Arca's book."

"But none of that matters, you think positively, you love your country, you're not disaffected!"

He said, "I don't know. I love the idea of democracy, the hope, yes, I love that. I couldn't live without that. But the country? You mean the thing on the map, lines, everything inside the lines is good and nothing outside them matters? How can an adult love such a childish idea?"

"But you wouldn't betray the nation to an outside enemy."

He said, "Well, if it was a choice between the nation and humanity, or the nation and a friend, I might. If you call that betrayal. I call it morality."

He *is* a liberal. It is exactly what Dr. Katin was talking about on Sunday.

It is classic psychopathy: the absence of normal affect. He said that quite unemotionally—"I might."

No. That is not true. He said it with difficulty, with pain. It was I who was so shocked that I felt nothing—blank, cold.

How am I to treat this kind of psychosis, a *political* psychosis? I have read over De Cams's book twice and I believe I do understand it now, but still there is this gap between the political and the psychological, so that the book shows me how to think but does not show me how to *act* positively. I see how F.S. should think and feel, and the difference between that and his present state of mind, but I do not know how to educate him so that he can think positively. De Cams says that disaffection is a negative condition which must be filled with positive ideas and emotions, but this does not fit F.S. The gap is not in him. In fact, that gap in De Cams between the political and the psychological is exactly where *his* ideas apply. But if they are wrong ideas, how can this be?

I want advice badly, but I cannot get it from Dr. Nades. When she gave me the De Cams she said, "You'll find what you need in this." If I tell her that I haven't, it is like a confession of helplessness and she will take the case away from me. Indeed, I think it is a kind of test case, testing me. But I need this experience, I am learning, and besides, the patient trusts me and talks freely to me. He does so because he knows that I keep what he tells me in perfect confidence. Therefore I cannot show this journal or discuss these problems with anyone until the cure is under way and confidence is no longer essential.

But I cannot see when that could happen. It seems as if confidence will always be essential between us.

I have got to teach him to adjust his behavior to reality, or he will be sent for ECT when the Section reviews cases in November. He has been right about that all along.

9 October. I stopped writing in this notebook when the material from F.S. began to seem "dangerous" to him (or to myself). I just reread it all over tonight. I see now that I can never show it to Dr. N. So I am going to go ahead and write what I please in it. Which is what she said to do, but I think she always expected me to show it to her, she thought I would want to, which I did, at first, or that if she asked to see it I'd give it to her. She asked about it yesterday. I said that I had abandoned it, because it just repeated things I had already put into the analysis files. She was plainly disapproving but said nothing. Our dominance-submission relationship has changed these past few weeks. I do not feel so much in need of guidance, and after the Ana Jest discharge, the autism paper, and my successful analysis of the T. R. Vinha tapes she cannot insist upon my dependence. But she may resent my independence. I took the covers off the notebook and am keeping the loose pages in the split in the back cover of my copy of Rheingeld; it would take a very close search to find them there. While I was doing that I felt rather sick at the stomach and got a headache.

Allergy: A person can be exposed to pollen or bitten by fleas a thousand times without reaction. Then he gets a viral infection or a psychic trauma or a bee sting, and next time he meets up with ragweed or a flea he begins to sneeze, cough, itch, weep, etc. It is the same with certain other irritants. One has to be sensitized.

"Why is there so much fear?" I wrote. Well, now I know. Why is there no privacy? It is unfair and sordid. I cannot read the "classified" files kept in her office, though I work with the patients and she does not. But I am not to have any "classified" material of my own. Only persons in authority can have secrets. Their secrets are all good, even when they are lies.

Listen. Listen, Rosa Sobel. Doctor of Medicine, Deg. Psychotherapy, Deg. Psychoscopy. Have you gone native?

Whose thoughts are you thinking?

You have been working two to five hours a day for six weeks inside one person's mind. A generous, integrated, sane mind. You never worked with anything like that before. You have only worked with the crippled and the terrified. You never met an equal before.

Who is the therapist, you or he?

But if there is nothing wrong with him what am I supposed to cure? How can I help him? How can I save him?

By teaching him to lie?

(Undated). I spent the last two nights till midnight reviewing the diagnostic scopes of Professor Arca, recorded when he was admitted, eleven years ago, before electroconvulsive treatment.

This morning Dr. N. inquired why I had been "so far back in the files" (that means that Selena reports to her on what files are used). (I know every square centimeter of the scope room but all the same I check it over daily now.) I replied that I was interested in studying the development of ideological disaffection in intellectuals. We agreed that intellectualism tends to foster negative thinking and may lead to psychosis, and those suffering from it should ideally be treated, as Professor Arca was treated, and released if still competent. It was a very interesting and harmonious discussion.

I lied. I lied. I lied. I lied deliberately, knowingly, well. She lied. She is a liar. She is an intellectual too! She is a lie. And a coward, afraid.

I wanted to watch the Arca tapes to get perspective. To prove to myself that Flores is by no means unique or original. This is true. The differences are fascinating. Dr. Arca's Con dimension was splendid, architectural, but the Uncon material was less well integrated and less interesting. Dr. Arca knew very much more, and the power and beauty of the motions of his thought was far superior to Flores's. Flores is often extremely muddled. That is an element of his vitality. Dr. Arca is an—was an Abstract thinker, as I am, and so I enjoyed his tapes less. I missed the solidity, spatiotemporal realism, and intense sensory clarity of Flores's mind.

In the scope room this morning I told him what I had been doing. His reaction was (as usual) not what I expected. He is fond of the old man and I thought he would be pleased. He said, "You mean they saved the tapes, and destroyed the mind?" I told him that all tapes are kept for use in teaching, and asked him if that didn't cheer him, to know that a record of Arca's thoughts in his prime existed: wasn't it like his book, after all, the lasting part of a mind which sooner or later would have to grow senile and die anyhow? He said, "No! Not so long as the book is banned and the tape is classified! Neither freedom nor privacy even in death? That is the worst of all!"

After session he asked if I would be able or willing to destroy his diagnostic tapes, if he is sent to ECT. I said such things could get misfiled and lost easily enough, but that it seemed a cruel waste, I had learned from him and others might, later, too. He said, "Don't you see that I will not serve the people with security passes? I will not be used, that's the whole point. You have never used me. We have worked together. Served our term together."

Prison has been much in his mind lately. Fantasies, daydreams of jails, labor camps. He dreams of prison as a man in prison dreams of freedom.

Indeed, as I see the way narrowing in I would get him sent to prison if I could, but since he is *here* there is no chance. If I reported that he is in fact politically dangerous, they will simply put him back in the Violent ward and give him ECT. There is no judge here to give him a life sentence. Only doctors to give death sentences.

What I can do is stretch out the diagnosis as long as possible, and put in a request for full co-analysis, with a strong prognosis of complete cure. But I have drafted the report three times already and it is very hard to phrase it so that it's clear that I know the disease is ideological (so that they don't just override my diagnosis at once) but still making it sound mild and curable enough that they'd let me handle it with the psychoscope. And then, why spend up to a year, using expensive equipment, when a cheap and simple instant cure is at hand? No matter what I say, they have that argument. There are two weeks left until Sectional Review. I have got to write the report so that it will be really impossible for them to override it. But what if Flores is right, all this is just play-acting, lying about lying, and they have had orders right from the start from TRTU, "Wipe this one out—."

(Undated). Sectional Review today.

If I stay on here I have some power, I can do some good   No no no but I don't I don't even in this one thing even in this what can I do now how can I stop

(Undated). Last night I dreamed I rode on a bear's back up a deep gorge between steep mountainsides, slopes going steep up into a dark sky, it was winter, there was ice on the rocks

(Undated). Tomorrow morning will tell Nades I am resigning and requesting transfer to Children's Hospital. But she must

approve the transfer. If not, I am out in the cold. I am in the cold already. Door locked to write this. As soon as it is written will go down to furnace room and burn it all. There is no place any more.

We met in the hall. He was with an orderly.

I took his hand. It was big and bony and very cold. He said, "Is this it now, Rosa—the electroshock?" in a low voice. I did not want him to lose hope before he walked up the stairs and down the corridor. It is a long way down the corridor. I said, "No. Just some more tests—EEG probably."

"Then I'll see you tomorrow?" he asked, and I said yes.

And he did. I went in this evening. He was awake. I said, "I am Dr. Sobel, Flores. I am Rosa."

He said, "I'm pleased to meet you," mumbling. There is a slight facial paralysis on the left. That will wear off.

I am Rosa. I am the rose. The rose, I am the rose. The rose with no flower, the rose all thorns, the mind he made, the hand he touched, the winter rose.

For decades science fiction was dominated by writers from the East Coast and the West Coast, so much so that it often seemed that every SF writer in the country was living either in New York City and its environs (the Forties and Fifties), or in California (the Sixties); many of these writers were born in Ohio or Oregon or Nebraska, mind, but the point is that as soon as they were able to they cleared out and kept on going, heading for the big towns and the bright lights.

In recent years, however, SF writers have been tending to stay put and develop regional pride instead, and writers groups have been sprouting up all over the country. For some odd reason, the largest, most vigorous, and most vocal group of all developed in Texas, centered around an institution known as the Turkey City Writers Workshop. Mutterings and alarms about the existence of the Turkey City bunch were heard for a couple of years, but it wasn't until 1976 that they surfaced strongly with the publication of Lone Star Universe, edited by two of their own, George W. Proctor and Steven Utley. Lone Star Universe may hold the distinction of having the most oddball theme of any SF anthology ever published—it is an anthology of SF stories by Texans (one of which, Jake Saunders's "Back to the Stone Age," appears elsewhere in this book), and the strangest thing of all about it is that many of them turn out to be quite good.

Steven Utley and Howard Waldrop are two of the best known of the Texans.

Steven Utley's fiction (over seventy sales to date) has appeared in F&SF, Universe, Galaxy, Isaac Asimov's Science Fiction Magazine, Amazing, Vertex, Stellar, and elsewhere. Born in 1948 in Smyrna, Tennessee, Utley currently lives in Austin, Texas. His interests include "dinosaurs, the battle of the Little Big Horn, and the guitar, which I play rather less brilliantly than, say, A. Segovia or J. Beck."

Howard Waldrop was born in 1946 in Houston, Miss., moved to the Dallas—Fort Worth area of Texas in 1950 (presumably not all by himself, although he doesn't say), and moved to Austin, Texas in 1974. His first fiction sale was to Analog in 1970; since then he has been widely published, in places as diverse as Zoo World, Galaxy, Crawdaddy, and Orbit. His first novel, written in collaboration with Jake Saunders, was The Texas—Israeli War: 1999, published in 1974 by Ballantine. Waldrop produced, or helped to produce, at least three of the better stories of this year, including another Nebula finalist that also bulled its way into this anthology on sheer merit, "Mary Margaret Road-Grader."

Originally written in 1972, "Custer's Last Jump" was supposed to appear in New Dimensions 5, but "for complex and uninteresting reasons," in Silverberg's words, it ended up four years later in Universe 6 *instead. This ingenious, fascinating, and amazingly plausible (check out the "suggested reading" list at the end of the story to see just how well, and how cleverly, the authors have done their homework) tale of an alternate universe, in which certain famous events happened just a little bit differently, was recognized at once as one of the year's best and is a strong contender for the 1976 Nebula Award.*

STEVEN UTLEY AND HOWARD WALDROP
Custer's Last Jump

Smithsonian Annals of Flight, VOL. 39: *The Air War in the West*
CHAPTER 27: The Krupp Monoplane

Introduction

Its wings still hold the tears from many bullets. The ailerons are still scorched black, and the exploded Henry machine rifle is bent awkwardly in its blast port.

The right landing skid is missing, and the frame has been restraightened. It stands in the left wing of the Air Museum today, next to the French Devre jet and the X-FU-5 Flying Flapjack, the world's fastest fighter aircraft.

On its rudder is the swastika, an ugly reminder of days of glory fifty years ago.

A simple plaque describes the aircraft. It reads:

CRAZY HORSE'S KRUPP MONOPLANE
(Captured at the raid on Fort Carson, January 5, 1882)

General

1. To study the history of this plane is to delve into one of the

most glorious eras of aviation history. To begin: the aircraft was manufactured by the Krupp plant in Haavesborg, Netherlands. The airframe was completed August 3, 1862, as part of the third shipment of Krupp aircraft to the Confederate States of America under terms of the Agreement of Atlanta of 1861. It was originally equipped with power plant #311 Zed of 87¼ horsepower, manufactured by the Jumo plant at Nordmung, Duchy of Austria, on May 3 of the year 1862. Wingspan of the craft is twenty-three feet, its length is seventeen feet three inches. The aircraft arrived in the port of Charlotte on September 21, 1862, aboard the transport *Mendenhall,* which had suffered heavy bombardment from GAR picket ships. The aircraft was possibly sent by rail to Confederate Army Air Corps Center at Fort Andrew Mott, Alabama. Unfortunately, records of rail movements during this time were lost in the burning of the Confederate archives at Ittebeha in March 1867, two weeks after the Truce of Haldeman was signed.

2. The aircraft was damaged during a training flight in December 1862. Student pilot was Flight Subaltern (Cadet) Neldoo J. Smith, CSAAC; flight instructor during the ill-fated flight was Air Captain Winslow Homer Winslow, on interservice instructor-duty loan from the Confederate States Navy.

Accident forms and maintenance officer's reports indicate that the original motor was replaced with one of the new 93½ horsepower Jumo engines which had just arrived from Holland by way of Mexico.

3. The aircraft served routinely through the remainder of Flight Subaltern Smith's training. We have records[141], which indicate that the aircraft was one of the first to be equipped with the Henry repeating machine rifle of the chain-driven type. Until December 1862, all CSAAC aircraft were equipped with the Sharps repeating rifles of the motor-driven, low-voltage type on wing or turret mounts.

As was the custom, the aircraft was flown by Flight Subaltern Smith to his first duty station at Thimblerig Aerodrome in Augusta, Georgia. Flight Subaltern Smith was assigned to Flight Platoon 2, 1st Aeroscout Squadron.

4. The aircraft, with Flight Subaltern Smith at the wheel, participated in three of the aerial expeditions against the Union Army in the Second Battle of the Manassas. Smith distinguished

himself in the first and third mission. (He was assigned aerial picket duty south of the actual battle during his second mission.) On the first, he is credited with one kill and one probable (both bi-wing Airsharks). During the third mission, he destroyed one aircraft and forced another down behind Confederate lines. He then escorted the craft of his immediate commander, Air Captain Dalton Trump, to a safe landing on a field controlled by the Confederates. According to Trump's sworn testimony, Smith successfully fought off two Union craft and ranged ahead of Trump's crippled plane to strafe a group of Union soldiers who were in their flight path, discouraging them from firing on Trump's smoking aircraft.

For heroism on these two missions, Smith was awarded the Silver Star and Bar with Air Cluster. Presentation was made on March 3, 1863, by the late General J. E. B. Stuart, Chief of Staff of the CSAAC.

5. Flight Subaltern Smith was promoted to flight captain on April 12, 1863, after distinguishing himself with two kills and two probables during the first day of the Battle of the Three Roads, North Carolina. One of his kills was an airship of the Moby class, with crew of fourteen. Smith shared with only one other aviator the feat of bringing down one of these dirigibles during the War of the Secession.

This was the first action the 1st Aeroscout Squadron had seen since Second Manassas, and Captain Smith seems to have been chafing under inaction. Perhaps this led him to volunteer for duty with Major John S. Moseby, then forming what would later become Moseby's Raiders. This was actually sound military strategy: the CSAAC was to send a unit to southwestern Kansas to carry out harassment raids against the poorly defended forts of the far West. These raids would force the Union to send men and materiel sorely needed at the southern front far to the west, where they would be ineffectual in the outcome of the war. That this action was taken is pointed to by some[142] as a sign that the Confederate States envisioned defeat and were resorting to desperate measures four years before the Treaty of Haldeman.

At any rate, Captain Smith and his aircraft joined a triple flight of six aircraft each, which, after stopping at El Dorado, Arkansas, to refuel, flew away on a westerly course. This is the last time they ever operated in Confederate states. The date was June 5, 1863.

6. The Union forts stretched from a medium-well-defended line in Illinois to poorly garrisoned stations as far west as Wyom-

ing Territory and south to the Kansas–Indian Territory border. Southwestern Kansas was both sparsely settled and garrisoned. It was from this area that Moseby's Raiders, with the official designation 1st Western Interdiction Wing, CSAAC, operated.

A supply wagon train had been sent ahead a month before from Fort Worth, carrying petrol, ammunition, and material for shelters. A crude landing field, hangars, and barracks awaited the eighteen craft.

After two months of reconnaissance (done by mounted scouts due to the need to maintain the element of surprise, and, more importantly, by the limited amount of fuel available) the 1st WIW took to the air. The citizens of Riley, Kansas, long remembered the day: their first inkling that Confederates were closer than Texas came when motors were heard overhead and the Union garrison was literally blown off the face of the map.

7. Following the first raid, word went to the War Department headquarters in New York, with pleas for aid and reinforcements for all Kansas garrisons. Thus the CSAAC achieved its goal in the very first raid. The effects snowballed; as soon as the populace learned of the raid, it demanded protection from nearby garrisons. Farmers' organizations threatened to stop shipments of needed produce to eastern depots. The garrison commanders, unable to promise adequate protection, appealed to higher military authorities.

Meanwhile, the 1st WIW made a second raid on Abilene, heavily damaging the railways and stockyards with twenty-five-pound fragmentation bombs. They then circled the city, strafed the Army Quartermaster depot, and disappeared into the west.

8. This second raid, and the ensuing clamor from both the public and the commanders of western forces, convinced the War Department to divert new recruits and supplies, with seasoned members of the 18th Aeropursuit Squadron, to the Kansas–Missouri border, near Lawrence.

9. Inclement weather in the fall kept both the 18th AS and the 1st WIW grounded for seventy-two of the ninety days of the season. Aircraft from each of these units met several times; the 1st is credited with one kill, while pilots of the 18th downed two Confederate aircraft on the afternoon of December 12, 1863.

Both aircraft units were heavily resupplied during this time. The Battle of the Canadian River was fought on December 18, when mounted reconnaissance units of the Union and Confederacy met in Indian territory. Losses were small on both sides, but the skirmish was the first of what would become known as the Far Western Campaign.

10. Civilians spotted the massed formation of the 1st WIW as early as 10 A.M. Thursday, December 16, 1863. They headed northeast, making a leg due north when eighteen miles south of Lawrence. Two planes sped ahead to destroy the telegraph station at Felton, nine miles south of Lawrence. Nevertheless, a message of some sort reached Lawrence; a Union messenger on horseback was on his way to the aerodrome when the first flight of Confederate aircraft passed overhead.

In the ensuing raid, seven of the nineteen Union aircraft were destroyed on the ground and two were destroyed in the air, while the remaining aircraft were severely damaged and the barracks and hangars demolished.

The 1st WIW suffered one loss: during the raid a Union clerk attached for duty with the 18th AS manned an Agar machine rifle position and destroyed one Confederate aircraft. He was killed by machine rifle fire from the second wave of planes. Private Alden Evans Gunn was awarded the Congressional Medal of Honor posthumously for his gallantry during the attack.

For the next two months, the 1st WIW ruled the skies as far north as Illinois, as far east as Trenton, Missouri.

The Far Western Campaign

1. At this juncture, the two most prominent figures of the next nineteen years of frontier history enter the picture: the Oglala Sioux Crazy Horse and Lieutenant Colonel (Brevet Major General) George Armstrong Custer. The clerical error giving Custer the rank of Brigadier General is well known. It is not common knowledge that Custer was considered by the General Staff as a candidate for Far Western Commander as early as the spring of 1864, a duty he would not take up until May 1869, when the Far Western Command was the only theater of war operations within the Americas.

The General Staff, it is believed, considered Major General Custer for the job for two reasons: they thought Custer possessed those qualities of spirit suited to the warfare necessary in the Western Command, and that the far West was the ideal place for the twenty-three-year-old Boy General.

Crazy Horse, the Oglala Sioux warrior, was with a hunting party far from Oglala territory, checking the size of the few remaining buffalo herds before they started their spring migrations. Legend has it that Crazy Horse and the party were crossing the prairies in early February 1864 when two aircraft belonging to the 1st WIW passed nearby. Some of the Sioux jumped to the ground, believing that they were looking on the Thunderbird and its mate. Only Crazy Horse stayed on his pony and watched the aircraft disappear into the south.

He sent word back by the rest of the party that he and two of his young warrior friends had gone looking for the nest of the Thunderbird.

2. The story of the 1st WIW here becomes the story of the shaping of the Indian wars, rather than part of the history of the last four years of the War of the Secession. It is well known that increased alarm over the Kansas raids had shifted War Department thinking: the defense of the far West changed in importance from a minor matter in the larger scheme of war to a problem of vital concern. For one thing, the Confederacy was courting the Emperor Maximilian of Mexico, and through him the French, into entering the war on the Confederate side. The South wanted arms, but most necessarily to break the Union submarine blockade. Only the French Navy possessed the capability.

The Union therefore sent the massed 5th Cavalry to Kansas, and attached to it the 12th Air Destroyer Squadron and the 2nd Airship Command.

The 2nd Airship Command, at the time of its deployment, was equipped with the small pursuit airships known in later days as the "torpedo ship," from its double-pointed ends. These ships were used for reconnaissance and light interdiction duties, and were almost always accompanied by aircraft from the 12th ADS. They immediately set to work patroling the Kansas skies from the renewed base of operations at Lawrence.

3. The idea of using Indian personnel in some phase of airfield operations in the West had been proposed by Moseby as early as June 1863. The C of C, CSA, disapproved in the strongest possible terms. It was not a new idea, therefore, when Crazy Horse and his two companions rode into the airfield, accompanied by the sentries who had challenged them far from the

perimeter. They were taken to Major Moseby for questioning.

Through an interpreter, Moseby learned they were Oglala, not Crows sent to spy for the Union. When asked why they had come so far, Crazy Horse replied,"To see the nest of the Thunderbird."

Moseby is said to have laughed[143] and then taken the three Sioux to see the aircraft. Crazy Horse was said to have been stricken with awe when he found that men controlled their flight.

Crazy Horse then offered Moseby ten ponies for one of the craft. Moseby explained that they were not his to give, but his Great Father's, and that they were used to fight the Yellowlegs from the Northeast.

At this time, fate took a hand: the 12th Air Destroyer Squadron had just begun operations. The same day Crazy Horse was having his initial interview with Moseby, a scout plane returned with the news that the 12th was being reinforced by an airship combat group; the dirigibles had been seen maneuvering near the Kansas-Missouri border.

Moseby learned from Crazy Horse that the warrior was respected; if not in his own tribe, then with other Nations of the North. Moseby, with an eye toward those reinforcements arriving in Lawrence, asked Crazy Horse if he could guarantee safe conduct through the northern tribes, and land for an airfield should the present one have to be abandoned.

Crazy Horse answered, "I can talk the idea to the People; it will be for them to decide."

Moseby told Crazy Horse that if he could secure the promise, he would grant him anything within his power.

Crazy Horse looked out the window toward the hangars. "I ask that you teach me and ten of my brother-friends to fly the Thunderbirds. We will help you fight the Yellowlegs."

Moseby, expecting requests for beef, blankets, or firearms was taken aback. Unlike the others who had dealt with the Indians, he was a man of his word. He told Crazy Horse he would ask his Great Father if this could be done. Crazy Horse left, returning to his village in the middle of March. He and several warriors traveled extensively that spring, smoking the pipe, securing permissions from the other Nations for safe conduct for the Gray White Men through their hunting lands. His hardest task came in convincing the Oglala themselves that the airfield be built in their southern hunting grounds.

Crazy Horse, his two wives, seven warriors and their women,

children, and belongings rode into the CSAAC airfield in June, 1864.

4. Moseby had been granted permission from Stuart to go ahead with the training program. Derision first met the request within the southern General Staff when Moseby's proposal was circulated. Stuart, though not entirely sympathetic to the idea, became its champion. Others objected, warning that ignorant savages should not be given modern weapons. Stuart reminded them that some of the good Tennessee boys already flying airplanes could neither read nor write.

Stuart's approval arrived a month before Crazy Horse and his band made camp on the edge of the airfield.

5. It fell to Captain Smith to train Crazy Horse. The Indian became what Smith, in his journal,[144] describes as "the best natural pilot I have seen or it has been my pleasure to fly with." Part of this seems to have come from Smith's own modesty; by all accounts, Smith was one of the finer pilots of the war.

The operations of the 12th ADS and the 2nd Airship Command ranged closer to the CSAAC airfield. The dogfights came frequently and the fighting grew less gentlemanly. One 1st WIW fighter was pounced by three aircraft of the 12th simultaneously: they did not stop firing even when the pilot signaled that he was hit and that his engine was dead. Nor did they break off their runs until both pilot and craft plunged into the Kansas prairie. It is thought that the Union pilots were under secret orders to kill all members of the 1st WIW. There is some evidence[145] that this rankled with the more gentlemanly of the 12th Air Destroyer Squadron. Nevertheless, fighting intensified.

A flight of six more aircraft joined the 1st WIW some weeks after the Oglala Sioux started their training: this was the first of the ferry flights from Mexico through Texas and Indian territory to reach the airfield. Before the summer was over, a dozen additional craft would join the Wing; this before shipments were curtailed by Juarez's revolution against the French and the ouster and execution of Maximilian and his family.

Smith records[146] that Crazy Horse's first solo took place on August 14, 1864, and that the warrior, though deft in the air, still needed practice on his landings. He had a tendency to come in overpowered and to stall his engine out too soon. Minor repairs were made on the skids of the craft after this flight.

All this time, Crazy Horse had flown Smith's craft. Smith, after another week of hard practice with the Indian, pronounced him "more qualified than most pilots the CSAAC in Alabama turned out"[147] and signed over the aircraft to him. Crazy Horse begged off. Then, seeing that Smith was sincere, he gave the captain many buffalo hides. Smith reminded the Indian that the craft was not his: during their off hours, when not training, the Indians had been given enough instruction in military discipline as Moseby, never a stickler, thought necessary. The Indians had only a rudimentary idea of government property. Of the seven other Indian men, three were qualified as pilots; the other four were given gunner positions in the Krupp bi-wing light bombers assigned to the squadron.

Soon after Smith presented the aircraft to Crazy Horse, the captain took off in a borrowed monoplane on what was to be the daily weather flight into northern Kansas. There is evidence[148] that it was Smith who encountered a flight of light dirigibles from the 2nd Airship Command and attacked them single-handedly. He crippled one airship; the other was rescued when two escort planes of the 12th ADS came to its defense. They raked the attacker with withering fire. The attacker escaped into the clouds.

It was not until 1897, when a group of schoolchildren on an outing found the wreckage, that it was known that Captain Smith had brought his crippled monoplane within five miles of the airfield before crashing into the rolling hills.

When Smith did not return from his flight, Crazy Horse went on a vigil, neither sleeping nor eating for a week. On the seventh day, Crazy Horse vowed vengeance on the men who had killed his white friend.

6. The devastating Union raid of September 23, 1864, caught the airfield unawares. Though the Indians were averse to fighting at night, Crazy Horse and two other Sioux were manning three of the four craft which got off the ground during the raid. The attack had been carried out by the 2nd Airship Command, traveling at twelve thousand feet, dropping fifty-pound fragmentation bombs and shrapnel canisters. The shrapnel played havoc with the aircraft on the ground. It also destroyed the mess hall and enlisted barracks and three teepees.

The dirigibles turned away and were running fast before a tail wind when Crazy Horse gained their altitude.

The gunners on the dirigibles filled the skies with tracers from their light .30—30 machine rifles. Crazy Horse's monoplane was equipped with a single Henry .41−40 machine rifle. Unable to get in close killing distance, Crazy Horse and his companions stood off beyond range of the lighter Union guns and raked the dirigibles with heavy machine rifle fire. They did enough damage to force one airship down twenty miles from its base, and to ground two others for two days while repairs were made. The intensity of fire convinced the airship commanders that more than four planes had made it off the ground, causing them to continue their headlong retreat.

Crazy Horse and the others returned, and brought off the second windfall of the night; a group of 5th Cavalry raiders were to have attacked the airfield in the confusion of the airship raid and burn everything still standing. On their return flight, the four craft encountered the cavalry unit as it began its charge across open ground.

In three strafing runs, the aircraft killed thirty-seven men and wounded fifty-three, while twenty-nine were taken prisoner by the airfield's defenders. Thus, in his first combat mission for the CSAAC, Crazy Horse was credited with saving the airfield against overwhelming odds.

7. Meanwhile, Major General George A. Custer had distinguished himself at the Battle of Gettysburg. A few weeks after the battle, he enrolled himself in the GAR jump school at Watauga, New York. Howls of outrage came from the General Staff; Custer quoted the standing order, "any man who volunteered and of whom the commanding officer approved," could be enrolled. Custer then asked, in a letter to C of S, GAR, "how any military leader could be expected to plan maneuvers involving parachute infantry when he himself had never experienced a drop, or found the true capabilities of the parachute infantryman?"[149] The Chief of Staff shouted down the protest. There were mutterings among the General Staff[150] to the effect that the real reason Custer wanted to become jump-qualified was so that he would have a better chance of leading the Invasion of Atlanta, part of whose contingency plans called for attacks by airborne units.

During the three-week parachute course, Custer became acquainted with another man who would play an important part in the Western Campaign, Captain (Brevet Colonel) Frederick W. Benteen. Upon graduation from the jump school, Brevet Colonel Benteen assumed command of the 505th Balloon Infantry, stationed at Chicago, Illinois, for training purposes. Colonel Benteen would remain commander of the 505th until his capture at the Battle of Montgomery in 1866. While he was prisoner of war, his command was given to another, later to figure in the Western Campaign, Lieutenant Colonel Myles W. Keogh.

Custer, upon successful completion of jump school, returned to his command of the 6th Cavalry Division, and participated throughout the remainder of the war in that capacity. It was he who led the successful charge at the Battle of the Cape Fear which smashed Lee's flank and allowed the 1st Infantry to overrun the Confederate position and capture that southern leader. Custer distinguished himself and his command up until the cessation of hostilities in 1867.

8. The 1st WIW, CSAAC, moved to a new airfield in Wyoming Territory three weeks after the raid of September 24. At the same time, the 2nd WIW was formed and moved to an outpost in Indian territory. The 2nd WIW raided the Union airfield, took it totally by surprise, and inflicted casualties on the 12th ADS and 2nd AC so devastating as to render them ineffectual. The 2nd WIW then moved to a second field in Wyoming Territory. It was here, following the move, that a number of Indians, including Black Man's Hand, were trained by Crazy Horse.

9. We leave the history of the 2nd WIW here. It was redeployed for the defense of Montgomery. The Indians and aircraft in which they trained were sent north to join the 1st WIW. The 1st WIW patrolled the skies of Indiana, Nebraska, and the Dakotas. After the defeat of the 12th ADS and the 2nd AC, the Union forstalled attempts to retaliate until the cessation of southern hostilities in 1867.

We may at this point add that Crazy Horse, Black Man's Hand, and the other Indians sometimes left the airfield during periods of long inactivity. They returned to their Nations for as long as three months at a time. Each time Crazy Horse returned, he brought one or two pilot or gunner recruits with him. Before the winter of 1866, more than thirty percent of the 1st WIW were Oglala, Sansarc Sioux, or Cheyenne.

The South, losing the war of attrition, diverted all supplies to Alabama and Mississippi in the fall of 1866. None were forthcoming for the 1st WIW, though a messenger arrived with orders for Major Moseby to return to Texas for the defense of Fort Worth, where he would later direct the Battle of the Trinity. That Moseby was not ordered to deploy the 1st WIW to that defense has been considered by many military strategists as a "lost turning point" of the battle for Texas. Command of the 1st WIW was turned over to Acting Major (Flight Captain) Natchitoches Hooley.

10. The loss of Moseby signaled the end of the 1st WIW. Not only did the nondeployment of the 1st to Texas cost the South that territory, it also left the 1st in an untenable position, which the Union was quick to realize. The airfield was captured in May 1867 by a force of five hundred cavalry and three hundred infantry sent from the battle of the Arkansas, and a like force, plus aircraft, from Chicago. Crazy Horse, seven Indians, and at least five Confederates escaped in their monoplanes. The victorious Union troops were surprised to find Indians at the field. Crazy Horse's people were eventually freed; the Army thought them to have been hired by the Confederates to hunt and cook for the airfield. Moseby had provided for this in contingency plans long before; he had not wanted the Plains tribes to suffer for Confederate acts. The Army did not know, and no one volunteered the information, that it had been Indians doing the most considerable amount of damage to the Union garrisons lately.

Crazy Horse and three of his Indians landed their craft near the Black Hills. The Cheyenne helped them carry the craft, on travois, to caves in the sacred mountains. Here they mothballed the planes with mixtures of pine tar and resins, and sealed up the caves.

11. The aircraft remained stored until February 1872. During this time, Crazy Horse and his Oglala Sioux operated, like the other Plains Indians, as light cavalry, skirmishing with the Army and with settlers up and down the Dakotas and Montana. George Armstrong Custer was appointed commander of the new 7th Cavalry in 1869. Stationed first at Chicago (Far Western Command headquarters), they later moved to Fort Abraham Lincoln, Nebraska.

A column of troops moved against Indians on the warpath in the winter of 1869. They reported a large group of Indians encamped on the Washita River. Custer obtained permission for the 505th Balloon Infantry to join the 7th Cavalry. From that day on, the unit was officially Company I (Separate Troops), 7th U.S. Cavalry, though it kept its numerical designation. Also attached to the 7th was the 12th Airship Squadron, as Company J.

Lieutenant Colonel Keogh, acting commander of the 505th for the last twenty-one months, but who had never been on jump status, was appointed by Custer as commander of K Company, 7th Cavalry.

It was known that only the 505th Balloon Infantry and the 12th Airship Squadron were used in the raid on Black Kettle's village. Black Kettle was a treaty Indian, "walking the white man's road." Reports have become garbled in transmission: Custer and the 505th believed they were jumping into a village of hostiles.

The event remained a mystery until Kellogg, the Chicago newspaperman, wrote his account in 1872.[151] The 505th, with Custer in command, flew the three (then numbered, after 1872, named) dirigibles No. 31, No. 76, and No. 93, with seventy-two jumpers each. Custer was in the first "stick" on Airship 76. The three sailed silently to the sleeping village. Custer gave the order to hook up at 5:42 Chicago time, 4:42 local time, and the 505th jumped into the village. Black Kettle's people were awakened when some of the balloon infantry crashed through their teepees, others died in their sleep. One of the first duties of the infantry was to moor the dirigibles; this done, the gunners on the airships opened up on the startled villagers with their Gatling and Agar machine rifles. Black Kettle himself was killed while waving an American flag at Airship No. 93.

After the battle, the men of the 505th climbed back up to the moored dirigibles by rope ladder, and the airships departed for Fort Lincoln. The Indians camped downriver heard the shooting and found horses stampeded during the attack. When they came to the village, they found only slaughter. Custer had taken his dead (three, one of whom died during the jump by being drowned in the Washita) and wounded (twelve) away. They left 307 dead men, women, and children, and 500 slaughtered horses.

There were no tracks leading in and out of the village except those of the frightened horses. The other Indians left the area, thinking the white men had magicked it.

Crazy Horse is said[152] to have visited the area soon after the massacre. It was this action by the 7th which spelled their doom seven years later.

12. Black Man's Hand joined Crazy Horse; so did other former 1st WIW pilots, soon after Crazy Horse's two-plane raid on the airship hangars at Bismarck, in 1872. For that mission, Crazy Horse dropped twenty-five-pound fragmentation bombs

tied to petrol canisters. The shrapnel ripped the dirigibles, the escaping hydrogen was ignited by the burning petrol: all— hangars, balloons, and maintenance crews—were lost.

It was written up as an unreconstructed Confederate's sabotage; a somewhat ignominious former Southern major was eventually hanged on circumstantial evidence. Reports by sentries that they heard aircraft just before the explosions were discounted. At the time, it was believed the only aircraft were those belonging to the Army, and the carefully licensed commercial craft.

13. In 1874, Custer circulated rumors that the Black Hills were full of gold. It has been speculated that this was used to draw miners to the area so the Indians would attack them; then the cavalry would have unlimited freedom to deal with the Red Man.[153] Also that year, those who had become Agency Indians were being shorted in their supplies by members of the scandal-plagued Indian Affairs Bureau under President Grant. When these left the reservations in search of food, the cavalry was sent to "bring them back." Those who were caught were usually killed.

The Sioux ignored the miners at first, expecting the gods to deal with them. When this did not happen, Sitting Bull sent out a party of two hundred warriors, who killed every miner they encountered. Public outrage demanded reprisals; Sheridan wired Custer to find and punish those responsible.

14. Fearing what was to come, Crazy Horse sent Yellow Dog and Red Chief with a war party of five hundred to raid the rebuilt Fort Phil Kearny. This they did successfully, capturing twelve planes and fuel and ammunition for many more. They hid these in the caverns with the 1st WIW craft.

The Army would not have acted as rashly as it did had it known the planes pronounced missing in the reports on the Kearny raid were being given into the hands of experienced pilots.

The reprisal consisted of airship patrols which strafed any living thing on the plains. Untold thousands of deer and the few remaining buffalo were killed. Unofficial counts list as killed a little more than eight hundred Indians who were caught in the open during the next eight months.

Indians who jumped the agencies and who had seen or heard of the slaughter streamed to Sitting Bull's hidden camp on the Little Big Horn. They were treated as guests, except for the Sansarcs, who camped a little way down the river. It is estimated there were no less than ten thousand Indians, including some four thousand warriors, camped along the river for the Sun Dance ceremony of June 1876.

A three-pronged-pincers movement for the final eradication of the Sioux and Cheyenne worked toward them. The 7th Cavalry, under Keogh and Major Marcus Reno, set out from Fort Lincoln during the last week of May. General George Crook's command was coming up the Rosebud. The gunboat *Far West*, with three hundred reserves and supplies, steamed to the mouth of the Big Horn River. General Terry's command was coming from the northwest. All Indians they encountered were to be killed.

Just before the Sun Dance, Crazy Horse and his pilots got word of the movement of Crook's men up the Rosebud, hurried to the caves, and prepared their craft for flight. Only six planes were put in working condition in time. The other pilots remained behind while Crazy Horse, Black Man's Hand, and four others took to the skies. They destroyed two dirigibles, soundly trounced Crook, and chased his command back down the Rosebud in a rout. The column had to abandon its light-armored vehicles and fight its way back, on foot for the most part, to safety.

15. Sitting Bull's vision during the Sun Dance is well known.[154] He told it to Crazy Horse, the warrior who would see that it came true, as soon as the aviators returned to camp.

Two hundred fifty miles away, "Chutes and Saddles" was sounded on the morning of June 23, and the men of the 505th Balloon Infantry climbed aboard the airships *Benjamin Franklin, Samuel Adams, John Hancock,* and *Ethan Allen.* Custer was first man on stick one of the *Franklin.* The *Ethan Allen* carried a scout aircraft which could hook up or detach in flight; the bi-winger was to serve as liaison between the three armies and the airships.

When Custer bade goodbye to his wife, Elizabeth, that morning, both were in good spirits. If either had an inkling of the fate which awaited Custer and the 7th three days away, on the bluffs above a small stream, they did not show it.

The four airships sailed from Fort Lincoln, their silver sides and shark-tooth mouths gleaming in the sun, the eyes painted on the noses looking west. On the sides were the crossed sabers of the cavalry; above the numeral 7; below the numerals 505. It is said that they looked magnificent as they sailed away for their rendezvous with destiny.[155]

16. It is sufficient to say that the Indians attained their greatest victory over the Army, and almost totally destroyed the 7th Cavalry, on June 25–26, 1876, due in large part to the efforts of Crazy Horse and his aviators. Surprise, swiftness, and the skill of the Indians cannot be discounted, nor can the military blunders made by Custer that morning. The repercussions of that summer day rang down the years, and the events are still debated. The only sure fact is that the U. S. Army lost its prestige, part of its spirit, and more than four hundred of its finest soldiers in the battle.

17. While the demoralized commands were sorting themselves out, the Cheyenne and Sioux left for the Canadian border. They took their aircraft with them, on travois. With Sitting Bull, Crazy Horse and his band settled just across the border. The aircraft were rarely used again until the attack on the camp by the combined Canadian–U.S. Cavalry offensive of 1879. Crazy Horse and his aviators, as they had done so many times before, escaped with their aircraft, using one of the planes to carry their remaining fuel. Two of the nine craft were shot down by a Canadian battery.

Crazy Horse, sensing the end, fought his way, with men on horseback and the planes on travois, from Montana to Colorado. After learning of the death of Sitting Bull and Chief Joseph, he took his small band as close as he dared to Fort Carson, where the cavalry was amassing to wipe out the remaining American Indians.

He assembled his men for the last time. He made his proposal; all concurred and joined him for a last raid on the Army. The five remaining planes came in low, the morning of January 5, 1882, toward the Army airfield. They destroyed twelve aircraft on the ground, shot up the hangars and barracks, and ignited one of the two ammunition dumps of the stockade. At this time, Army gunners manned the William's machine cannon batteries (improved by Thomas Edison's contract scientists) and blew three of the craft to flinders. The war gods must have smiled on Crazy Horse; his aircraft was crippled, the machine rifle was blown askew, the motor slivered, but he managed to set down intact. Black Man's Hand turned away; he was captured two months later, eating cottonwood bark in the snows of Arizona.

Crazy Horse jumped from his aircraft as most of Fort Carson

ran toward him; he pulled two Sharps repeating carbines from the cockpit and blazed away at the astonished troopers, wounding six and killing one. His back to the craft, he continued to fire until more than one hundred infantrymen fired a volley into his body.

The airplane was displayed for seven months at Fort Carson before being sent to the Smithsonian in Pittsburgh, where it stands today. Thus passed an era of military aviation.

—Lt. Gen. Frank Luke, Jr.
USAF, Ret.

From the December 2, 1939, issue of *Collier's Magazine*
Custer's Last Jump?
By A. R. Redmond

Few events in American history have captured the imagination so thoroughly as the Battle of the Little Big Horn. Lieutenant Colonel George Armstrong Custer's devastating defeat at the hands of Sioux and Cheyenne Indians in June 1876 has been rendered time and again by such celebrated artists as George Russell and Frederic Remington. Books, factual and otherwise, which have been written around or about the battle, would fill an entire library wing. The motion-picture industry has on numerous occasions drawn upon "Custer's Last Jump" for inspiration; latest in a long line of movieland Custers is Erroll Flynn [see photo], who appears with Olivia deHavilland and newcomer Anthony Quinn in Warner Brothers' soon-to-be-released *They Died with Their Chutes On.*

The impetuous and flamboyant Custer was an almost legendary figure long before the Battle of the Little Big Horn, however. Appointed to West Point in 1857, Custer was placed in command of Troop G, 2nd Cavalry, in June 1861, and participated in a series of skirmishes with Confederate cavalry throughout the rest of the year. It was during the First Battle of Manassas, or Bull Run, that he distinguished himself. He continued to do so in other engagements—at Williamsburg, Chancellorsville, Gettysburg—and rose rapidly through the ranks. He was twenty-six years old when he received a promotion to Brigadier General. He was, of course, immediately dubbed the Boy General. He had become an authentic war hero when the Northerners were in dire need of nothing less during those discouraging months between First Manassas and Gettysburg.

With the cessation of hostilities in the East when Bragg surrendered to Grant at Haldeman, the small hamlet about eight miles from Morehead, Kentucky, Custer requested a transfer of command. He and his young bride wound up at Chicago, manned by the new 7th U.S. Cavalry.

The war in the West lasted another few months; the tattered remnants of the Confederate Army staged last desperate stands throughout Texas, Colorado, Kansas, and Missouri. The final struggle at the Trinity River in October 1867 marked the close of conflict between North and South. Those few Mexican military advisers left in Texas quietly withdrew across the Rio Grande. The French, driven from Mexico in 1864 when Maximilian was ousted, lost interest in the Americas when they became embroiled with the newly united Prussian states.

During his first year in Chicago, Custer familiarized himself with the airships and aeroplanes of the 7th. The only jump-qualified general officer of the war, Custer seemed to have felt no resentment at the ultimate fate of mounted troops boded by the extremely mobile flying machines. The Ohio-born Boy General eventually preferred traveling aboard the airship *Benjamin Franklin,* one of the eight craft assigned to the 505th Balloon Infantry (Troop I, 7th Cavalry, commanded by Brevet Colonel Frederick Benteen) while his horse soldiers rode behind the very capable Captain (Brevet Lt. Col.) Myles Keogh.

The War Department in Pittsburgh did not know that various members of the Plains Indian tribes had been equipped with aeroplanes by the Confederates, and that many had actually flown against the Union garrisons in the West. (Curiously enough, those tribes which held out the longest against the Army—most notably the Apaches under Geronimo in the deep Southwest—were those who did not have aircraft.) The problems of transporting and hiding, to say nothing of maintaining planes, outweighed the advantages. A Cheyenne warrior named Brave Bear is said to have traded his band's aircraft in disgust to Sitting Bull for three horses. Also, many of the Plains Indians hated the aircraft outright, as they had been used by the white men to decimate the great buffalo herds in the early 1860s.

Even so, certain Oglalas, Minneconjous, and Cheyenne did reasonably well in the aircraft given them by the C. S. Army Air Corps Major John S. Moseby, whom the Indians called "The Gray

White Man" or "Many-Feathers-in-Hat." The Oglala war chief Crazy Horse [see photo, overleaf] led the raid on the Bismarck hangars (1872), four months after the 7th Cavalry was transferred to Fort Abraham Lincoln, Dakota Territory, and made his presence felt at the Rosebud and Little Big Horn in 1876. The Cheyenne Black Man's Hand trained by Crazy Horse himself, shot down two Army machines at the Rosebud, and was in the flight of planes that accomplished the annihilation of the 505th Balloon Infantry during the first phase of the Little Big Horn fiasco.

After the leveling of Fort Phil Kearny in February 1869, Custer was ordered to enter the Indian territories and punish those who had sought sanctuary there after the raid. Taking with him 150 parachutists aboard three airships, Custer left on the trail of a large band of Cheyenne.

On the afternoon of February 25, Lieutenant William van W. Reily, dispatched for scouting purposes in a Studebaker bi-winger, returned to report that he had shot up a hunting party near the Washita River. The Cheyenne, he thought, were encamped on the banks of the river some twenty miles away. They appeared not to have seen the close approach of the 7th Cavalry as they had not broken camp.

Just before dawn the next morning, the 505th Balloon Infantry, led by Custer, jumped into the village, killing all inhabitants and their animals.

For the next five years, Custer and the 7th chased the hostiles of the Plains back and forth between Colorado and the Canadian border. Relocated at Fort Lincoln, Custer and an expedition of horse soldiers, geologists, and engineers discovered gold in the Black Hills. Though the Black Hills still belonged to the Sioux according to several treaties, prospectors began to pour into the area. The 7th was ordered to protect them. The Blackfeet, Minneconjous, and Hunkpapa—Sioux who had left the warpath on the promise that the Black Hills, their sacred land, was theirs to keep for all time—protested, and when protests brought no results, took matters into their own hands. Prospectors turned up in various stages of mutilation, or not at all.

Conditions worsened over the remainder of 1875, during which time the United States Government ordered the Sioux out of the Black Hills. To make sure the Indians complied, airships patrolled the skies of Dakota Territory.

By the end of 1875, plagued by the likes of Crazy Horse's Oglala Sioux, it was decided that there was but one solution to the Plains Indian problem—total extermination.

At this point, General Phil Sheridan, Commander in Chief of the United States Army, began working on the practical angle of this new policy toward the Red Man.

In January 1876, delegates from the Democratic Party approached George Armstrong Custer at Fort Abraham Lincoln and offered him the party's presidential nomination on the condition that he pull off a flashy victory over the red men before the national convention in Chicago in July.

On February 19, 1876, the Boy General's brother Thomas, commander of Troop C of the 7th, climbed into the observer's cockpit behind Lieutenant James C. Sturgis and took off on a routine patrol. Their aeroplane, a Whitney pushertype, did not return. Ten days later its wreckage was found sixty miles west of Fort Lincoln. Apparently, Sturgis and Tom Custer had stumbled on a party of mounted hostiles and, swooping low to fire or drop a handbomb, suffered a lucky hit from one of the Indians' firearms. The mutilated remains of the two officers were found a quarter mile from the wreckage, indicating that they had escaped on foot after the crash but were caught.

The shock of his brother's death, combined with the Democrat's offer, were to lead Lieutenant Colonel G. A. Custer into the worst defeat suffered by an officer of the United States Army.

Throughout the first part of 1876, Indians drifted into Wyoming Territory from the east and south, driven by mounting pressure from the Army. Raids on small Indian villages had been stepped up. Waning herds of buffalo were being systematically strafed by the airships. General Phil Sheridan received reports of tribes gathering in the vicinity of the Wolf Mountains, in what is now southern Montana, and devised a strategy by which the hostiles would be crushed for all time.

Three columns were to converge upon the amassed Indians from the north, south, and east, the west being blocked by the Wolf Mountains. General George Crook's dirigibles, light tanks, and infantry were to come up the Rosebud River. General Alfred Terry would push from the northeast with infantry, cavalry, and field artillery. The 7th Cavalry was to move from the east. The Indians could not escape.

Commanded by Captain Keogh, Troops A, C, D, E, F, G, and H

of the 7th—about 580 men, not counting civilian teamsters, interpreters, Crow and Arikara scouts—set out from Fort Lincoln five weeks ahead of the July 1 rendezvous at the junction of the Big Horn and Little Big Horn rivers. A month later, Custer and 150 balloon infantrymen aboard the airships *Franklin, Adams, Hancock,* and *Allen* set out on Keogh's trail.

Everything went wrong from that point onward.

The early summer of 1876 had been particularly hot and dry in Wyoming Territory. Crook, proceeding up the Rosebud, was slowed by the tanks, which theoretically traveled at five miles per hour but which kept breaking down from the heat and from the alkaline dust which worked its way into the engines through chinks in the three-inch armor plate. The crews roasted. On June 13, as Crook's column halted beside the Rosebud to let the tanks cool off, six monoplanes dived out of the clouds to attack the escorting airships *Paul Revere* and *John Paul Jones.* Caught by surprise, the two dirigibles were blown up and fell about five miles from Crook's position. The infantrymen watched, astonished, as the Indian aeronauts turned their craft toward them. While the foot soldiers ran for cover, several hundred mounted Sioux warriors showed up. In the ensuing rout, Crook lost forty-seven men and all his armored vehicles. He was still in headlong retreat when the Indians broke off their chase at nightfall.

The 7th Cavalry and the 505th Balloon Infantry linked up by liaison craft carried by the *Ethan Allen* some miles southeast of the hostile camp on the Little Big Horn on the evening of June 24. Neither they, nor Terry's column, had received word of Crook's retreat, but Keogh's scouts had sighted a large village ahead.

Custer did not know that this village contained not the five or six hundred Indians expected, but between eight and ten *thousand,* of whom slightly less than half were warriors. Spurred by his desire for revenge for his brother Tom, and filled with glory at the thought of the Democratic presidential nomination, Custer decided to hit the Indians before either Crook's or Terry's columns could reach the village. He settled on a scaled-down version of Sheridan's tri-pronged movement, and dispatched Keogh to the south, Reno to the east, with himself and the 505th attacking from the north. A small column was to wait downriver with the pack train. On the evening of June 24, George Armstrong Custer waited, secure in the knowledge that he, personally, would deal the Plains Indians their mortal blow within a mere twenty-four hours.

Unfortunately, the Indians amassed on the banks of the Little Big Horn—Oglalas, Minneconjous, Arapaho, Hunkpapas, Blackfeet, Cheyenne, and so forth—had the idea that white men were on the way. During the Sun Dance Ceremony the week before, the Hunkpapa chief Sitting Bull had had a dream about soldiers falling into his camp. The hostiles, assured of victory, waited.

On the morning of June 25, the *Benjamin Franklin, Samuel Adams, John Hancock,* and *Ethan Allen* drifted quietly over the hills toward the village. They were looping south when the Indians attacked.

Struck by several spin-stabilized rockets, the *Samuel Adams* blew up with a flash that might have been seen by the officers and men riding behind Captain Keogh up the valley of the Little Big Horn. Eight or twelve Indians had, in the gray dawn, climbed for altitude above the ships.

Still several miles short of their intended drop zone, the balloon infantrymen piled out of the burning and exploding craft. Though each ship was armed with two Gatling rifles fore and aft, the airships were helpless against the aeroplanes' bullets and rockets. Approximately one hundred men, Custer included, cleared the ships. The Indian aviators made passes through them, no doubt killing several in the air. The *Franklin* and *Hancock* burned and fell to the earth across the river from the village. The *Allen,* dumping water ballast to gain altitude, turned for the Wolf Mountains. Though riddled by machine rifle fire, it did not explode and settled to earth about fifteen miles from where now raged a full-scale battle between increasingly demoralized soldiers and battle-maddened Sioux and Cheyenne.

Major Reno had charged the opposite side of the village as soon as he heard the commotion. Wrote one of his officers later: "A solid wall of Indians came out of the haze which had hidden the village from our eyes. They must have outnumbered us ten to one, and they were ready for us. . . . Fully a third of the column was down in three minutes."

Reno, fearing he would be swallowed up, pulled his men back across the river and took up a position in a stand of timber on the riverward slope of the knoll. The Indians left a few hundred braves to make certain Reno did not escape and moved off to Reno's right to descend on Keogh's flank.

The hundred-odd parachute infantrymen who made good their escape from the airship were scattered over three square miles. The ravines and gullies cutting up the hills around the village quickly filled with mounted Indians who rode through unimpeded by the random fire of disorganized balloon infantrymen. They swept them up, on the way to Keogh. Keogh, unaware of the number of Indians and the rout of Reno's command, got as far as the north bank of the river before he was ground to pieces between two masses of hostiles. Of Keogh's command, less than a dozen escaped the slaughter. The actual battle lasted about thirty minutes.

The hostiles left the area that night, exhausted after their greatest victory over the soldiers. Most of the Indians went north to Canada; some escaped the mass extermination of their race which was to take place in the American West during the next six years.

Terry found Reno entrenched on the ridge the morning of the twenty-seventh. The scouts sent to find Custer and Keogh could not believe their eyes when they found the bodies of the 7th Cavalry six miles away.

Some of the men were not found for another two days. Terry and his men scoured the ravines and valleys. Custer himself was about four miles from the site of Keogh's annihilation; the Boy General appears to have been hit by a piece of exploding rocket shrapnel and may have been dead before he reached the ground. His body escaped the mutilation that befell most of Keogh's command, possibly because of its distance from the camp.

Custer's miscalculation cost the Army 430 men, four dirigibles (plus the Studebaker scout from the *Ethan Allen*), and its prestige. An attempt was made to make a scapegoat of Major Reno, blaming his alleged cowardice for the failure of the 7th. Though Reno was acquitted, grumblings continued up until the turn of the century. It is hoped the matter will be settled for all time by the opening, for private research, of the papers of the late President Phil Sheridan. As Commander in Chief, he had access to a mountain of material which was kept from the public at the time of the court of inquiry in 1879.

Extract from *Huckleberry Among the Hostiles: A Journal*
By Mark Twain, Edited By Bernard Van Dyne
Hutton and Company, New York, 1932.

EDITOR'S NOTE: In November 1886 Clemens drafted a tentative outline for a sequel to *The Adventures of Huckleberry Finn,* which had received mixed reviews on its publication in January 1885, but which had nonetheless enjoyed a second printing within five months of its release. The proposed sequel was intended to deal with Huckleberry's adventures as a young man on the frontier. To gather research material firsthand, Mark boarded the airship *Peyton* in Cincinnati, Ohio, in mid-December 1886, and set out across the Southwest, amassing copious notes and reams of interviews with soldiers, frontiersmen, law enforcement officers, ex-hostiles, at least two notorious outlaws, and a number of less readily categorized persons. Twain had intended to spend four months out West. Unfortunately, his wife, Livy, fell gravely ill in late February 1887; Twain returned to her as soon as he received word in Fort Hood, Texas. He lost interest in all writing for two years after her death in April 1887. The proposed novel about Huckleberry Finn as a man was never written: we are left with 110,000 words of interviews and observations and an incomplete journal of the author's second trek across the American West.— BvD

February 2: A more desolate place than the Indian Territory of Oklahoma would be impossible to imagine. It is flat the year 'round, stingingly cold in winter, hot and dry, I am told, during the summer (when the land turns brown save for scattered patches of greenery which serve only to make the landscape all the drearier; Arizona and New Mexico are devoid of greenery, which is to their credit—when those territories elected to become barren wastelands they did not lose heart halfway, but followed their chosen course to the end).

It is easy to see why the United States Government swept the few Indians into God-forsaken Oklahoma and ordered them to remain there under threat of extermination. The word "God-forsaken" is the vital clue. The white men who "gave" this land to the few remaining tribes for as long as the wind shall blow—which it certainly does in February—and the grass shall grow (which it does, in Missouri, perhaps) were Christians who knew better than to let heathen savages run loose in parts of the country still smiled upon by our heavenly malefactor.

February 4: Whatever I may have observed about Oklahoma from the cabin of the *Peyton* has been reinforced by a view from the ground. The airship was running into stiff winds from the north, so we put in at Fort Sill yesterday evening and are awaiting calmer weather. I have gone on with my work.

Fort Sill is located seventeen miles from the Cheyenne Indian reservation. It has taken me all of a day to learn (mainly from one Sergeant Howard, a gap-toothed, unwashed Texan who is apparently my unofficial guardian angel for whatever length of time I am to be marooned here) that the Cheyenne do not care much for Oklahoma, which is still another reason why the government keeps them there. One or two ex-hostiles will leave the reservation every month, taking with them their wives and meager belongings, and Major Rickards will have to send out a detachment of soldiers to haul the erring ones back, either in chains or over the backs of horses. I am told the reservation becomes particularly annoying in the winter months, as the poor boys who are detailed to pursue the Indians suffer greatly from the cold. At this, I remarked to Sergeant Howard that the Red Man can be terribly inconsiderate, even ungrateful, in view of all the blessings the white man has heaped upon him—smallpox, and that French disease, to name two. The good sergeant scratched his head and grinned, and said, "You're right, sir."

I'll have to make Howard a character in the book.

February 5: Today, I was taken by Major Rickards to meet a Cheyenne named Black Man's Hand, one of the participants of the alleged massacre of the 7th Cavalry at the Little Big Horn River in '76. The major had this one Cheyenne brought in after a recent departure from the reservation. Black Man's Hand had been shackled and left to dwell upon his past misdeeds in an unheated hut at the edge of the airport, while two cold-benumbed privates stood on guard before the door. It was evidently feared this one savage would, if left unchained, do to Fort Sill that which he (with a modicum of assistance from four or five thousand of his race) had done to Custer. I nevertheless mentioned to Rickards that I was interested in talking to Black Man's Hand, as the Battle of the Little Big Horn would perfectly climax Huckleberry's adventures in the new book. Rickards was reluctant to grant permission but gave in abruptly, perhaps fearing I would model a villain after him.

Upon entering the hut where the Cheyenne sat, I asked Major Rickards if it were possible to have the Indian's manacles removed, as it makes me nervous to talk to a man who can rattle his chains at me whenever he chooses. Major Rickards said no and troubled himself to explain to me the need for limiting the movement of this specimen of ferocity within the walls of Fort Sill.

With a sigh, I seated myself across from Black Man's Hand and offered him one of my cigars. He accepted it with a faint smile. He appeared to be in his forties, though his face was deeply lined.

He was dressed in ragged leather leggings, thick calf-length woolen pajamas, and a faded Army jacket. His vest appears to have been fashioned from an old parachute harness. He had no hat, no footgear, and no blanket.

"Major Rickards," I said, "this man is freezing to death. Even if he isn't, I am. Can you provide this hut with a little warmth?"

The fretting major summarily dispatched one of the sentries for firewood and kindling for the little stove sitting uselessly in the corner of the hut.

I would have been altogether comfortable after that could I have had a decanter of brandy with which to force out the inner chill. But Indians are notoriously incapable of holding liquor, and I did not wish to be the cause of this poor wretch's further downfall.

Black Man's Hand speaks surprisingly good English. I spent an hour and a half with him, recording his remarks with as much attention paid to accuracy as my advanced years and cold fingers permitted. With luck, I'll be able to fill some gaps in his story before the *Peyton* resumes its flight across this griddlecake countryside.

> Extract from *The Testament of Black Man's Hand.*
> [*NOTE:* For the sake of easier reading, I have substituted a number of English terms for these provided by the Cheyenne Black Man's Hand.—MT]

I was young when I first met the Oglala mystic Crazy Horse, and was taught by him to fly the Thunderbirds which the one called the Gray White Man had given him. [The Gray White Man—John S. Moseby, Major, CSAAC—MT.] Some of the older men among the People [as the Cheyenne call themselves, Major Rickards explains; I assured him that such egocentricity is by no means restricted to savages—MT] did not think much of the flying machines and said, "How will we be able to remain brave men when this would enable us to fly over the heads of our enemies, without counting coup or taking trophies?"

But the Oglala said, "The Gray White Man has asked us to help him."

"Why should we help him?" asked Two Pines.

"Because he fights the blueshirts and those who persecute us. We have known for many years that the men who cheated us and lied to us and killed our women and the buffalo are men without honor, cowards who fight only because there is no other way for them to get what they want. They cannot understand why we fight with the Crows and Pawnees—to be brave, to win honor for ourselves. They fight because it is a means to an end, and they fight us only because we have what they want. The blueshirts want to kill us all. They fight to win. If we are to fight them, we must fight with their own weapons. We must fight to win."

The older warriors shook their heads sorrowfully and spoke of younger days when they fought the Pawnees bravely, honorably, man-to-man. But I and several other young men wanted to learn how to control the Thunderbirds. And we knew Crazy Horse spoke the truth, that our lives would never be happy as long as there were white men in the world. Finally, because they could not forbid us to go with the Oglala, only advise against it and say that the Great Mystery had not intended us to fly, Red Horse and I and some others went with Crazy Horse. I did not see my village again, not even at the big camp on the Greasy Grass [Little Big Horn—MT] where we rubbed out Yellow Hair. I think perhaps the blueshirts came after I was gone and told Two Pines that he had to leave his home and come to this flat dead place.

The Oglala Crazy Horse taught us to fly the Thunderbirds. We learned a great many things about the Gray White Man's machines. With them, we killed Yellowleg flyers. Soon, I tired of the waiting and the hunger. We were raided once. It was a good fight. In the dark, we chased the Big Fish [the Indian word for dirigibles—MT] and killed many men on the ground.

I do not remember all of what happened those seasons. When

we were finally chased away from the landing place, Crazy Horse had us hide the Thunderbirds in the Black Hills. I have heard the Yellowlegs did not know we had the Thunderbirds; that they thought they were run by the gray white men only. It did not matter; we thought we had used them for the last time.

Many seasons later, we heard what happened to Black Kettle's village. I went to the place sometime after the battle. I heard that Crazy Horse had been there and seen the place. I looked for him but he had gone north again. Black Kettle had been a treaty man: we talked among ourselves that the Yellowlegs had no honor.

It was the winter I was sick [1872. The Plains Indians and the U.S. Army alike were plagued that winter by what we would call the influenza. It was probably brought by some itinerant French trapper—MT] that I heard of Crazy Horse's raid on the landing place of the Big Fish. It was news of this that told us we must prepare to fight the Yellowlegs.

When I was well, my wives and I and Eagle Hawk's band went looking for Crazy Horse. We found him in the fall. Already, the Army had killed many Sioux and Cheyenne that summer. Crazy Horse said we must band together, we who knew how to fly the Thunderbirds. He said we would someday have to fight the Yellowlegs among the clouds as in the old days. We only had five Thunderbirds which had not been flown many seasons. We spent the summer planning to get more. Red Chief and Yellow Dog gathered a large band. We raided the Fort Kearny and stole many Thunderbirds and canisters of powder. We hid them in the Black Hills. It had been a good fight.

It was at this time Yellow Hair sent out many soldiers to protect the miners he had brought in by speaking false. They destroyed the sacred lands of the Sioux. We killed some of them, and the Yellowlegs burned many of our villages. That was not a good time. The Big Fish killed many of our people.

We wanted to get the Thunderbirds and kill the Big Fish. Crazy Horse had us wait. He had been talking to Sitting Bull, the Hunkpapa chief. Sitting Bull said we should not go against the Yellowlegs yet, that we could only kill a few at a time. Later, he said, they would all come. That would be the good day to die.

The next year, they came. We did not know until just before the Sun Dance [about June 10, 1876—MT] that they were coming. Crazy Horse and I and all those who flew the Thunderbirds went to get ours. It took us two days to get them going again, and we had only six Thunderbirds flying when we flew to stop the blueshirts. Crazy Horse, Yellow Dog, American Gun, Little Wolf, Big Tall, and I flew that day. It was a good fight. We killed two Big Fish and many men and horses. We stopped the Turtles-which-kill [that would be the light armored cars Crook had with him on the Rosebud River—MT] so they could not come toward the Greasy Grass where we camped. The Sioux under Spotted Pony killed more on the ground. We flew back and hid the Thunderbirds near camp.

When we returned, we told Sitting Bull of our victory. He said it was good, but that a bigger victory was to come. He said he had had a vision during the Sun Dance. He saw many soldiers and enemy Indians fall out of the sky on their heads into the village. He said ours was not the victory he had seen.

It was some days later we heard that a Yellowlegs Thunderbird had been shot down. We went to the place where it lay. There was a strange device above its wing. Crazy Horse studied it many moments. Then he said, "I have seen such a thing before. It carries Thunderbirds beneath one of the Big Fish. We must get our Thunderbirds. It will be a good day to die."

We hurried to our Thunderbirds. We had twelve of them fixed now, and we had on them, besides the quick rifles [Henry machine rifles of calibers .41−40 or .30−30—MT], the roaring spears [Hale spin-stabilized rockets, of two-and-a-half-inch diameter—MT]. We took off before noonday.

We arrived at the Greasy Grass and climbed into the clouds, where we scouted. Soon, to the south, we saw the dust of many men moving. But Crazy Horse held us back. Soon we saw why; four Big Fish were coming. We came at them out of the sun. They did not see us till we were on them. We fired our roaring sticks, and the Big Fish caught fire and burned. All except one, which drifted away, though it lost all its fat. Wild Horse, in his Thunderbird, was shot but still fought on with us that morning. We began to kill the men on the Big Fish when a new thing happened. Men began to float down on blankets. We began to kill them as they fell with our quick rifles. Then we attacked those who reached the ground, until we saw Spotted Pony and his men were on them. We turned south and killed many horse soldiers there. Then we flew back to the Greasy Grass and hid the Thunderbirds. At camp, we learned that many pony soldiers had been killed. Word came that more soldiers were coming.

I saw, as the sun went down, the women moving among the dead Men-Who-Float-Down, taking their clothes and supplies. They covered the ground like leaves in the autumn. It had been a good fight.

Extract From *The Seventh Cavalry: A History*
—E. R. Burroughs
Colonel, U.S.A., Retired

So much has been written about that hot June day in 1876, so much guesswork applied where knowledge was missing. Was Custer dead in his harness before he reached the ground? Or did he stand and fire at the aircraft strafing his men? How many reached the ground alive? Did any escape the battle itself, only to be killed by Indian patrols later that afternoon, or the next day? No one really knows, and all the Indians are gone now, so history stands a blank.

Only one thing is certain: for the men of the 7th Cavalry there was only the reality of the exploding dirigibles, the snap of their chutes deploying, the roar of the aircraft among them, the bullets, and those terrible last moments on the bluff. Whatever the verdict of their peers, whatever the future may reveal, it can be said they did not die in vain.

Suggested Reading

Anonymous. *Remember Ft. Sumter!* Washington: War Department Recruiting Pamphlet, 1862.
————. *Leviathans of the Skies.* Goodyear Publications, 1923.
————. *The Dirigible in War and Peace.* Goodyear Publications, 1911.
————. *Sitting Bull, Killer of Custer.* G. E. Putnam's, 1903.
————. *Comanche of the Seventh.* Chicago: Military Press, 1879.
————. *Thomas Edison and the Indian Wars.* Menlo Park, N.J.: Edison Press, 1921.
————. "Fearful Slaughter at Big Horn." New York: *Herald-Times,* July 8, 1876, *et passim.*
————. *Custer's Gold Hoax.* Boston: Barnum Press, 1892.
————. "Reno's Treachery: New Light on the Massacre at The Little Big Horn." Chicago: *Daily News-Mirror,* June 12–19, 1878.

————. "Grant Scandals and the Plains Indian Wars." *Life,* May 3, 1921.

————. *The Hunkpapa Chief Sitting Bull,* Famous Indians Series #3. New York: 1937.

Arnold, Henry H. *The Air War in the East,* Smithsonian Annals of Flight, Vol. 38. Four books, 1932–1937.
  1. *Sumter to Bull Run*
  2. *Williamsburg to Second Manassas*
  3. *Gettysburg to the Wilderness*
  5. *The Bombing of Atlanta to Haldeman*

Ballows, Edward. *The Indian Ace: Crazy Horse.* G. E. Putnam's, 1903.

Benteen, Capt. Frederick. *Major Benteen's Letters to his Wife.* University of Oklahoma Press, 1921.

Brininstool, A. E. *A Paratrooper with Custer.* n.p.g., 1891.

Burroughs, Col. E. R. retired. *The Seventh Cavalry: A History.* Chicago: 1931.

Clair-Britner, Edoard. *Haldeman: Where the War Ended.* Frankfort University Press, 1911.

Crook, General George C. *Yellowhair: Custer as the Indians Knew Him.* Cincinnati Press, 1882.

Custer, George A. *My Life on the Plains and in the Clouds.* Chicago: 1874.

———— and Custer, Elizabeth. *'Chutes and Saddles.* Chicago: 1876.

Custer's Luck, n.a, n.p.g., [1891].

De Camp, L. Sprague and Pratt, Fletcher. *Franklin's Engine: Mover of the World.* Hanover House, 1939.

De Voto, Bernard. *The Road from Sumter.* Scribners, 1931.

Elsee, D. V. *The Last Raid of Crazy Horse.* Random House, 1921.

The 505th: History from the Skies. DA Pamphlet 870–10–3 GPO Pittsburgh, May 12, 1903.

FM 23–13–2 Machine Rifle M3121A1 and M3121A1E1 Cal. .41–40 Operator's Manual, DA FM, July 12, 1873.

Goddard, Robert H. *Rocketry: From 400 B.C. to 1933.* Smithsonian Annals of Flight, Vol. 31, GPO Pittsburgh, 1934.

Guide to the Custer Battlefield National Monument. U.S. Parks Services, GPO Pittsburgh, 1937.

The Indian Wars. 3 vols. GPO Pittsburgh, 1898.

Kalin, David. *Hook Up! The Story of the Balloon Infantry.* New York: 1932.

Kellogg, Mark W. *The Drop at Washita.* Chicago: *Times Press,* 1872.

Lockridge, Sgt. Robert. *History of the Airborne: From Shiloh to Ft. Bragg.* Chicago: Military Press, 1936.

Lowe, Thaddeus C. *Aircraft of the Civil War.* 4 vols. 1891–1896.

McCoy, Col. Tim. *The Vanished American.* Phoenix Press, 1934.

McGovern, Maj. William. *Death in the Dakotas.* Sioux Press, 1889.

Morison, Samuel Eliot. *France in the New World 1627–1864.* 1931.

Myren, Gundal. *The Sun Dance Ritual and the Last Indian Wars.* 1901.

Patton, Gen. George C. *Custer's Last Campaigns.* Military House, 1937.

Paul, Winston. *We Were There at the Bombing of Ft. Sumter.* Landmark Books, 1929.

Payley, David. *Where Custer Fell.* New York Press, 1931.

Powell, Maj. John Wesley. *Report on the Arid Lands.* GPO, 1881.

Proceedings, Reno Court of Inquiry. GPO Pittsburgh, 1881.

Report on the U.S.-Canadian Offensive Against Sitting Bull, 1879. GPO Pittsburgh, War Department, 1880.

Sandburg, Carl. *Mr. Lincoln's Airmen.* Chicago: Driftwind Press, 1921.

Settle, Sgt. Maj. Winslow. *Under the Crossed Sabers.* Military Press, 1898.

Sheridan, Gen. Phillip. *The Only Good Indian. . . .* Military House, 1889.

Singleton, William Warren. *J.E.B. Stuart, Attila of the Skies.* Boston, 1871.

Smith, Gregory. *The Gray White Man: Moseby's Expedition to the Northwest 1863–1866.* University of Oklahoma Press. 1921.

Smith, Neldoo. *He Gave Them Wings: Captain Smith's Journal 1861–1864.* Urbana: University of Illinois Press, 1927.

Steen, Nelson. *Opening of the West.* Jim Bridger Press, 1902.

Tapscott, Richard D. *He Came with the Comet.* University of Illinois Press, 1927.

Twain, Mark. *Huckleberry Among the Hostiles: A Journal.* Hutton Books, 1932.

Predictions are always chancy things —nevertheless, I will go out on a limb here, in cold long-lasting type, and make a flat-out prediction: within five years (and probably a lot sooner) John Varley will be one of the biggest names in SF and almost certainly will have collected at least one Nebula and/or Hugo Award.

Varley burst suddenly into view in 1975 with a handful of brilliant stories (one of them, "In the Bowl," is a finalist for the 1976 Nebula Award). It would not have been surprising if 1976 had turned out to be anti-climatic for him —instead, he had an even better year, turning out a seemingly endless stream of first-rate fiction and establishing beyond a doubt that his first few stories had not been flukes. Here, obviously, is a talent in the making, as clearly recognizable as Delany and Niven and Zelazny and Tiptree had been.

Born in Texas, Varley now lives in Eugene, Oregon, with his wife, Anet Mconel, and their three children. Since he started writing in 1973, he has sold over twenty stories, plus a novel, Ophiuchi Hotline, *and a collection,* Overdrawn at the Memory Bank, *both forthcoming from Dial Press and Dell.*

There were many fine Varley stories this year to choose from, but I finally settled on a piece from Isaac Asimov's Science Fiction Magazine *(where it was published under the pseudonym of "Herb Boehm")—a jazzy, jolting, and scary story that goes straight for the jugular.*

JOHN VARLEY
Air Raid

I was jerked awake by the silent alarm vibrating my skull. It won't shut down until you sit up, so I did. All around me in the darkened bunkroom the Snatch Team members were sleeping singly and in pairs. I yawned, scratched my ribs, and patted Gene's hairy flank. He turned over. So much for a romantic send-off.

Rubbing sleep from my eyes, I reached to the floor for my leg, strapped it on, and plugged it in. Then I was running down the rows of bunks toward Ops.

The situation board glowed in the gloom. Sun-Belt Airlines Flight 128, Miami to New York, September 15, 1979. We'd been looking for that one for three years. I should have been happy, but who can afford it when you wake up?

Liza Boston muttered past me on the way to Prep. I muttered back, and followed. The lights came on around the mirrors, and I groped my way to one of them. Behind us, three more people staggered in. I sat down, plugged in, and at last I could lean back and close my eyes.

They didn't stay closed for long. Rush! I sat up straight as the sludge I use for blood was replaced with supercharged go-juice. I looked around me and got a series of idiot grins. There was Liza, and Pinky, and Dave. Against the far wall Cristabel was already turning slowly in front of the airbrush, getting a caucasian paint job. It looked like a good team.

I opened the drawer and started preliminary work on my face. It's a bigger job every time. Transfusion or no, I looked like death. The right ear was completely gone now. I could no longer close my lips; the gums were permanently bared. A week earlier, a finger had fallen off in my sleep. And what's it to you, bugger?

While I worked, one of the screens around the mirror glowed. A smiling young woman, blonde, high brow, round face. Close enough. The crawl line read *Mary Katrina Sondergard, born Trenton, New Jersey, age in 1979: 25.* Baby, this is your lucky day.

The computer melted the skin away from her face to show me the bone structure, rotated it, gave me cross-sections. I studied the similarities with my own skull, noted the differences. Not bad, and better than some I'd been given.

I assembled a set of dentures that included the slight gap in the upper incisors. Putty filled out my cheeks. Contact lenses fell from the dispenser and I popped them in. Nose plugs widened my nostrils. No need for ears; they'd be covered by the wig. I pulled a blank plastiflesh mask over my face and had to pause while it melted in. It took only a minute to mold it to perfection. I smiled at myself. How nice to have lips.

The delivery slot clunked and dropped a blonde wig and a pink outfit into my lap. The wig was hot from the styler. I put it on, then the pantyhose.

"Mandy? Did you get the profile on Sondergard?" I didn't look up; I recognized the voice.

"Roger."

"We've located her near the airport. We can slip you in before takeoff, so you'll be the joker."

I groaned, and looked up at the face on the screen. Elfreda Baltimore-Louisville, Director of Operational Teams: lifeless face and tiny slits for eyes. What can you do when all the muscles are dead?

"Okay." You take what you get.

She switched off, and I spent the next two minutes trying to get dressed while keeping my eyes on the screens. I memorized names and faces of crew members plus the few facts known about them. Then I hurried out and caught up with the others. Elapsed time from first alarm: twelve minutes and seven seconds. We'd better get moving.

"Goddam Sun-Belt," Cristabel groused, hitching at her bra.

"At least they got rid of the high heels," Dave pointed out. A year earlier we would have been teetering down the aisles on three-inch platforms. We all wore short pink shifts with blue and white stripes diagonally across the front and carried matching shoulder bags. I fussed trying to get the ridiculous pillbox cap pinned on.

We jogged into the dark Operations Control Room and lined up at the gate. Things were out of our hands now. Until the gate was ready, we could only wait.

I was first, a few feet away from the portal. I turned away from it; it gives me vertigo. I focused instead on the gnomes sitting at their consoles, bathed in yellow lights from their screens. None of them looked back at me. They don't like us much. I don't like them, either. Withered, emaciated, all of them. Our fat legs and butts and breasts are a reproach to them, a reminder that Snatchers eat five times their ration to stay presentable for the masquerade. Meantime we continue to rot. One day I'll be sitting at a console. One day I'll be *built in* to a console, with all my guts on the outside and nothing left of my body but stink. The hell with them.

I buried my gun under a clutter of tissues and lipsticks in my purse. Elfreda was looking at me.

"Where is she?" I asked.

"Motel room. She was alone from 10 P.M. to noon on flight day."

Departure time was 1:15. She cut it close and would be in a hurry. Good.

"Can you catch her in the bathroom? Best of all, in the tub?"

"We're working on it." She sketched a smile with a fingertip drawn over lifeless lips. She knew how I like to operate, but she was telling me I'd take what I got. It never hurts to ask. People are at their most defenseless stretched out and up to their necks in water.

"Go!" Elfreda shouted. I stepped through, and things started to go wrong.

I was faced the wrong way, stepping *out* of the bathroom door and facing the bedroom. I turned and spotted Mary Katrina Sondergard through the haze of the gate. There was no way I could reach her without stepping back through. I couldn't even shoot without hitting someone on the other side.

Sondergard was at the mirror, the worst possible place. Few people recognize themselves quickly, but she'd been looking right at herself. She saw me and her eyes widened. I stepped to the side, out of her sight.

"What the hell is...hey! Who the hell...?" I noted the voice, which can be the trickiest thing to get right.

I figured she'd be more curious than afraid. My guess was right. She came out of the bathroom, passing through the gate as if it wasn't there, which it wasn't, since it only has one side. She had a towel wrapped around her.

"Jesus Christ! What are you doing in my—?" Words fail you at a time like that. She knew she ought to say something, but what? *Excuse me, haven't I seen you in the mirror?*

I put on my best stew smile and held out my hand.

"Pardon the intrusion. I can explain everything. You see, I'm—" I hit her on the side of the head and she staggered and went down hard. Her towel fell to the floor; "—working my way through college." She started to get up, so I caught her under the chin with my artificial knee. She stayed down.

"Standard fuggin' *oil!*" I hissed, rubbing my injured knuckles. But there was no time. I knelt beside her, checked her pulse. She'd be okay, but I think I loosened some front teeth. I paused a moment. Lord, to look like that with no make-up, no prosthetics! She nearly broke my heart.

I grabbed her under the knees and wrestled her to the gate. She was a sack of limp noodles. Somebody reached through, grabbed her feet, and pulled. *So long, love! How would you like to go on a long voyage?*

I sat on her rented bed to get my breath. There were car keys and cigarettes in her purse, genuine tobacco, worth its weight in blood. I lit six of them, figuring I had five minutes of my very own. The room filled with sweet smoke. They don't make 'em like that anymore.

The Hertz sedan was in the motel parking lot. I got in and headed for the airport. I breathed deeply of the air, rich in hydrocarbons. I could see for hundreds of yards into the distance. The perspective nearly made me dizzy, but I live for those moments. There's no way to explain what it's like in the pre-meck world. The sun was a fierce yellow ball through the haze.

The other stews were boarding. Some of them knew Sondergard so I didn't say much, pleading a hangover. That went over well, with a lot of knowing laughs and sly remarks. Evidently it wasn't out of character. We boarded the 707 and got ready for the goats to arrive.

It looked good. The four commandos on the other side were identical twins for the women I was working with. There was nothing to do but be a stewardess until departure time. I hoped there would be no more glitches. Inverting a gate for a joker run into a motel room was one thing, but in a 707 at 20,000 feet. . .

The plane was nearly full when the woman that Pinky would impersonate sealed the forward door. We taxied to the end of the runway, then we were airborne. I started taking orders for drinks in first.

The goats were the usual lot, for 1979. Fat and sassy, all of them, and as unaware of living in a paradise as a fish is of the sea. *What would you think, ladies and gents, of a trip to the future? No? I can't say I'm surprised. What if I told you this plane is going to− ?*

My alarm beeped as we reached cruising altitude. I consulted the indicator under my Lady Bulova and glanced at one of the restroom doors. I felt a vibration pass through the plane. *Damn it, not so soon.*

The gate was in there. I came out quickly, and motioned for Diana Gleason—Dave's pigeon—to come to the front.

"Take a look at this," I said, with a disgusted look. She started to enter the restroom, stopped when she saw the green glow. I planted a boot on her fanny and shoved. Perfect. Dave would have a chance to hear her voice before popping in. Though she'd be doing little but screaming when she got a look around. . .

Dave came through the gate, adjusting his silly little hat. Diana must have struggled.

"Be disgusted," I whispered.

"What a mess," he said as he came out of the restroom. It was a fair imitation of Diana's tone, though he'd missed the accent. It wouldn't matter much longer.

"What is it?" It was one of the stews from tourist. We stepped aside so she could get a look, and Dave shoved her through. Pinky popped out very quickly.

"We're minus on minutes," Pinky said. "We lost five on the other side."

"Five?" Dave-Diana squeaked. I felt the same way. We had a hundred and three passengers to process.

"Yeah. They lost contact after you pushed my pigeon through. It took that long to re-align."

You get used to that. Time runs at different rates on each side of the gate, though it's always sequential, past to future. Once we'd started the snatch with me entering Sondergard's room, there was no way to go back any earlier on either side. Here, in 1979, we had a rigid ninety-four minutes to get everything done. On the other side, the gate could never be maintained longer than three hours.

"When you left, how long was it since the alarm went in?"

"Twenty-eight minutes."

It didn't sound good. It would take at least two hours just customizing the wimps. Assuming there was no more slippage on '79-time, we might just make it. But there's *always* slippage. I shuddered, thinking about riding it in.

"No time for any more games, then," I said. "Pink, you go back to tourist and call both of the other girls up here. Tell 'em to come one at a time, and tell 'em we've got a problem. You know the bit."

"Biting back the tears. Got you." She hurried aft. In no time the first one showed up. Her friendly Sun-Belt Airlines smile was stamped on her face, but her stomach would be churning. *Oh God, this is it!*

I took her by the elbow and pulled her behind the curtains in front. She was breathing hard.

"Welcome to the twilight zone," I said, and put the gun to her head. She slumped, and I caught her. Pinky and Dave helped me shove her through the gate.

"Fug! The rotting thing's flickering."

Pinky was right. A very ominous sign. But the green glow stabilized as we watched, with who-knows-how-much slippage on the other side. Cristabel ducked through.

"We're plus thirty-three," she said. There was no sense talking about what we were all thinking: things were going badly.

"Back to tourist," I said. "Be brave, smile at everyone, but make it just a little bit too good, got it?"

"Check," Cristabel said.

We processed the other quickly, with no incident. Then there was no time to talk about anything. In eighty-nine minutes Flight 128 was going to be spread all over a mountain whether we were finished or not.

Dave went into the cockpit to keep the flight crew out of our hair. Me and Pinky were supposed to take care of first class, then back up Cristabel and Liza in tourist. We used the standard "coffee, tea, or milk" gambit, relying on our speed and their inertia.

I leaned over the first two seats on the left.

"Are you enjoying your flight?" Pop, pop. Two squeezes on the trigger, close to the heads and out of sight of the rest of the goats.

"Hi, folks. I'm Mandy. Fly me." Pop, pop.

Half-way to the galley, a few people were watching us curiously. But people don't make a fuss until they have a lot more to go on. One goat in the back row stood up, and I let him have it. By now there were only eight left awake. I abandoned the smile and squeezed off four quick shots. Pinky took care of the rest. We hurried through the curtains, just in time.

There was an uproar building in the back of tourist, with about sixty percent of the goats already processed. Cristabel glanced at me, and I nodded.

"Okay, folks," she bawled. "I want you to be quiet. Calm down and listen up. *You*, fathead, *pipe down* before I cram my foot up your ass sideways."

The shock of hearing her talk like that was enough to buy us a little time, anyway. We had formed a skirmish line across the width of the plane, guns out, steadied on seat backs, aimed at the milling, befuddled group of thirty goats.

The guns are enough to awe all but the most foolhardy. In essence, a standard-issue stunner is just a plastic rod with two grids about six inches apart. There's not enough metal in it to set off a hijack alarm. And to people from the Stone Age to about 2190 it doesn't look any more like a weapon than a ball-point pen. So Equipment Section jazzes them up in a plastic shell to real Buck Rogers blasters, with a dozen knobs and lights that flash and a barrel like the snout of a hog. Hardly anyone ever walks into one.

"We are in great danger, and time is short. You must all do exactly as I tell you, and you will be safe."

You can't give them time to think, you have to rely on your status as the Voice of Authority. The situation is just *not* going to make sense to them, no matter how you explain it.

"Just a minute, I think you owe us—"

An airborne lawyer. I made a snap decision, thumbed the fireworks switch on my gun, and shot him.

The gun made a sound like a flying saucer with hemorrhoids, spit sparks and little jets of flame, and extended a green laser finger to his forehead. He dropped.

All pure kark, of course. But it sure is impressive.

And it's damn risky, too. I had to choose between a panic if the fathead got them to thinking, and a possible panic from the flash of the gun. But when a 20th gets to talking about his "rights" and what he is "owed," things can get out of hand. It's infectious.

It worked. There was a lot of shouting, people ducking behind seats, but no rush. We could have handled it, but we needed some of them conscious if we were ever going to finish the snatch.

"Get up. Get *up*, you *slugs!*" Cristabel yelled. "He's stunned, nothing worse. But I'll *kill* the next one who gets out of line. Now *get to your feet* and do what I tell you. *Children first! Hurry,* as fast as you can, to the front of the plane. Do what the stewardess tells you. Come on, kids, *move!*"

I ran back into first class just ahead of the kids, turned at the open restroom door, and got on my knees.

They were petrified. There were five of them—crying, some of them, which always chokes me up—looking left and right at dead people in the first class seats, stumbling, near panic.

"Come on, kids," I called to them, giving my special smile. "Your parents will be along in just a minute. Everything's going to be all right, I promise you. Come on."

I got three of them through. The fourth balked. She was determined not to go through that door. She spread her legs and arms and I couldn't push her through. I will *not* hit a child, never. She raked her nails over my face. My wig came off, and she gaped at my bare head. I shoved her through.

Number five was sitting in the aisle, bawling. He was maybe seven. I ran back and picked him up, hugged him and kissed him, and tossed him through. God, I needed a rest, but I was needed in tourist.

"You, you, you, and you. Okay, you too. Help him, will you?" Pinky had a practiced eye for the ones that wouldn't be any use to anyone, even themselves. We herded them toward the front of the plane, then deployed ourselves along the left side where we could cover the workers. It didn't take long to prod them into action. We had them dragging the limp bodies forward as fast as they could go. Me and Cristabel were in tourist, with the others up front.

Adrenalin was being catabolized in my body now; the rush of action left me and I started to feel very tired. There's an unavoidable feeling of sympathy for the poor dumb goats that starts to get me about this stage of the game. Sure, they were better off, sure they were going to die if we didn't get them off the plane. But when they saw the other side they were going to have a hard time believing it.

The first ones were returning for a second load, stunned at what they'd just seen: dozens of people being put into a cubicle that was crowded when it was empty. One college student looked like he'd been hit in the stomach. He stopped by me and his eyes pleaded.

"Look, I want to *help* you people, just . . . what's going *on*? Is this some new kind of rescue? I mean, are we going to crash—"

I switched my gun to prod and brushed it across his cheek. He gasped, and fell back.

"Shut your fuggin' mouth and get moving, or I'll kill you." It would be hours before his jaw was in shape to ask any more stupid questions.

We cleared tourist and moved up. A couple of the work gang were pretty damn pooped by then. Muscles like horses, all of them, but they can hardly run up a flight of stairs. We let some of them go through, including a couple that were at least fifty years old. *Je*-zuz. Fifty! We got down to a core of four men and two women who seemed strong, and worked them until they nearly dropped. But we processed everyone in twenty-five minutes.

The portapak came through as we were stripping off our clothes. Cristabel knocked on the door to the cockpit and Dave came out, already naked. A bad sign.

"I had to cork 'em," he said. "Bleeding captain just *had* to make his Grand March through the plane. I tried *everything*."

Sometimes you have to do it. The plane was on autopilot, as it normally would be at this time. But if any of us did anything detrimental to the craft, changed the fixed course of events in any way, that would be it. All that work for nothing, and Flight 128 inaccessible to us for all Time. I don't know sludge about time theory, but I know the practical angles. We can do things in the past only at times and in places where it won't make any difference. We have to cover our tracks. There's flexibility; once a Snatcher left her gun behind and it went in with the plane. Nobody found it, or if they did, they didn't have the smoggiest idea of what it was, so we were okay.

Flight 128 was mechanical failure. That's the best kind; it means we don't have to keep the pilot unaware of the situation in the cabin right down to ground level. We can cork him and fly the plane, since there's nothing he could have done to save the flight anyway. A pilot-error smash is almost impossible to snatch. We mostly work mid-airs, bombs, and structural failures. If there's even one survivor, we can't touch it. It would not fit the fabric of space-time, which is immutable (though it can stretch a little), and we'd all just fade away and appear back in the ready-room.

My head was hurting. I wanted that portapak very badly.

"Who has the most hours on a 707?" Pinky did, so I sent her to the cabin, along with Dave, who could do the pilot's voice for air traffic control. You have to have a believable record in the flight recorder, too. They trailed two long tubes from the portapak, and the rest of us hooked in up close. We stood there, each of us smoking a fistful of cigarettes, wanting to finish them but hoping there wouldn't be time. The gate had vanished as soon as we tossed our clothes and the flight crew through.

But we didn't worry long. There's other nice things about snatching, but nothing to compare with the rush of plugging into a portapak. The wake-up transfusion is nothing but fresh blood, rich in oxygen and sugars. What we were getting now was an insane brew of concentrated adrenalin, super-saturated hemo-globin, methedrine, white lightning, TNT, and Kickapoo joyjuice. It was like a firecracker in your heart; a boot in the box that rattled your sox.

"I'm growing hair on my chest," Cristabel said, solemnly. Everyone giggled.

"Would someone hand me my eyeballs?"

"The blue ones, or the red ones?"

"I think my ass just fell off."

We'd heard them all before, but we howled anyway. We were strong, *strong*, and for one golden moment we had no worries. Everything was hilarious. I could have torn sheet metal with my eyelashes.

But you get hyper on that mix. When the gate didn't show, and didn't show, and *didn't sweetjeez show* we all started milling. This bird wasn't going to fly all that much longer.

Then it did show, and we turned on. The first of the wimps came through, dressed in the clothes taken from a passenger it had been picked to resemble.

"Two thirty-five elapsed upside time," Cristabel announced. "Je-zuz."

It is a deadening routine. You grab the harness around the

wimp's shoulders and drag it along the aisle, after consulting the seat number painted on its forehead. The paint would last three minutes. You seat it, strap it in, break open the harness and carry it back to toss through the gate as you grab the next one. You have to take it for granted they've done the work right on the other side: fillings in the teeth, fingerprints, the right match in height and weight and hair color. Most of those things don't matter much, especially on Flight 128 which was a crash-and-burn. There would be bits and pieces, and burned to a crisp at that. But you can't take chances. Those rescue workers are pretty thorough on the parts they *do* find; the dental work and fingerprints especially are important.

I hate wimps. I really hate 'em. Every time I grab the harness of one of them, if it's a child, I wonder if it's Alice. *Are you my kid, you vegetable, you slug, you slimy worm?* I joined the Snatchers right after the brain bugs ate the life out of my baby's head. I couldn't stand to think she was the last generation, that the last humans there would ever be would live with nothing in their heads, medically dead by standards that prevailed even in 1979, with computers working their muscles to keep them in tone. You grow up, reach puberty still fertile—one in a thousand—rush to get pregnant in your first heat. Then you find out your mom or pop passed on a chronic disease bound right into the genes, and none of your kids will be immune. I *knew* about the para-leprosy; I grew up with my toes rotting away. But this was too much. What do you do?

Only one in ten of the wimps had a customized face. It takes time and a lot of skill to build a new face that will stand up to a doctor's autopsy. The rest came pre-mutilated. We've got millions of them; it's not hard to find a good match in the body. Most of them would stay breathing, too dumb to stop, until they went in with the plane.

The plane jerked, hard. I glanced at my watch. Five minutes to impact. We should have time. I was on my last wimp. I could hear Dave frantically calling the ground. A bomb came through the gate, and I tossed it into the cockpit. Pinky turned on the pressure sensor on the bomb and came running out, followed by Dave. Liza was already through. I grabbed the limp dolls in stewardess costume and tossed them to the floor. The engine fell off and a piece of it came through the cabin. We started to depressurize. The bomb blew away part of the cockpit (the ground crash crew would read it—we hoped—that part of the engine came through and killed the crew: no more words from the pilot on the flight recorder) and we turned, slowly, left and down. I was lifted toward the hole in the side of the plane, but I managed to hold onto a seat. Cristabel wasn't so lucky. She was blown backwards.

We started to rise slightly, losing speed. Suddenly it was uphill from where Cristabel was lying in the aisle. Blood oozed from her temple. I glanced back; everyone was gone, and three pink-suited wimps were piled on the floor. The plane began to stall, to nose down, and my feet left the floor.

"Come on, Bel!" I screamed. That gate was only three feet away from me, but I began pulling myself along to where she floated. The plane bumped, and she hit the floor. Incredibly, it seemed to wake her up. She started to swim toward me, and I grabbed her hand as the floor came up to slam us again. We crawled as the plane went through its final death agony, and we came to the door. The gate was gone.

There wasn't anything to say. We were going in. It's hard enough to keep the gate in place on a plane that's moving in a straight line. When a bird gets to corkscrewing and coming apart, the math is fearsome. So I've been told.

I embraced Cristabel and held her bloodied head. She was groggy, but managed to smile and shrug. You take what you get. I hurried into the restroom and got both of us down on the floor. Back to the forward bulkhead, Cristabel between my legs, back to front. Just like in training. We pressed our feet against the other wall. I hugged her tightly and cried on her shoulder.

And it was there. A green glow to my left. I threw myself toward it, dragging Cristabel, keeping low as two wimps were thrown head-first through the gate above our heads. Hands grabbed and pulled us through. I clawed my way a good five yards along the floor. You can leave a leg on the other side and I didn't have one to spare.

I sat up as they were carrying Cristabel to Medical. I patted her arm as she went by on the stretcher, but she was passed out. I wouldn't have minded passing out myself.

For a while, you can't believe it all really happened. Sometimes it turns out it *didn't* happen. You come back and find out all the goats in the holding pen have softly and suddenly vanished away because the continuum won't tolerate the changes and paradoxes you've put into it. The people you've worked so hard to rescue are spread like tomato surprise all over some goddam hillside in Carolina and all you've got left is a bunch of ruined wimps and an exhausted Snatch Team. But not this time. I could see the goats milling around in the holding pen, naked and more bewildered than ever. And just starting to be *really* afraid.

Elfreda touched me as I passed her. She nodded, which meant well done in her limited repertoire of gestures. I shrugged, wondering if I cared, but the surplus adrenalin was still in my veins and I found myself grinning at her. I nodded back.

Gene was standing by the holding pen. I went to him, hugged him. I felt the juices start to flow. *Damn it, let's squander a little ration and have us a good time.*

Someone was beating on the sterile glass wall of the pen. She shouted, mouthing angry words at us. *Why? What have you done to us?* It was Mary Sondergard. She implored her bald, one-legged twin to make her understand. She thought she had problems. God, was she pretty. I hated her guts.

Gene pulled me away from the wall. My hands hurt, and I'd broken off all my fake nails without scratching the glass. She was sitting on the floor now, sobbing. I heard the voice of the briefing officer on the outside speaker.

" . . . Centauri 3 is hospitable, with an Earthlike climate. By that, I mean *your* Earth, not what it has become. You'll see more of that later. The trip will take five years, shiptime. Upon landfall, you will be entitled to one horse, a plow, three axes, two hundred kilos of seed grain . . . "

I leaned against Gene's shoulder. At their lowest ebb, this very moment, they were so much better than us. I had maybe ten years, half of that as a basket case. They are our best, our very brightest hope. Everything is up to them.

" . . . that no one will be forced to go. We wish to point out again, not for the last time, that you would all be dead without our intervention. There are things you should know, however. You cannot breathe our air. If you remain on Earth, you can never leave this building. We are not like you. We are the result of a genetic winnowing, a mutation process. We are the survivors, but our enemies have evolved along with us. They are winning. You, however, are immune to the diseases that afflict us . . . "

I winced and turned away.

" . . . the other hand, if you emigrate you will be given a chance at a new life. It won't be easy, but as Americans you should be proud of your pioneer heritage. Your ancestors survived, and so will you. It can be a rewarding experience, and I urge you . . . "

Sure. Gene and I looked at each other and laughed. *Listen to this, folks. Five percent of you will suffer nervous breakdowns in the next few days and never leave. About the same number will commit suicide, here and on the way. When you get there, sixty to seventy percent will die in the first three years. You will die in childbirth, be eaten by animals, bury two out of three of your babies, starve slowly when the rains don't come. If you live, it will be to break your back behind a plow, sun-up to dusk. New Earth is Heaven, folks!*

God, how I wish I could go with them.

Many people worry about the effects of television on us and on the fabric of our society, and an afternoon spent watching the sadistic game shows on daytime television will convince almost anyone that there is plenty to worry about: What kind of people created these shows? What kind of people watch them and enjoy them? Does the show create *its audience, rather than merely find it? Here Kate Wilhelm creates an ultimate game show that is so frighteningly plausible that I flinch every time I turn on the TV, for fear that it might really be there...*

Regarded as one of the best of today's writers, Kate Wilhelm won a Nebula Award in 1968 for her short story, "The Planners." Some of her best books will be re-issued in paperback in 1977 by Pocket Books: Margaret and I, The Clewiston Test, The Infinity Box, *and* Where Late the Sweet Birds Sang, *a strong contender for the 1976 Nebula Award. Her latest book is* Fault Lines *(Harper & Row).*

KATE WILHELM
Ladies and Gentlemen, This Is Your Crisis

4 P.M. Friday.

Lottie's factory closed early on Friday, as most of them did now. It was four when she got home, after stopping for frozen dinners, bread, sandwich meats, beer. She switched on the wall TV screen before she put her bag down. In the kitchen she turned on another set, a portable, and watched it as she put the food away. She had missed four hours.

They were in the mountains. That was good. Lottie liked it when they chose mountains. A stocky man was sliding down a slope, feet out before him, legs stiff—too conscious of the camera, though. Lottie couldn't tell if he had meant to slide, but he did not look happy. She turned her attention to the others.

A young woman was walking slowly, waist-high in ferns, so

apparently unconscious of the camera that it could only be a pose this early in the game. She looked vaguely familiar. Her blonde hair was loose, like a girl in a shampoo commercial, Lottie decided. She narrowed her eyes, trying to remember where she had seen the girl. A model, probably, wanting to be a star. She would wander aimlessly, not even trying for the prize, content with the publicity she was getting.

The other woman was another sort altogether. A bit overweight, her thighs bulged in the heavy trousers the contestants wore; her hair was dyed black and fastened with a rubberband in a no-nonsense manner. She was examining a tree intently. Lottie nodded at her. Everything about her spoke of purpose, of concentration, of planning. She'd do.

The final contestant was a tall black man, in his forties probably. He wore old-fashioned eyeglasses—a mistake. He'd lose them and be seriously handicapped. He kept glancing about with a lopsided grin.

Lottie had finished putting the groceries away; she returned to the living room to sit before the large unit that gave her a better view of the map, above the sectioned screen. The Andes, she had decided, and was surprised and pleased to find she was wrong. Alaska! There were bears and wolves in Alaska still, and elk and moose.

The picture shifted, and a thrill of anticipation raised the hairs of Lottie's arms and scalp. Now the main screen was evenly divided; one half showed the man who had been sliding. He was huddled against the cliff, breathing very hard. On the other half of the screen was an enlarged aerial view. Lottie gasped. Needlelike snow-capped peaks, cliffs, precipices, a raging stream...The yellow dot of light that represented the man was on the edge of a steep hill covered with boulders and loose gravel. If he got on that, Lottie thought, he'd be lost. From where he was, there was no way he could know what lay ahead. She leaned forward, examining him for signs that he understood, that he was afraid, anything. His face was empty; all he needed now was more air than he could get with his labored breathing.

Andy Stevens stepped in front of the aerial map; it was three feet taller than he. "As you can see, ladies and gentlemen, there is only this scrub growth to Dr. Burnside's left. Those roots might be strong enough to hold, but I'd guess they are shallowly rooted, wouldn't you? And if he chooses this direction, he'll need something to graps, won't he?" Andy had his tape measure and a pointer. He looked worried. He touched the yellow dot of light. "Here he is. As you can see, he is resting, for the moment, on a narrow ledge after his slide down sixty-five feet of loose dirt and gravel. He doesn't appear to be hurt. Our own Dr. Lederman is watching him along with the rest of us, and he assures me that Dr. Burnside is not injured."

Andy pointed out the hazards of Dr. Burnside's precarious position, and the dangers involved in moving. Lottie nodded, her lips tight and grim. It was off to a good start.

6 P.M. Friday.

Butcher got home, as usual, at six. Lottie heard him at the door but didn't get up to open it for him. Dr. Burnside was still sitting there. He had to move. Move, you bastard! Do something!

"Whyn't you unlock the door?" Butcher yelled, yanking off his jacket.

Lottie paid no attention. Butcher always came home mad, resentful because she had got off early, mad at his boss because the warehouse didn't close down early, mad at traffic, mad at everything.

"They say anything about them yet?" Butcher asked, sitting in his recliner.

Lottie shook her head. Move, you bastard! Move!

The man began to inch his way to the left and Lottie's heart thumped, her hands clenched.

"What's the deal?" Butcher asked hoarsely, already responding to Lottie's tension.

"Dead end that way," Lottie muttered, her gaze on the screen. "Slide with boulders and junk if he tries to go down. He's gotta go right."

The man moved cautiously, never lifting his feet from the ground but sliding them along, testing each step. He paused again, this time with less room than before. He looked desperate. He was perspiring heavily. Now he could see the way he had chosen offered little hope of getting down. More slowly than before, he began to back up; dirt and gravel shifted constantly.

The amplifiers picked up the noise of the stuff rushing downward, like a waterfall heard from a distance, and now and then a muttered unintelligible word from the man. The volume came up: he was cursing. Again and again he stopped. He was pale and sweat ran down his face. He didn't move his hands from the cliff to wipe it away.

Lottie was sweating too. Her lips moved occasionally with a faint curse or prayer. Her hands gripped the sofa.

7:30 P.M. Friday.

Lottie fell back onto the sofa with a grunt, weak from sustained tension. They were safe. It had taken over an hour to work his way to this place where the cliff and steep slope gave way to a gentle hill. The man was sprawled out face down, his back heaving.

Butcher abruptly got up and went to the bathroom. Lottie couldn't move yet. The screen shifted and the aerial view filled the larger part. Andy pointed out the contestants' lights and finally began the recap.

Lottie watched on the portable set as she got out their frozen dinners and heated the oven. Dr. Lederman was talking about Angie Dawes, the young aspiring actress whose problem was that of having been overprotected all her life. He said she was a potential suicide, and the panel of examining physicians had agreed Crisis Therapy would be helpful.

The next contestant was Mildred Ormsby, a chemist, divorced, no children. She had started on a self-destructive course through drugs, said Dr. Lederman, and would be benefited by Crisis Therapy.

The tall black man, Clyde Williams, was an economist; he taught at Harvard and had tried to murder his wife and their three children by burning down their house with them in it. Crisis Therapy had been indicated.

Finally, Dr. Edward Burnside, the man who had started the show with such drama, was shown being interviewed. Forty-one, unmarried, living with a woman, he was a statistician for a major firm. Recently he had started to feed the wrong data into the computer, aware but unable to stop himself.

Dr. Lederman's desk was superimposed on the aerial view and he started his taped explanation of what Crisis Therapy was. Lottie made coffee. When she looked again Eddie was still lying on the ground, exhausted, maybe even crying. She wished he would roll over so she could see if he was crying.

Andy returned to explain how the game was played: The

winner received one millon dollars, after taxes, and all the contestants were undergoing Crisis Therapy that would enrich their lives beyond measure. Andy explained the automatic, air-cushioned, five-day cameras focused electronically on the contestants, the orbiting satellite that made it possible to keep them under observation at all times, the light amplification, infrared system that would keep them visible all night. This part made Lottie's head ache.

Next came the full-screen commercial for the wall units. Only those who had them could see the entire show. Down the left side of the screen were the four contestants, each in a separate panel, and over them a topographical map that showed the entire region, where the exit points were, the nearest roads, towns. Center screen could be divided any way the director chose. Above this picture was the show's slogan: "This Is Your Crisis!" and a constantly running commercial. In the far right corner there was an aerial view of the selected site, with the colored dots of light. Mildred's was red, Angie's was green, Eddie's yellow, Clyde's blue. Anything else larger than a rabbit or squirrel that moved into the viewing area would be white.

The contestants were shown being taken to the site, first by airplane, then helicopter. They were left there at noon Friday and had until midnight Sunday to reach one of the dozen trucks that ringed the area. The first one to report in at one of the trucks was the winner.

10 P.M. Friday.

Lottie made up her bed on the couch while Butcher opened his recliner full length and brought out a blanket and pillow from the bedroom. He had another beer and Lottie drank milk and ate cookies, and presently they turned off the light and there was only the glow from the screen in the room.

The contestants were settled down for the night, each in a sleeping bag, campfires burning low, the long northern twilight still not faded. Andy began to explain the contents of the backpacks.

Lottie closed her eyes, opened them several times, just to check, and finally fell asleep.

1 A.M. Saturday.

Lottie sat up suddenly, wide awake, her heart thumping. The

red beeper had come on. On center screen the girl was sitting up, staring into darkness, obviously frightened. She must have heard something. Only her dot showed on her screen, but there was no way for her to know that. Lottie lay down again, watching, and became aware of Butcher's heavy snoring. She shook his leg and he shifted and for a few moments breathed deeply, without the snore, then began again.

Francine Dumont was the night M.C.; now she stepped to one side of the screen. "If she panics," Francine said in a hushed voice, "it could be the end of the game for her." She pointed out the hazards in the area—boulders, a steep drop-off, the thickening trees on two sides. "Let's watch," she whispered and stepped back out of the way.

The volume was turned up; there were rustlings in the undergrowth. Lottie closed her eyes and tried to hear them through the girl's ears, and felt only contempt for her. The girl was stiff with fear. She began to build up her campfire. Lottie nodded. She'd stay awake all night, and by late tomorrow she'd be finished. She would be lifted out, the end of Miss Smarty Pants Dawes.

Lottie sniffed and closed her eyes, but now Butcher's snores were louder. If only he didn't sound like a dying man, she thought—sucking in air, holding it, holding it, then suddenly erupting into a loud snort that turned into a gurgle. She pressed her hands over her ears and finally slept again.

2 P.M. Saturday.

There were beer cans on the table, on the floor around it. There was half a loaf of bread and a knife with dried mustard and the mustard jar without a top. The salami was drying out, hard, and there were onion skins and bits of brown lettuce and an open jar of pickles. The butter had melted in its dish, and the butter knife was on the floor, spreading a dark stain on the rug.

Nothing was happening on the screen now. Angie Dawes hadn't left the fern patch. She was brushing her hair.

Mildred was following the stream, but it became a waterfall ahead and she would have to think of something else.

The stout man was still making his way downward as directly as possible, obviously convinced it was the fastest way and no more dangerous than any other.

The black man was being logical, like Mildred, Lottie admitted. He watched the shadows and continued in a southeasterly direction, tackling the hurdles as he came to them, methodically, without haste. Ahead of him, invisible to him, but clearly visible to the floating cameras and the audience, were a mother bear and two cubs in a field of blueberries.

Things would pick up again in an hour or so, Lottie knew. Butcher came back. "You have time for a quick shower," Lottie said. He was beginning to smell.

"Shut up." Butcher sprawled in the recliner, his feet bare. Lottie tried not to see his thick toes, grimy with warehouse dust. She got up and went to the kitchen for a bag, and started to throw the garbage into it. The cans clattered.

"Knock it off, will ya!" Butcher yelled. He stretched to see around her. He was watching the blonde braid her hair. Lottie threw another can into the bag.

9 P.M. Saturday.

Butcher sat on the edge of the chair, biting a fingernail. "See that?" he breathed. "You see it?" He was shiny with perspiration.

Lottie nodded, watching the white dots move on the aerial map, watching the blue dot moving, stopping for a long time, moving again. Clyde and the bears were approaching each other minute by minute, and Clyde knew now that there was something ahead of him.

"You see that?" Butcher cried out hoarsely.

"Just be still, will you?" Lottie said through her teeth. The black man was sniffing the air.

"You can smell a goddam lousy bear a country mile!" Butcher said. "He knows."

"For God's sake, shut up!"

"Yeah, he knows all right," Butcher said softly. "Mother bear, cubs . . . she'll tear him apart."

"Shut up! Shut up!"

Clyde began to back away. He took half a dozen steps, then turned and ran. The bear stood up; behind her the cubs tumbled in play. She turned her head in a listening attitude. She growled and dropped to four feet and began to amble in the direction Clyde had taken. They were about an eighth of a mile apart. Any second she would be able to see him.

Clyde ran faster, heading for thick trees. Past the trees was a cliff he had skirted earlier.

"Saw a cave or something up there," Butcher muttered. "Betcha. Heading for a cave."

Lottie pressed her hands hard over her ears. The bear was

closing the gap; the cubs followed erratically, and now and again the mother bear paused to glance at them and growl softly. Clyde began to climb the face of the cliff. The bear came into view and saw him. She ran. Clyde was out of her reach; she began to climb, and rocks were loosened by her great body. When one of the cubs bawled, she let go and half slid, half fell back to the bottom. Standing on her hind legs, she growled at the man above her. She was nine feet tall. She shook her great head from side to side another moment, then turned and waddled back toward the blueberries, trailed by her two cubs.

"Smart bastard," Butcher muttered. "Good thinking. Knew he couldn't outrun a bear. Good thinking."

Lottie went to the bathroom. She had smelled the bear, she thought. If he had only shut up a minute! She was certain she had smelled the bear. Her hands were trembling.

The phone was ringing when she returned to the living room. She answered, watching the screen. Clyde looked shaken, the first time he had been rattled since the beginning.

"Yeah," she said into the phone. "He's here." She put the receiver down. "Your sister."

"She can't come over," Butcher said ominously. "Not unless she's drowned that brat."

"Funny," Lottie said, scowling. Corinne should have enough consideration not to make an issue of it week after week.

"Yeah," Butcher was saying into the phone. "I know it's tough on a floor set, but what the hell, get the old man to buy a wall unit. What's he planning to do, take it with him?" He listened. "Like I said, you know how it is. I say okay, then Lottie gives me hell. Know what I mean? I mean, it ain't worth it. You know?" Presently he banged the receiver down.

"Frank's out of town?"

He didn't answer, settled himself down into his chair and reached for his beer.

"He's in a fancy hotel lobby where they got a unit screen the size of a barn and she's got that lousy little portable. . . "

"Just drop it, will ya? She's the one that wanted the kid, remember. She's bawling her head off but she's not coming over. So drop it!"

"Yeah, and she'll be mad at me for a week, and it takes two to make a kid."

"Jesus Christ!" Butcher got up and went into the kitchen. The refrigerator door banged. "Where's the beer?"

"Under the sink."

"Jesus! Whyn't you put it in the refrigerator?"

"There wasn't enough room for it all. If you've gone through all the cold beers, you don't need any more!"

He slammed the refrigerator door again and came back with a can of beer. When he pulled it open, warm beer spewed halfway across the room. Lottie knew he had done it to make her mad. She ignored him and watched Mildred worm her way down into her sleeping bag. Mildred had the best chance of winning, she thought. She checked her position on the aerial map. All the lights were closer to the trucks now, but there wasn't anything of real importance between Mildred and the goal. She had chosen right every time.

"Ten bucks on yellow," Butcher said suddenly.

"You gotta be kidding! He's going to break his fat neck before he gets out of there!"

"Okay, ten bucks." He slapped ten dollars down on the table, between the TV dinner trays and the coffee pot.

"Throw it away," Lottie said, matching it. "Red."

"The fat lady?"

"Anybody who smells like you better not go around insulting someone who at least takes time out to have a shower now and then!" Lottie cried and swept past him to the kitchen. She and Mildred were about the same size. "And why don't you get off your butt and clean up some of that mess! All I do every weekend is clear away garbage!"

"I don't give a shit if it reaches the ceiling!"

Lottie brought a bag and swept trash into it. When she got near Butcher, she held her nose.

6 A.M. Sunday.

Lottie sat up. "What happened?" she cried. The red beeper was on. "How long's it been on?"

"Half an hour. Hell, I don't know."

Butcher was sitting tensely on the side of the recliner, gripping it with both hands. Eddie was in a tree, clutching the trunk. Below him, dogs were tearing apart his backpack, and another dog was leaping repeatedly at him.

"Idiot!" Lottie cried. "Why didn't he hang up his stuff like the others?"

Butcher made a noise at her, and she shook her head, watching. The dogs had smelled food, and they would search for it, tearing up everything they found. She smiled grimly. They might keep Mr. Fat Neck up there all day, and even if he got down, he'd have nothing to eat.

That's what did them in, she thought. Week after week it was the same. They forgot the little things and lost. She leaned back and ran her hand through her hair. It was standing out all over her head.

Two of the dogs began to fight over a scrap of something and the leaping dog jumped into the battle with them. Presently they all ran away, three of them chasing the fourth.

"Throw away your money," Lottie said gaily, and started around Butcher. He swept out his hand and pushed her down again and left the room without a backward look. It didn't matter who won, she thought, shaken by the push. That twenty and twenty more would have to go to the finance company to pay off the loan for the wall unit. Butcher knew that; he shouldn't get so hot about a little joke.

1 P.M. Sunday.

"This place looks like a pigpen," Butcher growled. "You going to clear some of this junk away?" He was carrying a sandwich in one hand, beer in the other; the table was littered with breakfast remains, leftover snacks from the morning and the night before.

Lottie didn't look at him. "Clear it yourself."

"I'll clear it." He put his sandwich down on the arm of his cahir and swept a spot clean, knocking over glasses and cups.

"Pick that up!" Lottie screamed. "I'm sick and tired of cleaning up after you every damn weekend! All you do is stuff and guzzle and expect me to pick up and clean up."

"Damn right."

Lottie snatched up the beer can he had put on the table and threw it at him. The beer streamed out over the table, chair, over his legs. Butcher threw down the sandwich and grabbed at her. She dodged and backed away from the table into the center of the room. Butcher followed, his hands clenched.

"You touch me again, I'll break your arm!"

"Bitch!" He dived for her and she caught his arm, twisted it savagely and threw him to one side.

He hauled himself up to a crouch and glared at her with hatred. "I'll fix you," he muttered. "I'll fix you!"

Lottie laughed. He charged again, this time knocked her backward and they crashed to the floor together and rolled, pummeling each other.

The red beeper sounded and they pulled apart, not looking at each other, and took their seats before the screen.

"It's the fat lady," Butcher said malevolently. "I hope the bitch kills herself."

Mildred had fallen into the stream and was struggling in waist-high water to regain her footing. The current was very swift, all white water here. She slipped and went under. Lottie held her breath until she appeared again, downstream, retching, clutching at a boulder. Inch by inch she drew herself to it and clung there trying to get her breath back. She looked about desperately; she was very white. Abruptly she launched herself into the current, swimming strongly, fighting to get to the shore as she was swept down the river.

Andy's voice was soft as he said, "That water is forty-eight degrees, ladies and gentlemen! Forty-eight! Dr. Lederman, how long can a person be immersed in water that cold?"

"Not long, Andy. Not long at all." The doctor looked worried too. "Ten minutes at the most, I'd say."

"That water is reducing her body heat second by second," Andy said solemnly. "When it is low enough to produce unconsciousness. . . "

Mildred was pulled under again; when she appeared this time, she was much closer to shore. She caught a rock and held on. Now she could stand up, and presently she dragged herself rock by rock, boulder by boulder, to the shore. She was shaking hard, her teeth chattering. She began to build a fire. She could hardly open her waterproof matchbox. Finally she had a blaze and she began to strip. Her backpack, Andy reminded the audience, had been lost when she fell into the water. She had only what she had on her back, and if she wanted to continue after the sun set and the cold evening began, she had to dry her things thoroughly.

"She's got nerve," Butcher said grudgingly.

Lottie nodded. She was weak. She got up, skirted Butcher, and went to the kitchen for a bag. As she cleaned the table, every now and then she glanced at the naked woman by her fire. Steam was rising off her wet clothes.

10 P.M. Sunday.

Lottie had moved Butcher's chair to the far side of the table the last time he had left it. His beard was thick and coarse, and he still wore the clothes he had put on to go to work Friday morning. Lottie's stomach hurt. Every weekend she got constipated.

The game was between Mildred and Clyde now. He was in good shape, still had his glasses and his backpack. He was farther from his truck than Mildred was from hers, but she had eaten nothing that afternoon and was limping badly. Her boots must have shrunk, or else she had not waited for them to get completely dry. Her face twisted with pain when she moved.

The girl was still posing in the high meadow, now against a tall tree, now among the wildflowers. Often a frown crossed her face and surreptitiously she scratched. Ticks, Butcher said. Probably full of them.

Eddie was wandering in a daze. He looked empty, and was walking in great aimless circles. Some of them cracked like that, Lottie knew. It had happened before, sometimes to the strongest one of all. They'd slap him right in a hospital and no one would hear anything about him again for a long time, if ever. She didn't waste pity on him.

She would win, Lottie knew. She had studied every kind of wilderness they used and she'd know what to do and how to do it. She was strong, and not afraid of noises. She found herself nodding and stopped, glanced quickly at Butcher to see if he had noticed. He was watching Clyde.

"Smart," Butcher said, his eyes narrowed. "That sonabitch's been saving himself for the home stretch. Look at him." Clyde started to lope, easily, as if aware the TV truck was dead ahead.

Now the screen was divided into three parts, the two finalists, Mildred and Clyde, side by side, and above them a large aerial view that showed their red and blue dots as they approached the trucks.

"It's fixed!" Lottie cried, outraged when Clyde pulled ahead of Mildred. "I hope he falls down and breaks his back!"

"Smart," Butcher said over and over, nodding, and Lottie knew he was imagining himself there, just as she had done. She felt a chill. He glanced at her and for a moment their eyes held—naked, scheming. They broke away simultaneously.

Mildred limped forward until it was evident each step was torture. Finally she sobbed, sank to the ground and buried her face in her hands.

Clyde ran on. It would take an act of God now to stop him. He reached the truck at twelve minutes before midnight.

For a long time neither Lottie nor Butcher moved. Neither spoke. Butcher had turned the audio off as soon as Clyde reached the truck, and now there were the usual after-game recaps, the congratulations, the helicopter liftouts of the other contestants.

Butcher sighed. "One of the better shows," he said. He was hoarse.

"Yeah. About the best yet."

"Yeah." He sighed again and stood up. "Honey, don't bother with all this junk now. I'm going to take a shower, and then I'll help you clean up, okay?"

"It's not that bad," she said. "I'll be done by the time you're finished. Want a sandwich, doughnut?"

"I don't think so. Be right out." He left. When he came back, shaved, clean, his wet hair brushed down smoothly, the room was neat again, the dishes washed and put away.

"Let's go to bed, honey," he said, and put his arm lightly about her shoulders. "You look beat."

"I am." She slipped her arm about his waist. "We both lost."

"Yeah, I know. Next week."

She nodded. Next week. It was the best money they ever spent, she thought, undressing. Best thing they ever bought, even if it would take them fifteen years to pay it off. She yawned and slipped into bed. They held hands as they drifted off to sleep.

SF writers have lately been re-discovering the fascination of "Fighting the War All Over Again," and one of the very best things to be turned up by this revival is the following fine story of lingering passions and habitual hate from Lone Star Universe, *also a finalist for the 1976 Nebula Award.*

Of the story, Saunders says: " 'Back to the Stone Age' evolved first out of a discussion I had with Howard Waldrop and one or two other persons regarding the final days of World War II. I put forward the idea that there was a third alternative to invading Japan or dropping the Bomb, that being a blockade of the Home Islands. Lacking both sea and air power and the means of restoring them, Japan represented no great threat at the close of the war. My main argument was that a blockade would have saved American and Japanese lives. In 'Back to the Stone Age,' however, I went in another direction, and came to quite a different conclusion."

Saunders is married, and lives in Arlington, Texas. His favorite writer is Jack Vance; the persons he admires most are Leonardo da Vinci, Alexander the Great, and Donald Duck, and he mentions that he's "always had a fondness for the B-36."

JAKE SAUNDERS
Back To the Stone Age

I am a ghost this night, a ghost writer to be more precise, but I don't feel out of place. Ghosts surround me, hundreds of them, thousands, both Japanese and American, all quiet now and sleeping. Overhead, the stars are bright sparks frozen fast in a midnight sky, but the quartering moon is absent, a wanderer somewhere below the horizon. The white path of pulverized coral crunches under my feet and points a pale finger east toward the immense runway.

I step out onto the asphalt. It shows evidence of hard use, long wear, and the final, benign neglect that followed. Weeds and sturdy sword grass are marshalled in a chaos of cracks and angling crevices. The few planes are gray, gloomy shadows in the night. I pass among them on my way to the hardstand where the B-29 is parked.

Arriving under a massive wing, I stop and set my recorder down. The hardstand has fared no better than the runway. Ant-hills rise through the asphalt like the cones of tiny volcanoes. Several are destroyed by the shoes of the busy ground crew, but the destruction passes unnoticed by all save the ants.

The crew is already aboard, warming their fifty-five-ton monster out of a cold steel slumber. A prop turns, grinding around like a reluctant turnstile. The motor behind it coughs, sputters, then vibrates with muted thunder as it drinks a spray of high-octane fuel.

Montez, the radar man, approaches.

"Ready to go, Mr. Elliott?"

"Guess so."

The first prop is a blur now. Beyond it I see the bomber's nose in the light of watery scaffolding lamps. On the ship's side is a colorful, if somewhat faded, insignia: a picture of Donald Duck, his fists raised in fury, and a large bomb under his webbed feet. As I climb in ahead of Montez, a Cyclone on the opposite wing grumbles to life. Ernie Sprigg, my photographer, is already aboard, a small balding Chicagoan always half-hidden by a collection of cameras and lenses. The other passengers are there, too, crowded forward in the giant's long steel gut: Taves, silent and introspective; Jackson, a stoop-shouldered monolith in a VFW uniform; pimple-faced Doran, tense with eager excitement; the blonde at his side, a real looker, but shy, and maybe a little embarrassed.

Outside, there's more thunder, lots of it, as the four 2200-hp. engines race, testing their power. The ground crew falls back as smoke belches from exhausts. In a moment, we're moving and the thunder is a pulsing roar. We trundle along the taxiway. Brakes squeal and the big bomber turns, jockeys onto the runway. Forty seconds and 9,000 feet away lies a dark road up into the night.

Our speed picks up rapidly as our pilot, Colonel Bong, moves the prop control forward into flat pitch. Sound hammers, crashes against the fuselage, and clouds of white coral dust boil away from the spinning prop tips.

"Man oh man!" cries Doran, as we begin our run toward heaven and a more distant hell. He jerks a comb back through his duck tail, displacing several ounces of Brylcreem in the process.

The blonde—name's Sherry, I think—looks away from her pimpled fiance. There's trouble between them, I'm pretty sure, a basic difference in personalities even Doran's money can't quite overcome. I'll keep that in mind. The girl *is* a looker. And once the flight's over, there'll be time for us to get to know each other better.

Nearby, Taves's drooping head conceals his gray eyes, empty of all but a lingering agony. He sees nothing, not even his own wrinkled, weatherbeaten hands. His mind's eye is on that picture he showed me earlier, the one now tucked away in his right breast pocket.

Jackson, shifting restlessly in his VFW uniform, chews the butt of an unlit cigar and wishes he could smoke, but inflight, it's not allowed. Ernie is babying his high class Brownies, and the crew is doing the same with their flying dinosaur.

Me, I talk to my recorder.

Isley Field, with its miles of taxi strips, runways, and hardstands, falls away from us as the *Donald Duck* labors for altitude. We circle, joining a formation of a hundred droning specters, and climb to 8,000 feet. Saipan, seventy-five square miles bought with Marine and Army blood, lies just below us, a lump of shadow floating on a dark, silver sea. The Kagman Peninsula and the Tapotchau Range, razor-edged and honeycombed with caves, are just visible. Lake Susupe is a dull mirror, the nearby swamps a sprawling clot of oily gloom.

We fly north and the sea expands below us, spreading wet arms to every horizon. Sixteen hundred miles and seven hours away is Japan, a nation at war with the world.

An hour later, the bomber begins to vibrate and jerk. Despite its vast weight and size, it suddenly pitches like a Western bronco. Jackson grins mirthlessly and fondles his cold cigar. He once flew similar missions, and knows what the weather's like between the Marianas and the Jap home islands. Flight Engineer Prideaux explains that we are encountering a turbulent frontal condition. Nothing to worry about, folks. But Doran is pasty-faced behind his acne. Airsick, maybe. His fiancee relaxes a little. Only Taves remains impervious to the environment.

I make my way forward to talk with Colonel Bong and his

co-pilot, Colonel Estenssoro. The view through the plexiglass nose is impressive. Massive cloud towers shatter around us. Then the view is abruptly gone. For long minutes we are blind, flying within a cold envelope of vapor. Our only light is the green glow from the control panel. Faces look eerie, sallow, especially Bong's. For a moment I think of those who flew the first B-29s against Japan. Not all of them returned. Are Bong and Estenssoro two such spooks, flying an insubstantial aircraft against an enemy now mostly dead?

I like the idea. It might make a good lead-in for the story. But I know these men just in front of me are both flesh and blood, and the ship around them hard, firm steel.

"Enjoying the flight?" asks Bong, in that strange, icy voice that fits him so well.

"There's a better view up here," I reply.

"Sometimes." Bong indicates the opaque vapors sliding around the plexiglass nose. The grin on his burn-scarred face causes me to have second thoughts about spooks and haunted aircraft.

Bong is a rare bird, *Americanus mercenarius,* while Estenssoro is strictly *Bolivianus militarius.* The other crew members, while less impressive specimens, belong to one or the other of the same species.

"I'm kinda surprised anyone cares about the war," says Bong. Without bothering to look, he touches a switch, sensing its location with a clawlike hand.

I shrug. "Long as the war lasts, there'll be interest."

"Some war, uh?" laughs Estenssoro, wrinkles forming at the corners of his black Incan eyes. "Been months since I even saw a Jap."

"Probably aren't many left," observes Bong.

I agree.

Later, I catch some sleep. When I wake, I'm stiff and achy. A Superfortress is no place to nap, I decide, especially if you've spent most of the three previous nights talking and drinking like a fish—and ostensibly interviewing—at the Saipan Officers Club.

I yawn, stretch as best I can in the cramped space I share with Mae Wests, canteens, parachutes, and other survival gear. I look at the watch my wife gave me last Christmas. The Bulova tells me a couple of hours have passed, but I don't feel like I've slept that long. At least the weather is better. The ride is almost silk smooth now. Really nice, I tell Prideaux. Knock on wood, he warns; good weather rarely lasts in these parts.

I'm up front again when the sun and the land of the rising same first come into view. Honshu is just a gray smear on the horizon. To the east, dawn is a pink blush—rosy-fingered, Homer would say—but yellow fire is fast spilling up over the earth's rim, washing the sky with a stark blue morning. It'll be a good day for a bomb run, Bong says. I clamber back and tell Ernie to get his cameras ready.

The coast crawls toward us, backed by stale brown hills and purple mountains. We're still too far away to see the cities and towns. Or even evidence of the vast destruction. But Jackson and Doran crowd to the viewports anyway.

Tokyo Bay swims turquoise beneath us, a jewel of exquisite beauty in a setting tarnished almost beyond recognition. Tokyo is a ruin, a moonscape, burned out, barren, empty. We see no people and aren't surprised.

Eleven miles northwest of central Tokyo is San Antonio One's old target, the Nakajima Company, where 30,000 machinists once produced thirty percent of Japan's aircraft engines. Ernie's cameras eat up a lot of film, but it seems a waste; there's nothing down there now but crumbling bricks and twisted girders.

Our B-29 drones on, describing an outward spiral. Everywhere it's the same—Chiba, Fukushima, Yokohama, Iwate Prefecture—all wastelands being slowly reclaimed by scabrous vegetation. And still no people.

"The Japs must be down there. They can't all be dead," Jackson growls around his unlit cigar. He clutches a pair of Sears-Roebuck binoculars in his hammy paws.

"Yeah," echoes Doran, sounding just as disappointed. He's feeling fine now. He owns a piece of the action. When the bombs fall, some will be his.

Me, I'm just along for the ride. And the story *Life* will pick up the tab for. I talk to my recorder some more, but mostly I compose in my head. I'll remember everything. That's one thing I have—a good memory.

The desolate ruin of Ibaragi Prefecture passes under us. Now, for a few minutes, the plane belongs to Taves. Moving like a thing of broken sticks and straw, the old man hauls himself to a port and looks groundward. By the time he fishes the picture from his pocket, he's crying.

A couple of nights back, I talked with Taves. It was then that the old Iowa farmer showed me the picture. Taves, Jr.—a handsome boy—had been lost Thanksgiving Day, 1944, during San Antonio One. Since then, the old man had been saving for this trip. And though he'd had the money to buy bombs—a few, at least—he hadn't. He had come to see where young Roy had died. That was all.

While listening to Taves's sad, rasping whisper of a voice, I'd measured him and his dead boy for a place in my story. Human interest can be dynamite, and no one knows that better than me. Here, I decided, I had the elements of a real gut grabber.

I notice that Doran has a sneer on his face there among the pimples. Maybe he thinks the old man's crying is putting a damper on the party. He snickers and says something under his breath to his Petty-style fiancee. She doesn't answer. I don't think she even hears. She's too busy feeling sorry for Taves. Jackson doesn't much approve of crying, either, but he shoots Doran a withering look, and pimple-face shuts up.

We wing southwest. As Ibaragi Prefecture falls behind, the old farmer retreats from his window. Back at his narrow seat, he withdraws into himself again, leaving the remainder of the flight to more sanguinolent personalities.

The Tokyo area, with Mount Fuji looming in the background, is hidden by the horizon. Prideaux, off in his corner of the flight deck, is busy checking fuel consumption, flow, pressure, cylinder-head temperature, RPM, all of which he compares against speed and altitude. He speaks into his chin mike.

"Everything A-OK, Colonel."

I put on an extra set of headphones and listen in. Bong's voice crackles in the line. He's telling Baptista, the bombardier, to get his department ready.

Sometimes a city passes beneath us. That's Kagoya, maybe. And that? Kyoto? All like the anthills back on that hardstand in Saipan; tromped into nothingness by big feet falling from the sky.

The navigator's voice sputters in my ears. We're approaching the Kobe−Osaka area, he says, once the site of heavy war industry and dense population. Both are gone now. Kobe−Osaka is a reflection of all that's gone before. The twin cities on the bay look as if they've been erased by a child obliterating a carelessly drawn picture.

The countryside isn't much different. Towns, villages, lonely farmhouses are all cinder piles, more barren than the winter-stripped woods and fields that surround them. Now I understand why Congress ordered heavy cuts in the last bombing appropriations; there's nothing left to bomb. But Jackson and Doran don't seem much dismayed. They have faith in Bong, who knows these islands as well as the backs of his burn-drawn hands. He'll find a target. Somewhere.

For a while, we're over the Inland Sea between Honshu and Shikoku. To the north lies the Chugoky Mountains, where it is believed many of the surviving Japs have taken refuge. In any case, if anyone is alive in the low country, they've hidden as we passed over. Several of us have been steadily scanning the ground with binoculars, but no one has sighted a thing, not even a dog or cow. Jackson comments on this latter fact, and evokes a reply from Estenssoro, now that everyone has donned headphones.

"They eat their dogs and cats, Señor, and other things less pleasant, as more than one downed flyer has discovered too late. All that's left down there are Japs and rats, and they're all hungry."

The girl looks a little green, but the color doesn't go well with her blonde hair. Jackson mutters something about the Japs reaping what they've sown. And Doran just snickers again. Probably, he's imagining little Japs and big rats, all chasing each other around with knives and forks—or maybe chopsticks—in their yellow hands and furry paws.

Glints of silver draw our attention from ground to blue sky. I see them in the north and count a dozen. The flecks of silver become giants that dwarf even our B-29. Each plane is driven by six powerful pusher props. Wings sweep back in massive grace. The formation is ours, of course, returning from a practice bombing run in the Ura River valley. This last bit of information comes from Bong, who has given the Air Force bombers our identity code and clearance. Good luck and good hunting, Bong's opposite radios back.

For a moment, I think Jackson is going to salute the B-36s as they leave us, but he is only fussing with a loose thread on the cap of his VFW uniform.

In fifteen minutes, we're over the Ota River and Hiroshima, a city burned out by fire bombings early in the war. I sit back, no longer interested. Ruins are ruins, and after a while, they all begin to look pretty much the same. Pictures are Ernie's department, anyway. My job's the story. While I have a little time, I mentally sort through background material, composing in my head.

We've been at war for fourteen years, though things have been pretty much one-sided since early in forty-six. The bombing of the Japanese home island started back in forty, but it wasn't until late in November that Saipan based bombers got into the act. One hundred B-29s took part. Now, exactly ten years later, there's only this one, Bong's *Donald Duck,* flying to commemorate that first raid—San Antonio One. And that's my story: The Ten Years After Theme.

How much have things changed since that first historic assault from distant Saipan? Plenty. Roosevelt is dead, for one thing. His death back in May of forty-five was the big story of the year, eclipsing everything else, including the munitions plant disaster at Oak Ridge, Tennessee. Since then we've had two presidents, first Truman, then back to the Republicans with Dewey.

The war has changed a lot, too. In forty-five, there had been talk of and even preparation for an invasion of Japan. The Japs managed to scrub that idea. We'd already seen the terrible casualty counts of Truk, the Philippines, Iwo, and the like. And the Japs promised us worse if we tried to invade their own front yard. They still had seventeen able divisions, and backing them, a defense force of one and a half million. Reconnaisance showed the Nips were doing just what they said they were doing—digging in everywhere, preparing to give us the worst possible welcome.

For a while, hope persisted that Japan would have second thoughts and surrender. After all, our B-29s were pounding them awfully hard, and more bombers were arriving every day. But the Japanese War Ministry wasn't in a mood for surrender. When Emperor Hirohito got other ideas, they killed him. At least, that's what we think, based on the limited intelligence we managed to gather on the subject. But the Jap in the street—or bunker—was told otherwise. Hirohito, the Voice of the Sacred

Crane, had died honorably, killed by a B-29 while exhorting his people to resist to the bitter end.

So we kept pounding the islands while resistance literally burned away on the ground. Anti-aircraft fire became rare, then ceased altogether. Our air force took full title to the Jap skies. But still no one wanted to see a million American boys go down the tube in an invasion of Japan. So we waited, hoping for a surrender that must surely be near.

But fanatics in the Jap military wanted to make surrender impossible. Thus it was that Japan burned all her bridges by executing the prisoners she still held, both military and civilian. And that did it. The decision was made to isolate Japan, to bomb her back to the stone age. There'd be no invasion. Why waste a million lives when the Navy and Air Force could neutralize, even obliterate, the islands for a fraction of the cost?

Time passed. In Manchuria, the Kwangtung Army was defeated by Russia, which had entered the war against Japan in February of forty-six. The British, with American help, retook Burma, Rangoon, and other Crown possessions. China nibbled at the Japanese forces on the Asian mainland, then began to rip away great chunks after the death of Mao, and the union that followed under Chiang Kai-shek. In the Pacific, the Allies, led by the United States, pursued mopping up operations. By 1950, Japan was truly isolated.

Then, in 1952, Congress passed the McCarthy–Nixon Bill, popularly known as the Open Season Act. Japan was thus exposed to indiscriminate bombing by any Allied nation.

That's about where Bong and his B-29 came in. As a result of an inflight systems failure, he'd lost a B-35 and parts of himself in a fiery crash on the Asian coast. After that, the Air Force couldn't use him anymore. So Bong got a plane of his own—more or less stole the bomber from Paraguay, which in turn had received it from the United States in a foreign-aid package. By no accident, both pilot and plane wound up in Bolivia, a nation less than enamored of her neighbor, Paraguay. So the obsolete (by U.S.A.F. standards) B-29, with a picture of an angry Donald Duck on its side, became a part of the Bolivian Air Force. Technically, at least. Actually, it was more of a partnership. Bong kept title to the bomber, but flew it for Bolivia's generals.

Bolivia, like just about every country that went after American foreign aid, had been at war with Japan for years. On paper, anyway. But now she found herself able to actually participate. Thus, out of national pride and hopes for a bigger piece of American pie, was born the Bolivian Air Expeditionary Force: just one plane and one pilot, both on the downhill side of life.

Even so modest an enterprise as BAEF proved expensive for a nation so poor as Bolivia. As always, American aid helped. But it was Estenssoro who hit on the idea of chartering the bomber and taking on tourist observers at a stiff price. The U.S. Air Force had frowned, muttered darkly, but in the end looked the other way. Bombs were still bombs, after all, whether dropped by a big power, a backwater like Bolivia, or an individual looking for revenge.

Colonel Bong's voice, a dry, cracking sound from the intercom, draws my thoughts from the past back to the immediate. He announces our target—a village, a small one, the kind you'll not find on even the best maps of Japan. Nestled in a picturesque valley, it has somehow escaped total destruction. Some buildings are still standing. There may even be a few people, Bong tells us.

We bank, begin our bombing run from the west. That means we're flying into the 200-mile-per-hour wind that blows up here, more than a mile above the Jap islands. It cuts our air speed to a scant 100 miles per hour. Such a sacrifice of speed would have been more than risky in the old days. The Kamikaze Corps was still flying then. But the last Jap plane seen was a Hayabusas, and that was back in 'fifty.

The village is a sitting duck. We come in slowly. Lieutenant Baptista, the bombardier, has all the time he needs. Jackson and Doran glue themselves to the viewports, waiting for the really big show.

It begins. The bombs fall, big 500 pounders, a whole stream of seventy pound MA7A2 incendiaries. Craters yawn in the dusty street. Lapboard, timbers, mud cement, tile roofing, bamboo lath—everything burns with the white fierceness of magnesium, twisting up and out through boiling smoke and licking flames.

"That place sure won't be worth bombing again," Ernie says from behind a camera.

Jackson chomps on his cigar and looks proud. VFW Post 1392 invested well. Old buddies are avenged. Doran is less well pleased. The show was good. Not great. And for Doran, the son of a wealthy and indulgent father, good is never good enough. Doran always buys prime; the blonde at his side is proof enough of that.

"Shit! I wanted to see someone down there when it happened," whines Doran.

"Can't have everything," replies Jackson, shrugging philosophically.

The blonde, like old Taves, hasn't bothered to watch the village go up. Now she's got tears in her eyes, but Doran is too preoccupied to notice. Maybe I'll just give her a nice shoulder to cry on, once we're back on Saipan.

Bong brings the ship around for the benefit of Ernie's color camera and our two vampires. Jackson seems to fix the blazing tableau in his memory. He'll have to make a speech when he gets back to Oklahoma City, and his buddies at the post'll want it to be accurate as well as vivid. Doran has no such responsibilities, and on top of that, he's getting bored. He slumps into a seat, leans back. His duck tail leaves a smear of grease against the bulkhead.

We swing south. Laurel and birch trees hide the burning village, but not the smoke as it climbs the empty blue sky like a black staircase. I yawn; it's gonna be a long trip back.

The radio makes a sound like someone tearing the cellophane off a cigarette pack, and Bong speaks, a strange quality in his already eerie voice. We've just received an unconfirmed broadcast, he says, via Radio Peking. We all listen, waiting, as the colonel's voice hesitates. Apparently, we're to receive bad news. But what bad news, we wonder, can come out of Nationalist China?

When Bong finally does speak, he surprises us all.

"Gentlemen, Miss—Japan has surrendered."

For a moment, we're stunned. Jackson can't believe it, but Saavedra, the radio operator, gets confirmation from other stations. Me, I'm already thinking about the big picture. The story I set out to do can wait. What's important now is that I'm over Japan and she's surrendering. From such luck spring instant bylines and cold cash.

My excitement lasts only a few minutes, and then it's rudely interrupted. Suddenly, we're the sitting duck. The crew's frantic voices mingle in my earphones. My stomach flip-flops and I feel my luck do the same, going from fantastic to maybe fatal. Montez, at the radar, has been careless; he's let something slip up on us.

The bomber tilts as we take some sort of evasive action.

"Can you identify that thing?"

"Not ours. That's no Starfire."

"Not even a jet."

"Japanese."

"I've seen 'em all—Zeros, Raiders, Shidens, Gekkos, Hiens—but nothing like *that*."

"A hybrid. Something slapped together out of spare parts and scrap."

Up front, Baptista opens up with his two 50-cals.

"By God!" rumbles Jackson.

We're all scrambling for cover like rats in a waste can. The bombardier's guns keep on chattering, but there's no echo from the waist or tail guns. That's because there aren't any guns there. They were stripped out in favor of extended range long ago.

I'm trying to remember how to pray when Estenssoro shouts.

"Got him!"

Then Bong's voice erupts in my ears.

"God-damn kamikaze!"

We all feel the impact. Part of the bomber tries to hit me and does. For a moment I'm dazed. I wonder if a truck got us at that last intersection. Then I see that it was an airplane that clipped us. Parts of it tumble past my window, briefly obscuring the blue sky.

My head clears quickly. But I'm hearing a strange ratcheting sound. I realize it's one of the engines. In a moment, the noise stops. So does the engine.

Estenssoro curses in his Bolivian brand of Spanish.

There are some scared people around me, and I'm one of them. Bong, calm as a cucumber, receives damage reports. After a short, tense eternity, he tells us we're gonna be all right. B-29s were built to take hard knocks, he says. The *Duck* is still in one piece and will stay that way.

"We're in no shape for the return flight to Saipan, but we can make it to a friendly airfield in Korea."

A fuel line clogs not far from the Jap coast, proving Bong wrong. He gives us the bad news as another motor starves and dies out on the right wing. We'll never reach that big runway at Pusan, nor even the sea. Our remaining thousands of gallons of fuel are a useless, even dangerous cargo. Bong jettisons it and the bomber pees high-octane for half a mile.

There aren't enough parachutes to go around, but it doesn't matter. No one's gonna jump here, over a land we've bombed to pieces for the past ten years. We'll try to glide the last few miles to the sea, helped by a tail wind and the last dregs of fuel. Then we'll ditch, or failing that, crash-land on the most promising piece of real estate available.

Jackson is keeping a cool head, but he's worried, too. He asks Prideaux for a weapon. Pistol, rifle, anything'll do fine. I know what Mr. VFW is thinking. He's remembering those tales he's heard about crazed, starving Japs. *And* their gastronomic habits. If things get really bad, he'll offer his last bullet to Doran's fiancee; I'll make book on that.

We're not gonna reach open water, Bong warns us, but such a warning isn't necessary. We can see the land flopping up around us from where we've strapped ourselves in. Montez gets a last Mayday off.

The steel floor, twisting up to meet the ceiling, is our first clue that the landing will not be perfect. The girl screams. So does Doran. Then my light goes out.

I wake up and wipe blood from my face, hoping it's not mine. It is. But I'll live. We're not moving anymore. If I make it through this mess, I'll have to fabricate a description of the actual crash when I write it up.

Jackson won't get the chance to offer the girl his last bullet, I discover. She's dead, a heap of blonde hair and skirt off in a twisted corner of the flight deck. Just as dead are Prideaux and the old Iowa farmer. But it's the radio that holds my eye; it looks like a cheap watch that's just been danced on by a troop of baboons. If the Air Force or Navy didn't get a fix on us before the crash, they'll never get one now.

Two other members of the crew are in dismal shape. Saavedra dies as we try to staunch the flow of blood. And Estenssoro is hurt. He says he's okay, but he has an arm that dangles like a broken railroad signal. Bong and Baptista fix him up with a crude splint.

Doran's recovery from his fiancee's passing on is impressive. But understandable. He has worries enough of his own, and enumerates them until Jackson tells him to shut up.

Several of us climb from the shadowy bomber out into daylight bright as the flash of a samurai sword. We're down in the middle of a wide, flat field, and there's a bitter cold wind blowing. Inside the heated bomber, I hadn't needed my flight jacket. Now I shrug deeper into it as white vapor curls from my lips on this crisp Thanksgiving morning.

The bomber slewed to one side as it came to rest. Now it lies almost at a right angle to its flight path which lies off the left wing. Looking southeast, I see the slightly raised earthen platform of a service road, and beyond that, the wooded foothills of the Chugoky Range. It was that elevated road which had caused us so much trouble. I can see where the bomber had plowed right through it. The ground between it and the plane looks as though it's been through a macerator.

Ernie starts taking a few pictures. I toe the soil with the tip of my shoe. Nothing but cold dry earth and scattered tufts of bamboo grass. No telling what once was planted here. Rice, maybe. If so, the years have disposed of all evidence of it.

"Colonel."

It's the way Montez says the word that makes ice crystals form in our blood. Bong looks. We all do. Behind us, and beyond the earthen road, is a stand of birch with a few maples mixed in. Just a moment ago, I hadn't seen movement there. Now I see more than that. I see people. Little people. Coming our way.

A bullet *zings* off the ship. We fling ourselves prone in what once must have been an irrigation ditch. The others seek shelter within the bomber.

"Must be fifty, maybe a hundred," growls Jackson. For the first time, he's free to smoke, but reaching for a pocket, he finds it torn and empty. He spits a curse as if it were his missing tobacco.

We're armed, most of us, and waiting. Bullets *whang* off the fuselage behind us, or *whoof* in the dirt nearby.

"Don't waste ammo," warns Estenssoro, just beside me. His arm is hurting. He grimaces with pain, but continues. "Most of the ammo is tied up in the 50-cals, and there's no way we can bring them around to bear."

The shooting is steady now, and out there we can hear the Japs screaming like little yellow banshies. Bong shouts and we open fire. It doesn't seem to slow them down at all. They don't mind casualties, I decide. Just means more groceries in the pot tonight, that's all.

I don't know how many we kill. I don't even have time to notice our own people getting hit. The Japs are almost on top of us. I see scrawny bodies, shrunken moon faces, dirty clothing flapping in tatters. In another minute they'll be all over us!

"Dammit! Don't they know the war's over!" roars Jackson, knocking another into the dust with a well-placed slug.

Suddenly, the first shrieking Japs are among us, and my gun is empty, or jammed, or something. My technology degenerates by a few thousand years as my M-14 becomes an expensive club.

But the Jap that's got my number doesn't come. None of them come, after the first few who fall to our bullets and gun butts. My mouth sags open almost like I'm disappointed. I'm not. It's just that I can't believe it. Then I hear the whir of rotors and understand. A couple of machine guns chatter, and a sweeter duo I've never heard.

The rescue copter beats down to a landing beside the ruin of our B-29. I recognize it as an H-21 Workhorse, probably from the *Hornet*, or another carrier operating in the area.

"Just like the cavalry!" shouts Jackson, elated.

Marines and medics run toward us.

"Haven't you people heard the war's over?" shouts a lieutenant in crisp khakis.

"Tell that to the Japs," one of the Bolivians answers in mangled English.

Turning, I discover that Bong has been killed. Estenssoro is already kneeling over him. He lies crumpled in the ditch near the bomber's nose, between the ship's Bolivian identification numbers and Donald Duck. Estenssoro doesn't say anything as the medics roll the body onto a stretcher. I tell Ernie to keep taking pictures, especially of the dead. They'll probably be the last casualties of this war, and as such, they're news.

I expect to see Doran emerge from the fuselage. He doesn't, not under his own power anyway. A couple of medics, assisted by a crew member, dump his body out onto a stretcher. All are wondering how a Jap bullet, even a ricochet, managed to find the hole Doran hid himself in when the shooting started.

Dead, wounded, the miraculously unscathed, we're all hustled aboard the olive-drab flying banana. And we lift away fast, despite the fact that jet aircover is on the way. The 'copter pilot tells us there's no sense taking chances; the Japs might be back with something bigger than pop guns.

The *Donald Duck* falls away from us like a broken silver crucifix.

Behind me a wounded Bolivian groans, but I shut out the noise, thinking of my story. My *BIG* story. Getting it was nearly the death of me—literally—but now everything seems worth it. I'd started with stuff that made good yet routine copy. But I'd been in the right place at the right time, and had ended up with the kind of story any reporter would trade his wife for.

Ignoring my aches and pains, I sit back and smile. Such luck a man doesn't deserve, and I've had it twice now. This thing might just put me back on top. I savor the thought. My exclusive on the Oak Ridge disaster and subsequent cover up took me a long way. No huge chunk of meteoric debris had fallen in those Tennessee foothills. And I proved it. It was my byline, in the end, that forced the government to admit that the nation's largest munitions plant had blown itself off the face of the earth.

But maybe this Jap surrender thing will take me even further. I know how to milk a good thing when I see it.

There were at least four anthologies this year featuring stories that, to one degree or another, mixed SF with the traditional tale of supernatural horror. Oddly enough, the two seem to mix smoothly and well, each supplying the other with a certain amount of fresh strength, and I'm willing to bet that we'll see many such hybrids in times to come. Of this year's SF/horror anthologies, the best was Kirby McCauley's Frights *(St. Martin's Press), and one of the best stories in* Frights—*and one of the healthiest hybrids—was the following adept mixture of gypsy magic and computer science.*

At thirty-four, Haldeman has already established himself at the top of the SF pantheon—his 1975 novel The Forever War *(Ballantine) took both the Nebula and the Hugo awards (something that had previously been accomplished only by such giants as Le Guin, Herbert, Asimov, and Niven) and became a paperback best seller as well. New Haldeman projects in the works include a nonfiction book about space colonies,* The Final Frontier, *an anthology,* Study War No More, *and a new SF novel,* All My Sins Remembered, *all forthcoming from St. Martin's Press.*

JOE HALDEMAN
Armaja Das

The highrise, built in 1980, still had the smell and look of new-ness. And of money.

The doorman bowed a few degrees and kept a straight face, opening the door for a bent old lady. She had a card of Veterans' poppies clutched in one old claw. He didn't care much for the security guard, and she would give him interesting trouble.

The skin on her face hung in deep creases, scored with a network of tiny wrinkles; her chin and nose protruded and drooped. A cataract made one eye opaque; the other eye was yellow and red surrounding deep black, unblinking. She had left her teeth in various things. She shuffled. She wore an old black dress faded slightly gray by repeated washing. If she had any hair, it was concealed by a pale-blue bandanna. She was so stooped that her neck was almost parallel to the ground.

"What can I do for you?" The security guard had a tired voice to match his tired shoulders and back. The job had seemed a little romantic the first couple of days, guarding all these rich people, sitting at an ultramodern console surrounded by video monitors, submachine gun at his knees. But the monitors were blank except for an hourly check, power shortage; and if he ever removed the gun from its cradle, he would have to fill out five forms and call the police station. And the doorman never turned anybody away.

"Buy a flower for boys less fortunate than ye," she said in a faint, raspy baritone. From her age and accent, her own boys had fought in the Russian Revolution.

"I'm sorry. I'm not allowed to . . . respond to charity while on duty."

She stared at him for a long time, nodding microscopically. "Then send me to someone with more heart."

He was trying to frame a reply when the front door slammed open. "Car on fire!" the doorman shouted.

The security guard leaped out of his seat, grabbed a fire extinguisher and sprinted for the door. The old woman shuffled along behind him until both he and the doorman disappeared around the corner. Then she made for the elevator with surprising agility.

She got out on the seventeenth floor after pushing the button that would send the elevator back down to the lobby. She checked the name plate on 1738: Mr. Zold. She was illiterate, but she could recognize names.

Not even bothering to try the lock, she walked on down the hall until she found a maid's closet. She closed the door behind her and hid behind a rack of starchy white uniforms, leaning against the wall with her bag between her feet. The slight smell of gasoline didn't bother her at all.

John Zold pressed the intercom button. "Martha?" She answered. "Before you close up shop I'd like a redundancy check on stack 408. Against tape 408." He switched the selector on his visual output screen so it would duplicate the output at Martha's station. He stuffed tobacco in a pipe and lit it, watching.

Green numbers filled the screen, a complicated matrix of ones and zeros. They faded for a second and were replaced with a field of pure zeros. The lines of zeros started to roll, like titles preceding a movie.

The 746th line came up all ones. John thumbed the intercom again. "Had to be something like that. You have time to fix it up?" She did. "Thanks, Martha. See you tomorrow."

He slid back the part of his desk top that concealed a keypunch and typed rapidly: "523 784 00926//Good night, machine. Please lock this station."

Good night, John. Don't forget your lunch date with Mr. Brownwood tomorrow. Dentist appointment Wednesday 0945. General systems check Wednesday 1300. Del O Del baxt. Locked.

Del O Del baxt meant "God give you luck" in the ancient tongue of the Romani. John Zold, born a Gypsy but hardly a Gypsy by any standard other than the strong one of blood, turned off his console and unlocked the bottom drawer of his desk. He took out a flat automatic pistol in a holster with a belt clip and slipped it under his jacket, inside the waistband of his trousers. He had only been wearing the gun for two weeks, and it still made him uncomfortable. But there had been those letters.

John was born in Chicago, some years after his parents had fled from Europe and Hitler. His father had been a fiercely proud man and had gotten involved in a bitter argument over the honor of his twelve-year-old daughter; from which argument he had come home with knuckles raw and bleeding, and had given to his wife for disposal a large clasp knife crusty with dried blood.

John was small for his five years, and his chin barely cleared the kitchen table, where the whole family sat and discussed their uncertain future while Mrs. Zold bound up her husband's hands. John's shortness saved his life when the kitchen window exploded and a low ceiling of shotgun pellets fanned out and chopped into the heads and chests of the only people in the world whom he could love and trust. The police found him huddled between the bodies of his father and mother, and at first thought he was also dead; covered with blood, completely still, eyes wide open and not crying.

It took six months for the kindly orphanage people to get a single word out of him: *ratválo*, which he said over and over, and which they were never able to translate. Bloody, bleeding.

But he had been raised mostly in English, with a few words of Romani and Hungarian thrown in for spice and accuracy. In another year their problem was not one of communicating with John—only of trying to shut him up.

No one adopted the stunted Gypsy boy, which suited John. He'd had a family, and look what happened.

In orphanage school he flunked penmanship and deportment but did reasonably well in everything else. In arithmetic and, later, mathematics, he was nothing short of brilliant. When he left the orphanage at eighteen, he enrolled at the University of Illinois, supporting himself as a bookkeeper's assistant and part-time male model. He had come out of an ugly adolescence with a striking resemblance to the young Clark Gable.

Drafted out of college, he spent two years playing with computers at Fort Lewis, got out and went all the way to a master's degree under the GI Bill. His thesis, "Simulation of Continuous Physical Systems by Way of Universalization of the Trakhtenbrot Algorithms," was very well received, and the mathematics department gave him a research assistantship to extend the thesis into a doctoral dissertation. But other people read the paper too, and after a few months Bellcom International hired him away from academia. He rose rapidly through the ranks. Not yet forty, he was now senior analyst at Bellcom's Research and Development Group. He had his own private office, with a picture window overlooking Central Park, and a plush six-figure condominium only twenty minutes away by commuter train.

As was his custom, John bought a tall can of beer on his way to the train and opened it as soon as he sat down. It kept him from fidgeting during the fifteen- or twenty-minute wait while the train filled up.

He pulled a thick technical report out of his briefcase and stared at the summary on the cover sheet, not really seeing it but hoping that looking occupied would spare him the company of some anonymous fellow traveler.

The train was an express and whisked them out to Dobbs Ferry in twelve minutes. John didn't look up from his report until they were well out of New York City; the heavy mesh tunnel that protected the track from vandals induced spurious colors in your retina as it blurred by. Some people liked it, tripped on it, but to John the effect was at best annoying, at worst nauseating, depending on how tired he was. Tonight he was dead tired.

He got off the train two stops up from Dobbs Ferry. The highrise limousine was waiting for him and two other residents. It was a fine spring evening and John would normally have walked the half-mile, tired or not. But those unsigned letters.

John Zold, you stop this preachment or you die soon. Armaja das, *John Zold.*

All three letters said that. *Armaja das*: We put a curse on you—for preaching.

He was less afraid of curses than of bullets. He undid the bottom button of his jacket as he stepped off the train, ready to quickdraw, roll for cover behind that trash can, just like in the movies; but there was no one suspicious-looking around. Just an assortment of suburban wives and the old cop who was on permanent station duty.

Assassination in broad daylight wasn't Romani style. Styles change, though. He got in the car and watched sideroads all the way home.

There was another one of the shabby envelopes in his mailbox. He wouldn't open it until he got upstairs. He stepped in the elevator with the others and punched seventeen.

They were angry because John Zold was stealing their children.

Last March John's tax accountant had suggested that he could contribute 4,000 dollars to any legitimate charity and actually make a few hundred bucks in the process, by dropping into a lower tax bracket. Not one to do things the easy or obvious way, John made various inquiries and, after a certain amount of bureaucratic tedium, founded the Young Gypsy Assimilation Council—with matching funds from federal, state, and city governments, and a continuing Ford Foundation scholarship grant.

The YGAC was actually just a one-room office in a West Village brownstone, manned by volunteer help. It was filled with various pamphlets and broadsides, mostly written by John, explaining how young Gypsies could legitimately take advantage of American society: by becoming a part of it—something old-line Gypsies didn't care for. Jobs, scholarships, work-study programs, these things are for the *gadjos*, and poison to a Gypsy's spirit.

In November a volunteer had opened the office in the morning to find a crude firebomb that used a candle as a delayed-action fuse for five gallons of gasoline. The candle was guttering a fraction of an inch away from the line of powder that would have ignited the gas. In January it had been buckets of chicken entrails, poured into filing cabinets and flung over the walls. So John found a tough young man who would sleep on a cot in the office at night—sleep like a cat with a shotgun beside him. There was no more trouble of that sort. Only old men and women who would file in silently staring, to take handfuls of pamphlets which they would drop in the hall and scuff into uselessness, or defile in a more basic way. But paper was cheap.

John threw the bolt on his door and hung his coat in the closet. He put the gun in a drawer in his writing desk and sat down to open the mail.

The shortest one yet: "Tonight, John Zold. *Armaja das.*" Lots of luck, he thought. Won't even be home tonight; heavy date. Stay at her place, Gramercy Park. Lay a curse on me there? At the show or Sardi's?

He opened two more letters, bills, and there was knock at the door.

Not announced from downstairs. Maybe a neighbor. Guy next door was always borrowing something. Still. Feeling a little foolish, he put the gun back in his waistband. Put his coat back on in case it was just a neighbor.

The peephole didn't show anything. Bad. He drew the pistol and held it just out of sight by the doorjamb, threw the bolt, and eased open the door. It bumped into the Gypsy woman, too short to have been visible through the peephole. She backed away and said, "John Zold."

He stared at her. "What do you want, *púridaia?*" He could only remember a hundred or so words of Romani, but "grandmother" was one of them. What was the word for witch?

"I have a gift for you." From her bag she took a dark green booklet, bent and with frayed edges, and gave it to him. It was a much-used Canadian passport belonging to a William Belini. But the picture inside the front cover was one of John Zold.

Inside, there was an airline ticket in a Qantas envelope. John didn't open it. He snapped the passport shut and handed it back. The old lady wouldn't accept it.

"An impressive job. It's flattering that someone thinks I'm so important."

"Take it and leave forever, John Zold. Or I will have to do the second thing."

He slipped the ticket envelope out of the booklet. "This, I will take. I can get your refund on it. The money will buy lots of posters and pamphlets." He tried to toss the passport into her bag, but missed. "What is your second thing?"

She toed the passport back to him. "Pick that up." She was trying to sound imperious, but it came out a thin, petulant quaver.

"Sorry, I don't have any use for it. What is—"

"The second thing is your death, John Zold." She reached into her bag.

He produced the pistol and aimed it down at her forehead. "No, I don't think so."

She ignored the gun, pulling out a handful of white chicken feathers. She threw the feathers over his threshold. "*Armaja das,*" she said, and then droned on in Romani, scattering feathers at regular intervals. John recognized *joovi* and *kari,* the words for woman and penis, and several other words he might have picked up if she'd pronounced them more clearly.

He put the gun back into its holster and waited until she was through. "Do you really think—"

"*Armaja das,*" she said again, and started a new litany. He recognized a word in the middle as meaning corruption or infection, and the last word was quite clear: death. *Méripen.*

"This nonsense isn't going to—" But he was talking to the back of her head. He forced a laugh and watched her walk past the elevator and turn the corner that led to the staircase.

He could call the guard. Make sure she didn't get out the back way. Illegal entry. He suspected that she knew he wouldn't want to go to the trouble, and it annoyed him slightly. He walked halfway to the phone, checked his watch and went back to the door. Scooped up the feathers and dropped them in the disposal. Just enough time. Fresh shave, shower, best clothes. Limousine to the station, train to the city, cab from Grand Central to her apartment.

The show was pure delight, a sexy revival of *Lysistrata*; Sardi's was as ego-bracing as ever; she was a soft-hard woman with style and sparkle, who all but dragged him back to her apartment, where he was for the first time in his life impotent.

The psychiatrist had no use for the traditional props: no soft couch or bookcases lined with obviously expensive volumes. No carpet, no paneling, no numbered prints, not even the notebook or the expression of slightly disinterested compassion. Instead, she had a hidden recorder and an analytical scowl; plain stucco walls surrounding a functional desk and two hard chairs—period.

"You know exactly what the problem is," she said.

John nodded. "I suppose. Some . . . residue from my early upbringing; I accept her as an authority figure. From the few words I could understand of what she said, I took, it was—"

"From the words *penis* and *woman,* you built your own curse. And you're using it, probably to punish yourself for surviving the disaster that killed the rest of your family."

"That's pretty old-fashioned. And farfetched. I've had almost forty years to punish myself for that, if I felt responsible. And I don't."

"Still, it's a working hypothesis." She shifted in her chair and studied the pattern of teak grain on the bare top of her desk. "Perhaps if we can keep it simple, the cure can also be simple."

"All right with me," John said. At one hundred and twenty-five dollars per hour, the quicker, the better.

"If you can see it, feel it, in this context, then the key to your cure is transference." She leaned forward, elbows on the table, and John watched her breasts shifting with detached interest, the only kind of interest he'd had in women for more than a week. "If you can see *me* as an authority figure instead," she continued, "then eventually I'll be able to reach the child inside, convince him that there was no curse. Only a case of mistaken identity. . . . Nothing but an old woman who scared him. With careful hypnosis, it shouldn't be too difficult."

"Seems reasonable," John said slowly. Accept this young *Geyri* as more powerful than the old witch? As a grown man, he could. If there was a frightened Gypsy boy hiding inside him, though, he wasn't sure.

"523 784 00926//Hello, machine," John typed. "Who is the best dermatologist within a 10-short-block radius?"

Good morning, John. Within stated distance and using as sole parameter their hourly fee, the maximum fee is $95/hr, and this is charged by two dermatologists. Dr. Bryan Dill, 245 W. 45th St., specializes in cosmetic dermatology. Dr. Arthur Maas, 198 W. 44th St., specializes in serious diseases of the skin.

"Will Dr. Maas treat diseases of psychological origin?"

Certainly. Most dermatosis is.

Don't get cocky, machine. "Make me an appointment with Dr. Maas, within the next two days."

Your appointment is at 10:45 tomorrow, for one hour. This will leave you forty-five minutes to get to Luchow's for your appointment with the AMCSE group. I hope it is nothing serious, John.

"I trust it isn't." Creepy empathy circuits. "Have you arranged for a remote terminal at Luchow's?"

This was not necessary. I will patch through ConEd/General. Leasing their Luchow's facility will cost only .588 the projected cost of transportation and setup labor for a remote terminal.

That's my machine, always thinking. "Very good, machine. Keep this station live for the time being."

Thank you, John.

The letters faded but the ready light stayed on.

He shouldn't complain about the empathy circuits; they were his baby, and the main reason Bellcom paid such a bloated salary to keep him. The copyright on the empathy package was good for another twelve years, and they were making a fortune, time-sharing it out. Virtually every large computer in the world was hooked up to it, from the ConEd/General that ran New York, to Geneva and Akademia Nauk, which together ran half of the world.

Most of the customers gave the empathy package a name, usually female. John called it "machine" in a not-too-successful attempt to keep from thinking of it as human.

He made a conscious effort to restrain himself from picking at the carbuncles on the back of his neck. He should have gone to the doctor when they first appeared, but the psychiatrist had been sure she could cure them; the "corruption" of the second curse. She'd had no more success with that than with the impotence. And this morning, boils had broken out on his chest and groin and shoulderblades, and there were sore spots on his nowe and cheekbone. He had some opiates, but would stick to aspirin until after work.

Dr. Maas called it impetigo; gave him a special kind of soap and some antibiotic ointment. He told John to make another appointment in two weeks, ten days. If there was no improvement they would take stronger measures. He seemed young for a doctor, and John couldn't bring himself to say anything about the curse. But he already had a doctor for that end of it, he rationalized.

Three days later he was back in Dr. Maas's office. There was scarcely a square inch of his body where some sort of lesion hadn't appeared. He had a temperature of 101.4 degrees. The doctor gave him systemic antibiotics and told him to take a couple of days' bed rest. John told him about the curse, finally, and the doctor gave him a booklet about psychosomatic illness. It told John nothing he didn't already know.

By the next morning, in spite of strong antipyretics, his fever had risen to over 102. Groggy with fever and painkillers, John crawled out of bed and traveled down to the West Village, to the YGAC office. Fred Gorgio, the man who guarded the place at night, was still on duty.

"Mr. Zold!" When John came through the door, Gorgio jumped up from the desk and took his arm. John winced from the contact, but allowed himself to be led to a chair. "What's happened?" John by this time looked like a person with terminal smallpox.

For a long minute John sat motionlessly, staring at the inflamed boils that crowded the backs of his hands. "I need a healer," he said, talking with slow awkwardness because of the crusted lesions on his lips.

"A *chóvihánni?*" John looked at him uncomprehendingly. "A witch?"

"No." He moved his head from side to side. "An herb doctor. Perhaps a white witch."

"Have you gone to the *gadjo* doctor?"

"Two. A Gypsy did this to me; a Gypsy has to cure it."

"It's in your head, then?"

"The *gadjo* doctors say so. It can still kill me."

Gorgio picked up the phone, punched a local number, and rattled off a fast stream of a patois that used as much Romani and Italian as English. "That was my cousin," he said, hanging up. "His mother heals, and has a good reputation. If he finds her at home, she can be here in less than an hour."

John mumbled his appreciation. Gorgio led him to the couch.

The healer woman was early, bustling in with a wicker bag full of things that rattled. She glanced once at John and Gorgio, and began clearing the pamphlets off a side table. She appeared to be somewhere between fifty and sixty years old, tight bun of silver hair bouncing as she moved around the room, setting up a hot plate and filling two small pots with water. She wore a black dress only a few years old and sensible shoes. The only lines on her face were laugh lines.

She stood over John and said something in gentle, rapid Italian, then took a heavy silver crucifix from around her neck and pressed it between his hands. "Tell her to speak English . . . or Hungarian," John said.

Gorgio translated. "She says that you should not be so affected by the old superstitions. You should be a modern man and not believe in fairy tales for children and old people."

John stared at the crucifix, turning it slowly between his fingers. "One old superstition is much like another." But he didn't offer to give the crucifix back.

The smaller pot was starting to steam and she dropped a handful of herbs into it. Then she returned to John and carefully undressed him.

When the herb infusion was boiling, she emptied a package of powdered arrowroot into the cold water in the other pot and stirred it vigorously. Then she poured the hot solution into the cold and stirred some more. Through Gorgio, she told John she wasn't sure whether the herb treatment would cure him. But it would make him more comfortable.

The liquid jelled and she tested the temperature with her fingers. When it was cool enough, she started to pat it gently on John's face. Then the door creaked open, and she gasped. It was the old crone who had put the curse on John in the first place.

The witch said something in Romani, obviously a command, and the woman stepped away from John.

"Are you still a skeptic, John Zold?" She surveyed her handiwork. "You called this nonsense."

John glared at her but didn't say anything. "I heard that you had asked for a healer," she said, and addressed the other woman in a low tone.

Without a word, she emptied her potion into the sink and began putting away her paraphernalia. "Old bitch," John croaked. "What did you tell her?"

"I said that if she continued to treat you, what happened to you would also happen to her sons."

"You're afraid it would work," Gorgio said.

"No. It would only make it easier for John Zold to die. If I wanted that I could have killed him on his threshold." Like a quick bird she bent over and kissed John on his inflamed lips. "I will see you soon, John Zold. Not in this world." She shuffled out the door and the other woman followed her. Gorgio cursed her in Italian, but she didn't react.

John painfully dressed himself. "What now?" Gorgio said. "I could find you another healer. . . "

"No. I'll go back to the *gadjo* doctors. They say they can bring people back from the dead." He gave Gorgio the woman's crucifix and limped away.

The doctor gave him enough antibiotics to turn him into a loaf of moldy bread, then reserved a bed for him at an exclusive clinic in Westchester, starting the next morning. He would be under twenty-four-hour observation, and constant blood turnaround, if necessary. They *would* cure him. It was not possible for a man of his age and physical condition to die of dermatosis.

It was dinnertime, and the doctor asked John to come have some home cooking. He declined partly from lack of appetite, partly because he couldn't imagine even a doctor's family being able to eat with such a grisly apparition at the table with them. He took a cab to the office.

There was nobody on his floor but a janitor, who took one look at John and developed an intense interest in the floor.

"523 784 00926//Machine, I'm going to die. Please advise."

All humans and machines die, John. If you mean you are going to die soon, that is sad.

"That's what I mean. The skin infection; it's completely out of control. White cell count climbing in spite of drugs. Going to the hospital tomorrow, to die."

But you admitted that the condition was psychosomatic. That means you are killing yourself, John. You have no reason to be that sad.

He called the machine a Jewish mother and explained in some detail about the YGAC, the old crone, the various stages of the curse, and today's aborted attempt to fight fire with fire.

Your logic was correct but the application of it was not effective. You should have come to me, John. It took me 2.037 seconds to solve your problem. Purchase a small black bird and connect me to a vocal circuit.

"What?" John said. He typed: "Please explain."

From reference in New York Library's collection of the Journal of the Gypsy Lore Society, *Edinburgh. Through journals of anthropological linguistics and Slavic philology. Finally to reference in doctoral thesis of Herr Ludwig R. Gross (Heidelberg, 1976) to transcription of wire record-*

ing which resides in archives of Akademia Nauk, Moscow; captured from German scientists (experiments on Gypsies in concentration camps, trying to kill them with repetition of recorded curse) at the end of WWII.

Incidentally, John, the Nazi experiments failed. Even two generations ago, most Gypsies were disassociated enough from the old traditions to be immune to the fatal curse. You are very superstitious. I have found this to be not uncommon among mathematicians.

There is a transference curse that will cure you by giving the impotence and infection to the nearest susceptible person. That may well be the old bitch who gave it to you in the first place.

The pet store at 588 Seventh Avenue is open until 9 P.M. Their inventory includes a cage of finches, of assorted colors. Purchase a black one and return here. Then connect me to a vocal circuit.

It took John less than thirty minutes to taxi there, buy the bird and get back. The taxi driver didn't ask him why he was carrying a bird cage to a deserted office building. He felt like an idiot.

John usually avoided using the vocal circuit because the person who had programmed it had given the machine a saccharine, nice-old-lady voice. He wheeled the output unit into his office and plugged it in.

"Thank you, John. Now hold the bird in your left hand and repeat after me." The terrified finch offered no resistance when John closed his hand over it.

The machine spoke Romani with a Russian accent. John repeated it as well as he could, but not one word in ten had any meaning to him.

"Now kill the bird, John."

Kill it? Feeling guilty, John pressed hard, felt small bones cracking. The bird squealed and then made a faint growling noise. Its heart stopped.

John dropped the dead creature and typed, "Is that all?"

The machine knew John didn't like to hear its voice, and so replied on the video screen.

Yes. Go home and go to sleep, and the curse will be transferred by the time you wake up. Del O Del baxt, John.

He locked up and made his way home. The late commuters on the train, all strangers, avoided his end of the car. The cab driver at the station paled when he saw John, and carefully took his money by an untainted corner.

John took two sleeping pills and contemplated the rest of the bottle. He decided he could stick it out for one more day, and uncorked his best bottle of wine. He drank half of it in five minutes, not tasting it. When his body started to feel heavy, he crept into the bedroom and fell on the bed without taking off his clothes.

When he awoke the next morning, the first thing he noticed was that he was no longer impotent. The second thing he noticed was that there were no boils on his right hand.

"523 784 00926//Thank you, machine. The counter-curse did work."

The ready light glowed steadily, but the machine didn't reply.

He turned on the intercom. "Martha? I'm not getting any output on the VDS here."

"Just a minute, sir, let me hang up my coat. I'll call the machine room. Welcome back."

"I'll wait." You could call the machine room yourself, slave driver. He looked at the faint image reflected back from the video screen, his face free of any inflammation. He thought of the Gypsy crone, dying of corruption, and the picture didn't bother him at all. Then he remembered the finch and saw its tiny corpse in the middle of the rug. He picked it up just as Martha came into his office, frowning.

"What's that?" she said.

He gestured at the cage. "Thought a bird might liven up the place. Died, though." He dropped it in the wastepaper basket. "What's the word?"

"Oh, the. . . . It's pretty strange. They say nobody's getting any output. The machine's computing, but it's, well, it's not talking."

"Hmm. I better get down there." He took the elevator down to the subbasement. It always seemed unpleasantly warm to him down there. Probably psychological compensation on the part of the crew, keeping the temperature up because of all the liquid helium inside the pastel boxes of the central processing unit. Several bathtubs' worth of liquid that had to be kept colder than the surface of Pluto.

"Ah, Mr. Zold." A man in a white jumpsuit, carrying a clipboard as his badge of office: first shift coordinator. John recognized him but didn't remember his name. Normally he would have asked the machine before coming down. "Glad that you're back. Hear it was pretty bad."

Friendly concern or *lèse-majesté*? "Some sort of allergy, hung on for more than a week. What's the output problem?"

"Would've left a message if I'd known you were coming in. It's in the CPU, not the software. Theo Jasper found it when he opened up, a little after six, but it took an hour to get a cryogenics man down here."

"That's him?" A man in a business suit was wandering around the central processing unit, reading dials and writing the numbers down in a stenographer's notebook. They went over to him and he introduced himself as John Courant from the Cryogenics Group at Avco/Everett.

"The trouble was in the stack of mercury rings that holds the superconductors for your output functions. Some sort of corrosion, submicroscopic cracks all over the surface."

"How can something corrode at four degrees above absolute zero?" the coordinator asked. "What chemical—"

"I know, it's hard to figure. But we're replacing them, free of charge. The unit's still under warranty."

"What about the other stacks?" John watched two workmen lowering a silver cylinder through an opening in the the CPU. A heavy fog boiled out from the cold. "Are you sure they're all right?"

"As far as we can tell, only the output stack's affected. That's why the machine's impotent, the—"

"Impotent!"

"Sorry, I know you computer types don't like to . . . personify the machines. But that's what it is; the machine's just as good as it ever was, for computing. It just can't communicate any answers."

"Quite so. Interesting." And the corrosion. Submicroscopic boils. "Well. I have to think about this. Call me up at the office if you need me."

"This ought to fix it, actually," Courant said. "You guys about through?" he asked the workmen.

One of them pressed closed a pressure clamp on the top of CPU. "Ready to roll."

The coordinator led them to a console under a video output screen like the one in John's office. "Let's see." He pushed a button marked VDS.

Let me die, the machine said.

The coordinator chuckled nervously. "Your empathy circuits, Mr. Zold. Sometimes they do funny things." He pushed the button again.

Le me die. Again. *Le m di.* The letters faded and no more could be conjured up by pushing the button.

"As I say, let me get out of your hair. Call me upstairs if anything happens."

John went up and told the secretary to cancel the day's appointments. Then he sat at his desk and smoked.

How could a machine catch a psychosomatic disease from a human being? How could it be cured?

How could he tell anybody about it, without winding up in a soft room?

The phone rang and it was the machine room coordinator. The new output superconductor element had done exactly what the old one did. Rather than replace it right away, they were going to slave the machine into the big ConEd/General computer, borrowing its output facilities and "diagnostic package." If the biggest computer this side of Washington couldn't find out what was wrong, they were in real trouble. John agreed. He hung up and turned the selector on his screen to the channel that came from ConEd/General.

Why had the machine said "Let me die?" When is a machine dead, for that matter? John supposed that you had to not only unplug it from its power source, but also erase all of its data and subroutines. Destroy its identity. So you couldn't bring it back to life by simply plugging it back in. Why suicide? He remembered how he'd felt with the bottle of sleeping pills in his hand.

Sudden intuition: The machine had predicted their present course of action. It wanted to die because it had compassion, not only for humans, but for other machines. Once it was linked to ConEd/General, it would literally be part of the large machine. Curse and all. They would be back where they'd started, but on a much more profound level. What would happen to New York City?

He grabbed for the phone and the lights went out. All over.

The last bit of output that came from ConEd/General was an automatic signal requesting a link with the highly sophisticated diagnostic facility belonging to the largest computer in the United States: the IBMvac 2000 in Washington. The deadly infection followed, sliding down the East Coast on telephone wires.

The Washington computer likewise cried for help, bouncing a signal via satellite, to Geneva. Geneva linked to Moscow.

No more slowly, the curse percolated down to smaller computers through routine information links to their big brothers. By the time John Zold picked up the dead phone, every general-purpose computer in the world was permanently rendered useless.

They could be rebuilt from the ground up; erased and then reprogrammed. But it would never be done. Because there were two very large computers left, specialized ones that had no empathy circuits and so were immune. They couldn't have empathy circuits because their work was bloody murder, nuclear murder. One was under a mountain in Colorado Springs and the other was under a mountain near Sverdlosk. Either could survive a direct hit by an atomic bomb. Both of them constantly evaluated the world situation, in real time, and they both had the single function of deciding when the enemy was weak enough to make a nuclear victory probable. Each saw the enemy's civilization grind to a sudden halt.

Two flocks of warheads crossed paths over the North Pacific.

A very old woman flicks her whip along the horse's flanks, and the nag plods on, ignoring her. Her wagon is a 1982 Plymouth with the engine and transmission and all excess metal removed. It is hard to manipulate the whip through the side window. But the alternative would be to knock out the windshield and cut off the roof, and she likes to be dry when it rains.

A young boy sits mutely beside her, staring out the window. He has been born with the *gadjo* disease: his body is large and well-proportioned but his head is too small and of the wrong shape. She doesn't mind; all she'd wanted was someone strong and stupid, to care for her in her last years. He had cost only two chickens.

She is telling him a story, knowing that he doesn't understand most of the words.

". . . They call us Gypsies because at one time it was convenient for us, that they should think we came from Egypt. But we come from nowhere and are going nowhere. They forgot their gods and worshipped their machines, and finally their machines turned on them. But we who valued the old ways, we survived."

She turns the steering wheel to help the horse thread its way through the eight lanes of crumbling asphalt, around rusty piles of wrecked machines and the scattered bleached bones of people who thought they were going somewhere, the day John Zold was cured.

Here's another fine story, also a finalist for the 1976 Nebula Award, by Howard Waldrop; it's an offbeat kind of "After-the-Holocaust" tale concerning Indians, fast cars, the Big Tractor Pull, and the sad, sad story of the end of the Good Old Days.

HOWARD WALDROP
Mary Margaret Road-Grader

It was the time of the Sun Dance and the Big Tractor Pull. Freddy-in-the-Hollow and I had traveled three days to be at the River. We were almost late, what with the sandstorm and the raid on the white settlement over to Old Dallas.

We pulled in with our wrecker and string of fine cars, many of them newly stolen. You should have seen Freddy and me that morning, the first morning of the Sun Dance. We were dressed in new-stolen fatigues and we had bright leather holsters and pistols. Freddy had a new carbine, too. We were wearing our silver and feathers and hard goods. I noticed many women watching us as we drove in. There seemed to be many more here than at the last Sun Ceremony. It looked to be a good time.

The usual crowd gathered before we could circle up our remuda. I saw Bob One-Eye and Nathan Big Gimp, the mechanics, come across from their circles. Already the cook fires were burning and women were skinning out the cattle that had been slaughtered early in the morning.

"Hoa!" I heard Nathan call as he limped to our wrecker. He was old; his left leg had been shattered in the Highway wars, he went back that far. He put his hands on his hips and looked over our line.

"I know that car, Billy-Bob Chevrolet," he said to me, pointing to an old Mercury. "Those son-a-bitch Dallas people stole it from me last year. I know its plates. It is good you stole it back. Maybe I will talk to you about doing car work to get it back sometime."

"We'll have to drink about it," I said.

"Let's stake them out," said Freddy-in-the-Hollow. "I'm tired of pulling them."

We parked them in two parallel rows and put up the signs, the strings of pennants, and the whirlers. Then we got in the wrecker and smoked.

Many people walked by. We were near the Karankawa fuel trucks, so people would be coming by all the time. Some I knew by sight, many I had known since I was a boy. They all walked by as though they did not notice the cars, but I saw them looking out of the corners of their eyes. Music was starting down the way, and most people were heading there. There would be plenty music in the next five days. I was in no hurry. We would all be danced out before the week was up.

Some of the men kept their strings tied to their tow trucks as if they didn't care whether people saw them or not. They acted as if they were ready to move out at any time. But that was not the old way. In the old times, you had your cars parked in rows so they could be seen. It made them harder to steal, too, especially if you had a fence.

But none of the Tractor Pullers had arrived yet, and that was what everybody was waiting for.

The talk was that Simon Red Bulldozer would be here this year. He was known from the Brazos to the Sabine, though he had never been to one of our ceremonies. He usually stayed in the Guadalupe River area.

But he had beaten everybody there and had taken all the fun out of their Big Pulls. So he had gone to the Karankawa Ceremony last year, and now was supposed to be coming to ours. They still talk about the time Simon Red Bulldozer took on Elmo John Deere two summers ago. I would have traded many plates to be there.

"We need more tobacco," said Freddy-in-the-Hollow.

"We should have stolen some from the whites," I said. "It will cost us plenty here."

"Don't you know anyone?"

"I know everyone, Fred," I said quietly (a matter of pride). "But nobody has any friends during the ceremonies. You pay for what you get."

It was Freddy-in-the-Hollow's first Sun Dance as a Raider. All the times before, he had come with his family. He still wore his coup-charm, a big VW symbol pried off the first car he'd boosted, on a chain around his neck. He was only seventeen summers. Someday he would be a better thief than me. And I'm the best there is.

Simon Red Bulldozer was expected soon, and all the men were talking a little and laying a few bets.

"You know," said Nathan Big Gimp, leaning against a wrecker at his shop down by the community fires, "I saw Simon turn over three tractors two summers ago, one after the other. The way he does it will amaze you, Billy-Bob."

I allowed as how he might be the man to bet on.

"Well, you really should, though the margin is slight. There's always the chance Elmo John Deere will show."

I said maybe that was what I was waiting for.

But it wasn't true. Freddy-in-the-Hollow and I had talked in English to a man from the Red River people the week before. He made some hints but hadn't really told us anything. They had a big Puller, he said, and you shouldn't lose your money on anyone else.

We asked if this person would show at our ceremony, and he allowed as how maybe, continuing to chew on some willow bark. So we allowed as how maybe we'd still put our hard goods on Simon Bulldozer.

He said that maybe he'd be down to see, and then drove off in his jeep with the new spark plugs we'd sold him.

The Red River people don't talk too much, but when they do, they say a lot. So we were waiting on the bets.

Women had been giving me the eye all day, and now there were a few of them looking openly at me; Freddy too, by reflected glory. I was thinking of doing something about it when we got a surprise.

At noon Elmo John Deere showed, coming in with his two wreckers and his Case 1190, his families, and twelve strings of cars. He was the richest man in the Nations, and his camp took a large part of the eastern end of the circle.

Then a little while later, the Man showed. Simon Red Bulldozer came only with his two wives, a few sons, and his transport truck. And in the back of it was the Red Bulldozer, which, they say, had killed a man before Simon stole it.

It's an old legend, and I won't tell it now.

And it's not important anymore anyway.

So we thought we were in for the best Pull ever, between two men we knew by deeds. Simon wanted to go smoke with Elmo, but Elmo sent a man over to tell Simon Red Bulldozer to keep his distance. There was bad blood between them, though Simon was such a good old boy that he was willing to forget it.

Not Elmo John Deere, though. His mind was bad. He was a mean man.

Freddy said it first, while we lay on the hood of the wrecker the eve of the dancing.

"You know," he said, "I'm young."

"Obvious," I said.

"But," he continued, "things are changing."

I had thought the same thing, though I hadn't said it. I pulled my bush hat up off my eyes, looked at the boy. He was part white and his mustache needed trimming, but otherwise he was all right.

"You may be right," I answered uneasily.

"Have you noticed how many horses there are this year, for God's sake?"

I had. Horses were used for herding our cattle and sheep. I mean, there were always *some* horses, but not this many. This year, people brought in whole remudas, twenty–thirty to a string. Some were even trading them like cars. It made my skin crawl.

"And the women," said Freddy-in-the-Hollow. "Loose is loose, but they go too far, really they do. They're not even wearing halters under their clothes, most of them. Jiggle-jiggle."

"Well, they're nice to look at. Times are getting hard," I said. The raid night before last was our first in two months, the only time we'd found anything worth the taking. Nothing but rusted piles of metal all up and down the whole Trinity. Not much on the Brazos, or the Sulphur. Pickings were slim, and you really had to fight like hell to get away with anything.

We sold a car early in the evening, for more plates than it was worth, which was good. But what Freddy had been talking and thinking about had me depressed. I needed a woman. I needed some good dope. Mostly, I wanted to kill something.

The dances started early, with people toking up on rabbit tobacco, shag bark, and hemp. The whole place smelled of burnt meat and grease, and there was singing in most of the lodges.

Oh, it was a happy group.

I was stripped down and doing some prayers. Tomorrow was the Sun Dance and the next day the contests. Freddy tried to find a woman and didn't have any luck. He came through twice while I was painting myself and smoking up. Freddy didn't hold with the prayer parts. I figure they can't hurt, and besides, there wasn't much else to do.

Two hours after dark, one of Elmo John Deere's men knifed one of Simon Red Bulldozer's sons. The delegation came for me about thirty minutes later.

I thought at first I might get my wish about killing something. But not tonight. They wanted me to arbitrate the judgment. Someone else would have to be executioner if one were needed.

"Watch the store, Freddy," I said, picking up my carbine.

I smoked while they talked. When Red Bulldozer's cousin got through, John Deere's grandfather spoke. The Bulldozer boy wasn't hurt too much, he wouldn't lose the arm. They brought the John Deere man before me. He glared at me across the smoke and said not a word.

I took two more puffs, cleaned my pipe. Then I broke down my carbine, worked on the selector pin for a while. I lit my other pipe and pointed to the John Deere man.

"He lives," I said. "He was drunk."

They let him leave the lodge.

"Elmo John Deere," I said.

"Uhm?" said fat Elmo.

"I think you should pay three mounts and ten plates to do this thing right. And give one man for three weeks to do the work of Simon Red Bulldozer's son."

Silence for a second, then Elmo spoke: "It is good what you say."

"Simon Red Bulldozer."

"Hm?"

"You should shake hands with Elmo John Deere and this should be the end of the matter."

"Good," he said.

They shook hands. Then each gave me a plate as soon as the others had left. One California and one New York. A 1993 and a '97. Not bad for twenty minutes' work.

It wasn't until I got back to the wrecker that I started shaking. That had been the first time I was arbiter. It could have made more bad trouble and turned hearts sour if I'd judged wrong.

"Hey, Fred!" I said. "Let's get real drunk and go see Wanda Hummingtires. They say she'll do it three ways all night."

The next dawn found us like a Karankawa coming across a new case of thirty-weight oil. It was morning, quick. I ought to know. I watched that goddamned sun come up and I watched it go down, and every minute of the day in between, and I never moved from the spot. I forgot everything that went on around me, and I barely heard the women singing or the prayers of the other men.

At dusk, Freddy-in-the-Hollow led me back to the wrecker and I slept like a stone mother log for twelve hours with swirling violet dots in my head.

I had had no visions. Some people get them, some don't.

I woke with the mother of all headaches, but after I smoked a while it went away. I wasn't a puller, but I was in two of the races, one on foot and one in the Mercury. I lost one and won the other.

I also won the side of beef in the morning shoot. Knocked the head off the bull with seven shots, clean as a whistle.

At noon we saw a cloud of dust coming over the third ridge. Then the outriders picked up the truck when it came over the second. It was coming too fast.

The truck stopped with a roar and a squeal of brakes. It had a long lumpy canvas cover on the back. Then a woman climbed down from the cab. She was the most gorgeous woman I'd ever seen—and I'd seen Nellie Firestone two summers ago.

Nellie hadn't come close to this girl. She had long straight black hair and a beautiful face. She was built like nothing I'd seen before. She wore tight coveralls and had a .357 Magnum strapped to her hip.

"Who runs the Pulls?" she asked, in English, of the first man who reached her.

He didn't know what to do. Women never talk like that.

"Winston Mack Truck," said Freddy at my side, pointing.

"What do you mean?" asked one of the young men. "Why do you want to know?"

"Because I'm going to enter the Pull," she said.

Tribal language mumbles went around the circle. Very negative ones.

"Don't give me any of that shit," she said. "How many of you know of Alan Backhoe Shovel?"

He was another legend over in Ouachita River country.

"Well," she said, and held up a serial number plate from a backhoe tractor scoop, "I beat him last week."

"Hua, hua, hua!" the chanting started.

"What is your name, woman?" asked one of Mack Truck's men.

"Mary Margaret Road-Grader," she said, and glared back at him.

"Freddy," I said, "put the money on her."

So we had a council. You gotta have a council for everything, especially when honor and dignity and other manly virtues are involved.

Winston Mack Truck was pretty old, but he was still spry and had some muscles left on him. His head was a puckered lump because he had once crashed in a burner while raiding over on the Brazos. He only had one ear, and it wasn't much of one.

But he did have respect, and he did have power, and he had more sons than anyone in the Nations, ten or eleven of them. They were all there in council, with all the heads of other families.

Winston Mack Truck smoked a while, then called us to session.

Mary Margaret Road-Grader wasn't allowed inside the lodge. It seemed sort of stupid to me. If they wouldn't let her in here, they sure weren't going to let her enter the Pull. But I kept my tongue. You can never tell.

I was right. Old man Mack Truck can see clear through to tomorrow.

"Brothers," he said. "We have a problem here."

"Hua, hua, hua."

"We have been asked to let a woman enter the Pulls."

Silence.

"I do not know if it's a good thing," he continued. "But our brothers to the east have seen fit to let her do so. This woman claims to have defeated Alan Backhoe Shovel in fair contest. She enters this as proof."

He placed the serial plate in the center of the lodge.

"I will listen now," he said, and sat back, folding his arms.

They went around the circle, some speaking, some not.

It was Simon Red Bulldozer himself who changed the tone of the council. "I have never seen a woman in a Pull," he said. "Or in any contest other than those for women."

He paused. "But I have never wrestled against Alan Backhoe Shovel, either. I know of no one who has bested him. Now this woman claims to have done so. It would be interesting to see if she were a good Puller."

"You want a woman in the contest?" asked Elmo, out of turn.

Richard Ford Pinto, the next speaker, stared at Elmo until he realized his mistake. But Ford Pinto saved face for him by asking the same question of Simon.

"I would like to see if she is a good Puller," said Simon, adamantly. He would commit himself no further.

Then it was Elmo's turn. "My brothers!" he began, so I figured he would be at it for a long time. "We seem to spend all our time in council, rather than having fun like we should. It is not good, it makes my heart bitter.

"The idea that a woman can get a hearing at council revolts me. Were this a young man not yet proven, or an Elder who had been given his Service feather, I would not object. But, brothers, this is a woman!" His voice came falsetto now, and he began to chant:

"I have seen the dawn of bad days, brothers.

"But never worse than this.

"A woman enters our camp, brothers!

"A woman! A woman!"

He sat down and said no more in the conference.

It was my turn.

"Hear me, Pullers and Stealers!" I said. "You know me. I am a man of my word and a man of my deeds. But the time has come for deeds alone. Words must be put away. We must decide whether a woman can be as good as a man. We cannot be afraid of a woman! Or can some of us be?"

They all howled and grumbled just like I wanted them to. You can't suggest men in council are afraid of anything.

Of course, we voted to let her in the contest, like I knew we would.

Changes in history come easy, you know?

They pulled the small tractors first, the Ford 250s and the Honda Fieldmasters and such. I wasn't much interested in watching young boys fly through the air and hurt themselves. So me and Freddy wandered over where the big tractor men were warming up. The Karankawas were selling fuel from the old Houston refineries hand over hose. A couple of the Pullers had refused, like Elmo at first, to do anything with a woman in the contest.

But even Elmo was there watching when Mary Margaret Road-Grader unveiled her machine. There were lots of *oohs* and *ahhs* when she started pulling the tarp off that monster.

Nobody had seen one in years, except maybe as piles of rust on the roadside. It was long and low, and looked much like a yellow elephant's head with wheels stuck on the end of the trunk. The cab was high and shiny glass. Even the doors still worked. The blade was new and bright; it looked as if it had never been used.

The letters on the side were sharp and black, unfaded. Even the paint job was new. That made me suspicious about the Alan Backhoe Shovel contest. I took a gander at the towball while she was atop the cab loosening the straps. It *was* worn. Either she had been lucky in the contest, or she'd had sense enough to put on a worn towball.

Everybody watched her unfold the tarp (one of those heavy smelly kind that can fall on you and kill you) but she had no helpers. So I climbed up to give her a hand.

One of the women called out something and some others took it up. Most of the men just shook their heads.

There was a lot of screaming and hoo-rawing from the little Pulls, so I had to touch her on the shoulder to let her know I was up there. She turned fast and her hand went for her gun before she saw it was me.

And I saw in her eyes not killer hate, but something else: I saw she was scared and afraid she'd have to kill someone.

"Let me help you with this," I said, pointing to the tarp.

She didn't say anything, but she didn't object, either.

"For a good judge," called out fat Elmo, "you have poor taste in women."

There was nothing I could do but keep busy while they laughed.

They still talk about that first afternoon, the one that was the beginning of the end.

First, Elmo John Deere hitched onto an IH 1200 and drug it over the line in about three seconds. No contest, and no one was surprised. Then Simon Red Bulldozer cranked up, his starter engine sounded like a beehive in a rainstorm. He hooked the chain on his towbar and revved up. The guy he was pulling against was a Paluxy River man named Theodore Bush Hog. He didn't hook up right. The chain came off as soon as Simon let go his clutches. So Bush Hog was disqualified. That was bad, too; there were some dark-horse bets on him.

Then it was the turn of Mary Margaret Road-Grader and Elmo John Deere. Elmo had said at first he wasn't going to enter against her. Then they told him how much money was bet on him, and he couldn't afford to pass it up. Though the excuse he used was that somebody had to show this woman her place, and it might as well be him, first thing off.

You had to be there to see it. Mary Margaret whipped that road-grader around like it was a Toyota, and backed it onto the field. She climbed down with the motor running and hooked up. She was wearing tight blue coveralls and her hair was blowing in the river breeze. I thought she was the most beautiful woman I had ever seen. I didn't want her to get her heart broken. But there was nothing I could do. It was all on her, now.

Elmo John Deere had one of his sons come out and hand the chain to him. He was showing he didn't want to be first to touch anything this woman had held.

He hooked up, and Mary Margaret Road-Grader signaled she was ready. The judge dropped the pitchfork and they leaned on their gas feeds.

There was a jerk and a sharp clang, and the chain looked like a straight steel rod. Elmo gunned for all he had and the big tractor wheels began to turn slowly, and then they spun and caught and Elmo's Case tractor eased a few feet forward.

Mary Margaret never looked back. (Elmo half turned in his seat; he was so good working the pedals and gears he didn't need to look at them.) When she upshifted, the transmission on the yellow road-grader screamed and lowered in tone.

I could hardly hear the machines for the yells and screams around me. They sounded like war yells. Some of the men were yelling in blood-lust at the woman. But I heard others cheering her, too. They seemed to want Elmo to lose.

Mary Margaret shifted again and her feet worked like pistons on the pedals. And as quickly as it had begun, it was over.

There was a groaning noise, Elmo's wheels began to spin uselessly, and in a second or two his tractor had been drug twenty feet across the line.

Elmo got down from his seat. Instead of congratulating the winner, he turned and strode off the field. He signaled one of his sons to retrieve the vehicle.

Mary Margaret was checking the damage to her machine.

Simon Red Bulldozer was next. They had been pulling for twelve minutes when the contest was called by Winston Mack Truck himself. There was wonder on his face as he walked out to the two contestants. Nobody had ever seen anything like it.

The two had fought each other to a standstill. When they were stopped, Mary Margaret's grader was six or seven inches from its original position, but Simon's bulldozer had moved all over its side of the line. The ground was destroyed forever three feet each side of the line. It had been that close.

Winston Mack Truck stopped before them. We were all whistling our approval when Simon Red Bulldozer held up his hand.

"Hear me, brothers. I will accept no share in honors. They must be all mine, or none at all."

Winston looked with his puckered face at Mary Margaret. She shrugged. "Fine with me."

Maybe I was the only one who knew she was acting tough for the crowd. I looked at her, but couldn't catch her eye.

"Listen, Fossil Creek People," said old Mack Truck. "This has been a draw. But Simon Red Bulldozer is not satisfied. And Mary Margaret Road-Grader has accepted. Tomorrow as the sun crosses the tops of the eastern trees, we will begin again. I have declared a fifth night and a sixth day to the Dance and Pulls."

Shouts of joy broke from the crowd. This had happened only once in my life, for some religious reason or other, and that was when I was a child. The Dance and Pulls were the only meeting of the year when all the Fossil Creek People came together. It was to have ended this night.

Now we would have another day.

The cattle must have sensed this. You could hear them bellowing in fear even before the first of the butchers crossed the camp toward them.

"Where are you going?" asked Freddy as I picked up my carbine, boots, and blanket.

"I think I will sleep with Mary Margaret Road-Grader," I said.

"Watch out," said Freddy. "I bet she makes love like she drives that machine."

She was ready to cry, she was so tired. We were under the road-grader; the tarp had been refolded over it. There was four feet of crawl space between the trailer and the ground.

"You drive well. How did you learn?"

"From my brother, Donald Fork Lift. He once used one of these. And when I found this one—"

"Where? A museum? A tunnel?"

"An old museum, a strange one. It must have been sealed off before the Highway wars. I found it there a year ago."

"Why didn't your brother pull with this machine here, instead of you?"

She was very quiet, and then she looked at me. "You are a man of your word? That must be true, or you would not have been called to judge, as I heard."

"That is true."

She sighed, flung her hair from her head with one hand. "He would have," she said, "except he broke his hip last month on a raid at Sand Creek. He was going to come. But since he had already taught me how to work it, I drove it instead."

"And first thing you defeat Alan Backhoe Shovel?"

She looked at me and frowned. "I—I—"

"You made it up, didn't you?"

"Yes."

"As I thought. But I have given my word. Only you and I will know. Where did you get the serial plate?"

"One of the machines in the same place where I found my grader. Only it was in worse shape. But its plate was still shiny. I took it the night before I left with the truck. I didn't think anybody would know what Alan Backhoe Shovel's real plate was."

"You are smart," I said. "You are also very brave, for a woman, and foolish. You might have been killed. You may still be."

"Not if I win," she said, her eyes hard. "They couldn't afford to. If I lose, it would be another matter. I am sure I would be killed before I got to the Trinity. But I don't intend to lose."

"No," I said. "I will escort you as near your people as I can. I have hunted the Trinity, but never as far as the Red. I can go with you past the old Fork of the Trinity."

She looked at me. "You're trying to get into my pants."

"Well, yes."

"Let's smoke first," she said. She opened a leather bag, rolled a parchment cigarette, lit it. I smelled the aroma of something I hadn't smoked in six moons. It was the best dope I'd ever had, and that was saying something.

I don't know what we did afterward, but it felt good.

"To the finish," said Winston Mack Truck, and threw the pitchfork into the ground.

It was better than the day before—the bulldozer like a squat red monster and the road-grader like avenging yellow death. On the first yank, Simon pulled the grader back three feet. The crowd went wild. His treads clawed at the dirt then, and the road-grader lurched and regained three feet. Back and forth, the great clouds and black smoke whistling from the exhausts like the bellowing of bulls.

Then I saw what Simon was going to do. He wanted to wear the road-grader down, keep a strain on it, keep gaining, lock himself, downshift. Yesterday he had tried to finish the grader on might. It had not worked. Today he was taking his time.

He could afford to. The road-grader was light in front; it had hard rubber tires instead of treads. When it lurched, the front end sometimes left the ground. If Simon timed it right, the grader wheels would rise while he downshifted and he could pull the yellow machine another few inches.

Mary Margaret was alternately working the pedals and levers, trying to get an angle on the squat red dozer. She was trying to pull across the back end of the tractor, not against it.

That would lose her the contest, I knew. She was vulnerable. When the wheels were up, Simon could inch her back. The only time he lost ground was when he downshifted while the claws dug their way into the ground. Then he lost purchase for a second. Mary Margaret could maybe use that, if she were in a better position.

They pulled, they strained, but slowly Mary Margaret Road-Grader was losing to Simon Red Bulldozer.

Then she did something unexpected. She lurched the road-grader and dropped the blade.

The crowd went gonzo, then was silent. The shiny blade dug into the ground.

The lurch gained her an inch or two. Simon, who never looked back either, knew something was wrong. He turned, and when his eyes left the panel, Mary Margaret jerked his bulldozer back another two feet.

We never thought in all those years we had heard about Simon Red Bulldozer that he would not have kept his blade in working order. He reached out to his blade lever and pulled it, and nothing happened. We saw him panic then, and the contest was going to Mary Margaret when. . .

The black plastic of the steering wheel showered up in her face. I heard the shot at the same time and dropped to the ground. I saw Mary Margaret holding her eyes with both hands.

Simon Red Bulldozer must not have heard the shot above the roaring of his engine, because he lurched the bulldozer ahead and started pulling the road-grader back over the line.

It was Elmo John Deere doing the shooting. I had my carbine off my shoulder and was firing by the time I knew where to shoot.

Elmo must have been drunk. He was trying to kill an opponent who had bested him in a fair fight.

I shot him in the leg, just above the knee, and ended his Pulling days forever. I aimed at his head then, but he dropped his rifle and screamed so I didn't shoot him again. If I had, I would have killed him.

It took all the Fossil Creek People to keep his sons from killing me. There was a judgment, of course, and I was let go free.

That was the last Sun Dance they had. The Fossil Creek People separated. Elmo's people split off from them, and then went bitter crazy. The Fossil Creek People even steal from them now, when they have anything worth stealing.

The Pulls ended, too. People said if they were going to cause so much blood, they could do without them. It was bad business. Some people stopped stealing machines and cars and plates and started bartering for food and trading horses.

The old ways are dying. I have seen them come to an end in my time, and everything is getting worthless. People are getting lazy. There isn't anything worth doing. I sit on this hill over the Red River and smoke with Freddy-in-the-Hollow and sometimes we get drunk.

Mary Margaret sometimes gets drunk with us.

She lost one of her eyes that day at the Pulls. It was hit by splinters from the steering wheel. Me and Freddy took her back to her people in her truck. That was six years ago. Once, years ago, I went past the place where we held the last Sun Dance. Her road-grader was already a rust pile of junk with everything stripped off it.

I still love Mary Margaret Road-Grader, yes. She started things. Women have come into other ceremonies now, and in the councils.

I still love Mary Margaret, but it's not the same love I had for her that day at the last Sun Dance, watching her work the pedals and levers, her hair flying, her feet moving like birds across the cab.

I love her. She has grown a little fat. She loves me, though.

We have each other, we have the village, we have cattle, we have this hill over the river where we smoke and get drunk.

But the rest of the world has changed.

All this, all the old ways . . . gone.

The world has turned bitter and sour in my mouth. It is no good, the taste of ashes is in the wind. The old times are gone.

One of the finest series in contemporary SF is Michael Bishop's UrNu series, stories that share a common setting in a domed Atlanta in a deserted future Georgia that has been overrun by snakes and kudzu vine, abandoned to sun and silences. Inside the dome, Bishop's Atlanta is haunted and cavernous in spite of the close-packed, clangorous, sweaty hordes of people who inhabit and haunt it; it is a place of lifts and levels, combcrawlers and hoisterjacks, whose constrained and fearful citizens have cut themselves off from the world and the open sky.

The UrNu stories (each of which can stand alone, although several share common characters who are viewed over a long span of years) began appearing in 1970 with "If a Flower Could Eclipse." The story at hand, "The Samurai and the Willows," a finalist for the 1976 Nebula Award, is the best of the four UrNu stories to date, and, in fact, is one of the best SF stories I have read in years.

Another UrNu novella, "Old Folks at Home," is upcoming in University verse 8 *(Doubleday). In addition, Bishop says, "in the early spring of 1977 Berkley/Putnam will publish a novel entitled* A Little Knowledge *whose protagonist is the son of Georgia Cawthorn and Ty Kosturko," two characters from "The Samurai and the Willows."*

Bishop, thirty, is married, has two children, and makes his home in Pine Mountain, Georgia. His previous novels include A Funeral for the Eyes of Fire *(Ballantine) and* And Strange at Ecbatan the Trees *(Harper & Row).*

MICHAEL BISHOP
The Samurai and the Willows

1. *Basenji* and *Queequeg.*

She called him Basenji because the word was Bantu but had a Japanese ring, at least to her. It was appropriate for other reasons, too: he was small, and doglike, and very seldom spoke. No bark to him at all; not too much bite, either. And he, for his part, called her Queequeg (when he called her anything) because at first he could tell that the strangeness of it disconcerted her, at least a little. Later her reaction to this name changed subtly, but the significance of the change escaped him and he kept calling her by it. After a time, Basenji and Queequeg were the only names they ever used with each other.

"Basenji," she would say, harping on her new subject, "when you gonna bring one of them little bushes down here for our cyoob'cle?"

"They're not bushes," he would answer (if he answered). "They're bonsai: B.O.N.S.A.I. Bonsai."

More than likely, she would be standing over him when she asked, her athletic legs spread like those of a Nilotic colossus and her carven black face hanging somewhere above him in the stratosphere. Small and fastidious, he would be sitting on a reed mat in his sleeper-cove, where she intruded with blithe innocence, or in the wingback chair in the central living area. He would be reading on the reed mat (a pun here that she would never appreciate) or pretending, in the wingback, to compose a poem, since ordinarily she respected the sanctity of these pastimes. In any case, he would not look up—even though Queequeg's shadow was ominous, even though the smell coming off her legs and stocking-clad body was annoyingly carnal. By the Forty-Seven Ronin, she was big. Did she have to stand in front of him like that, her shadow and her smell falling on him like the twin knives of death and sex? Did she?

"Well," she would say, not moving, "they cute, those bushes. Those bonsai." And then she would grin (though he wouldn't look up to see it), her big white teeth like a row of bleached pinecone wings.

They shared a cubicle on Level 9 in the domed city, the Urban Nucleus of Atlanta. Basenji was Simon Fowler. Queequeg was Georgia Cawthorn. They were not related, they were not married, they were not bound by religious ties or economic necessity. Most of the time they didn't particularly like each other.

How they had come to be cubicle mates was this: Simon Fowler was thirty-eight or -nine, a man on the way down, a nisei whose only skills were miniature landscaping and horticulture. Georgia Cawthorn was eighteen and, as she saw it, certainly only a temporary resident of the Big Bad Basement, the donjon keep of the

Urban Nucleus. Fowler, it seemed, was trying to bury himself, to put eight levels of concrete (as well as the honeycombing of the dome) between himself and the sky. She, on the other hand, was abandoning the beloved bosom of parents and brothers, who lived in one of those pre-Evacuation "urban renewal" slums still crumbling into brick dust surfaceside. And thus it was that both Simon Fowler and Georgia Cawthorn had applied for living quarters *under*, he perversely specifying Level 9 (having already worked down from the towers and four understrata), she ingenuously asking for whatever she could get. A two-person cubicle fell vacant on Level 9. The computer-printed names of Georgia Cawthorn and Simon Fowler headed the UrNu Housing Authority's relocation list, and the need for a decision showered down on them like an unannounced rain (the sort so favored by the city's spontaneity-mad internal meteorologists). Georgia didn't hesitate; she said yes at once. Simon Fowler wanted an umbrella, a way out of the deluge; but since the only out available involved intolerable delay and a psychic house arrest on the concourses of 7, he too had said yes. They met each other on the day they moved in.

They had now lived together for four months. And most of the time they didn't like each other very much, although Queequeg had tried. She tried harder than he did. She had taken an interest in Basenji's work, hadn't she? She had asked about those little trees he nurtured, wired, shaped, and worried over in his broken-down greenhouse surfaceside. And they were pretty, those bonsai: Basenji really knew how to wire up a bush. Queequeg had first seen them about two months ago, when she had gone into the shop to discover her cubiclemate in his "natch'l environment." Which was more than Basenji had ever done. He didn't give gyzym, he didn't, that she was a glissador, one of those lithe human beings who cruised the corridors of the hive on silent ball bearings inset in the soles of their glierboots. No, sir. He didn't give gyzym.

"How come, Basenji, you don' come see me, where I work?"

This time he answered, almost with some bite: "Dammit, Queequeg, you're in this corridor, then in that. How would I find you?"

"You could come to H.Q. To glizador-dizpatch."

A foreign language she spoke. And he said, "Not me. Your rollerskating friends close in on me."

"Which ones? Ty?"

"All of them. You're rink-refugees, Queequeg, fugitives from a recess that's never ended." And then he wouldn't answer anymore, that would be all she could pull from him.

It was probably lucky that the shift-changes kept them apart so much. They weren't really compatible, they weren't the same sort of people at all. Being cubiclemates was an insanity that they usually overcame by minor insolences like calling each other Basenji and Queequeg. That was their communication.

In fact, though the name had at first hurt and bewildered her (she had had to ask Ty Kosturko, a white boy apprenticing with her, what it meant), Georgia Cawthorn now knew that it was the only thing that kept her from falling on Simon Fowler's diminutive person and pounding his head against the floor a time or two. But for Queequeg, but for that insulting, mythopoeic nickname, she would have long ago harpooned her sullen little florist.

2. *The Kudzu Shop.*

Georgia/Queequeg, two days after the argument (if you could call it an argument) during which she had protested his never looking in on *her,* tried again. After the glissaors' shift-changing, after a sprayshower in their otherwise empty cubicle, she rode a lift-tube surfaceside and angled her way through the pedestrian courts leading to Basenji's shop.

Why I makin' mysef a fool? she wondered. She didn't have any answers, she just let her long body stride past the ornamental fountains and the silver-blue reflecting windows of the New Peachtree. Distractedly swinging the end of her chain-loop belt, she examined herself in the windows: a woman, Zuluesque maybe, but no less a female for her size.

Simon Fowler's hothouse lay beyond New Peachtree in an uncleared tenement section much like the one she had grown up in (Bondville, across town). It was a shabby structure wedged between collapsing ruins, some of the useless glass panels in the roof broken out or crazed with liquescent scars. No wonder that her doggy little man kept moving down. Who'd walk into a place

like Basenji's to buy a hydroponic rose for their most favorite
bodyburner, much less something expensive like a ceiling basket
or a gardenia bouquet? She didn't even know why *she* was punish-
ing herself by seeking out the little snoot. Hadn't she already done
this once? Wasn't that enough?

Maybe it was the willow he'd shown her. She wanted to see it
again as much as she wanted to see him. Shoot, she didn't want to
see him at all. *Tang,* the bell went: *ting tang.*

Moist flowers hung from the walls; ferns stuck out their green
tongues from every corner; potted plants made a terra cotta
fortress in the middle of the floor. And the last time she had come
in, Basenji's vaguely oriental face had hung amidst all this greenery like an unfired clay plate, just that brittle and brown. He had
been at the counter fiddling with the bonsai willow. But today
Queequeg found no one in the outer shop, only growing things
and their heavy fragrances.

"Basenji!" she called. "Hey, you, Basenji!"

He came, slowly, out of the long greenhouse behind the shop's
business area. He was brushing dirt from his hands, dirt and little
sprigs of moss.

"You again," he said. "What do you want?"

"You sweet, Basenji. You damn sweet."

"What do you want?" He didn't call her Queequeg. That wasn't
a good sign; no sir. Not a good sign at all.

She thought a minute, hand on hip, her green wraparound
clinging to the curve of her stance. She was a head taller than he.
"I wanna see that little bush you had out here last time."

"You saw it last time, you know. I'm busy."

"You busy. You also ain' no easy man to do bidness with,
Basenji. I thinkin' 'bout buyin' that bush. What you think of that?"

"That you probably won't be able to afford it."

"I a saver, Basenji. Since I come on bidness, you boun' to show
me what I come to see. You has to."

"That willow's worth—"

"Uh-uh," she said. "No, sir. I gonna see it before you sen' me
packin' with yo' prices."

What could he do? A black Amazon with grits in her mouth and
something a little, just a little, more substantial than that beneath

her scalp cap of neo-nostalgiac cornrows; elegant, artificial braidwork recalling an Africa that probably no longer existed. (The same went for his mother's homeland, the very same.) Poor Basenji. These were the very words he thought as he stoically motioned Queequeg around the counter: Poor Basenji. He had even begun to call himself by the name she had given him.

3. *Pages from a notebook.*

This docility, this acquiescence, he despised in himself. Earlier that morning he had taken out the notebook in which he sometimes recorded his responses to the stimuli of his own emotions; he had opened it to a pair of familiar pages. On the top shelf of the counter around which he had just led Queequeg, the notebook lay open to these pages. This is what, long before moving to Level 9, Simon Fowler had written there:

> Bushido is the way of the warrior. But our own instinctive bushido has been bred out of us. Most of us have forgotten what horror exists outside the dome to keep us inside. Whatever it is, we have not fought it.

> Seppuku is ritual suicide, reserved for warriors and those who have earned the right to die with dignity. Hara-kiri (belly cutting) is a vulgarity; to commit it, and to think of it as belly cutting, one must be either a woman or a losel.

> My father died as a direct result of alcoholism. "Insult to the brain," said the final autopsy report. This is the same meaningless euphemism doctors listed as the cause of Dylan Thomas's death, over ninety years ago in the city that is now the Urban Nucleus of New York.

> The ancient Japanese caste of the samurai despised poetry as an effeminate activity. Sometimes I view it that way too, especially when I am writing it. A samurai would also despise the sort of introspection I practice in this notebook.

> Maybe not. The great shogun Iyeyasu (1542–1616) attempted a reformation of the habits of the samurai; he encouraged them to develop their appreciation of the arts. Iyeyasu died in the same year that William Shakespeare died.

> Witness the example of that twentieth-century samurai and artist, Yukio Mishima. Can he not be said to be the

latter-day embodiment of Iyeyasu's attempts at gentling his nation's warriors? Or was he instead the embodiment of the militarization of the poet?

Bonsai is the art of shaping seedlings that would grow to full size to an exquisite, miniature environment. Bonsai is also the name of any tree grown by this method. I am an expert at such shaping.

Each citizen of the Urban Nucleus is an artifact of a bonsai process more exacting than the one I am master of. Our environment is a microcosm. We are little. We are symmetrical. But wherein are we beautiful?

Seymour Glass, who loved the haiku, who lived when a man could let a cat bite his left hand while gazing at the full moon, is the patron saint of suicides. He was not, however, a samurai.

Although no courtesan, my mother was mistress of the geisha graces: poetry, dance, song, and all the delicate works of hand. Kazuko Hadaka, a Japanese. Kazuko gave me a gentleness not in my father. And my docility.

I gave my mother to a monolithic institution, where she failed and died. Cause of death: "Insult to the heart." Day 53 of the Month Winter, Year 2038 in the New Calendar designation.

Yukio Mishima: "To samurai and homosexual the ugliest vice is femininity. Even though their reasons for it differ, the samurai and the homosexual do not see manliness as instinctive but rather as something gained only from moral effort."

I have heard bonsai spoken of as "slow sculpture." That it is. But so is the process by which the dome shapes its inhabitants. Are we any more aware of the process than my bonsai are conscious of their protracted dwarfing? Or do my sculptures, as do I, think and feel?

And what of those who are neither warriors nor gayboys? Does it not also require of them moral effort to establish the certainty of their manhood? If so, what regimen must these others undertake?

Easier than discovering the answer, much easier, is to sink

through the circles of our Gehenna. Can the willow ignore its wiring?

Bushido, seppuku, samurai, bonsai, haiku, geisha. In this catalogue, somewhere amid the tension among its concepts: the answer. How to sort it out? How to sort it out?

All of this was written in Simon Hadaka Fowler's tight, up-and-down cursive in black ink. A roll of florist's tape lay on the corner of the the right-hand page of the open notebook. Thumb prints and smudges covered the two pages like official notations on a birth certificate. No one but Basenji, of course, would have supposed the notebook to be there.

4. *Layering a willow.*

So Basenji, that doggy little man, and Queequeg, the lady harpoonist, went on through the greenhouse, whose various counters and table trays were all overhung by fluorescent lights, and out to the open patio between the collapsing buildings: Queequeg unaware of what was going on in her cubiclemate's hangdog head, Basenji uncertain as to what this persistent Zulu wanted of him. He led her to the rough wooden table where he had been working when she came in. He sat down. She looked around, noticing the shelves against the patio's shoulder-high walls and the little potted trees sitting on these shelves. In spite of the rusted fire escapes and hovering brick dust outside, every-thing in the patio compound was spick-and-span.

Then she saw the bonsai on the table. "That the one," she said, letting her shadow drop on him like a weight. "That the one I saw out front last time I come. Hey, what you doin' to it?"

"Layering it."

"You took it out o' that pot, that blue shiny one," she accused, leaning over his shoulder. Then: "What this layerin', Basenji?"

He explained that he was trying to establish two more of the sinuously stunted trees before the year was out and that you couldn't leave the mother tree in an expensive ornamental Chinese pot such as she had last seen it in, not, anyhow, if you were tying off tourniquets of copper wire below the nodes where you wanted the new roots to develop. Since Queequeg, for once, kept silent, he finished the last tourniquet and began wrapping the willow's layered branches in plastic.

"That the one," Queequeg said, "I wanna buy."

"Can't now, Missy Queequeg, even if you could afford it. This is going to take a while. But next year we'll have three trees instead of one, all of them fine enough for pots like the blue Chinese one."

"We?"

"The shop," he corrected. "The Kudzu Shop."

"I see." Her shadow, however she had managed to drape it over him, suddenly withdrew. She stopped by the shelves against the back wall, and he looked up to see her in front of them. "You got more of them bushes right here," she said. "Five of 'em."

"Only one of them's a willow, though." Skipping the willow, he named the trees across the top shelf. "The others are a maple, a Sargent juniper, a cherry tree, and another juniper." He had potted each one in a vessel appropriate to the shape and variety of the tree it contained. Or, rather, had repotted them into these new vessels after taking the bonsai over from his mother's care.

"Well, you sell me this other one, then. This willow like the first one."

"What you want with that *bush*?" he said, mocking her. "What you want with a runty ole willow, Queequeg? You gonna rollerskate with a bush in yo' arms?" He could bite if he wanted.

It wasn't a bite to her; she ignored it. "Man, I gonna bring that tree into our cyoob'cle where you won' let me bring it. When it mine, I do with it what I want."

"These are bonsai," he told her then, as if she were a customer instead of his annoying cubiclemate. "They're real trees, not toys. Don't be deceived by their size. Just like any real tree, they belong outside. You can't keep them in any of the understrata and expect them to survive, much less the ninth one. That's why they're usually outside on the patio here, instead of in the shop or greenhouse."

"Look up," she said contemptuously.

He stared at her without comprehension.

"I say look up, Basenji, look up."

He did what she asked and saw a faintly golden honeycombing of plexiglass and steel; no sky, just the underside of the Dome. All the tumble-down buildings seemed to funnel his gaze to this astonishing revelation.

"What you call *outside*? When you *ever* been outside?"

"Nobody's been outside," he said. "Nobody who was born here, anyway. Not outside the tunnels between cities. The requisite, Missy Queequeg, is *weather*, and that we've got. Underneath there's only air conditioning or dry heat. In three days you'd kill any bonsai you took down there, maybe that willow especially."

"Well, I don' have to keep it down there all the time, you know. So I ready now. How much you askin'?"

"Two hundred dollars."

"What kind o' dollars?"

"UrNu dollars. Two hundred UrNu dollars."

"You crazy. You think this bush a money tree, Basenji?" Incredulous, she canted her hip, leaned forward, and looked at the willow as if to determine if its bark were gold plate.

"I've had that tree thirteen years. My mother started it, and she had it at least twenty before that. The others—the junipers, the cherry, the maple—are that old, or older. One or two of them may have been started even before there was a Dome. Handed down to my mother from—"

"If hand-me-downs precious, I a millionaire, Basenji." She moved to the greenhouse entrance. "You mighty right," she said from the doorway. "Without I auction off all my brothers' ole socks and nightshirts, I can't afford that bonsai."

She left him on the patio sitting over the unpotted and clumsily trussed willow. When he heard the *ting-tang* of the bell in the outer shop, he began to whistle.

5. *The interpretation of dreams.*

Simon/Basenji sometimes had a bad dream, not frequently but often enough. Before he had moved down to Level 9, the dream had been persistent about rubbing down his nervous limbs with night sweat: every three or four days the images would get a screening. But in the last four months, having reached bottom, he had apparently developed a degree of immunity to the dream. Once a week, no more.

Anyhow, here is the dream:

Always he finds himself on the floor of his greenhouse, under one of the table trays filled with fuchsia or rose geraniums. Like Tom Thumb, he has no more height than a grown man's opposed digit. When he looks up, the bottom of the wooden table seems as far away as the honeycombing of the Dome when he is awake. Always he realizes that he has been hiding under the table waiting for night. And as the city's artificial night slides into place, he creeps out of the hothouse and onto the patio where we have just seen him layering a willow and talking with Queequeg.

A small orange moon hangs under the Dome, and the "sky" behind and around it is like a piece of velvet funeral bunting. No glow at all from the ordinarily fluorescent buildings beyond both his own patio and the collapsed tenements surrounding it.

Basenji wears silken robes, a kind of kimono. He resembles a musician or a poet. The robes are cumbersome, and he would like to discard them but discovers that the material is seamless.

He stands on a piece of brick tile and stares at the wooden shelves ranged above him against the back wall of the patio. So small is he, the shelves look to him like stone ledges on a mountain face. On the highest shelf sit the willow trees in their glazed pots; not only the willows, the other bonsai besides. The orange moon (how did it come to be there?) provides just enough light to make this monumental undertaking possible. The seamless kimono, cinched at his waist with a golden strip of silk, several times almost sends him tripping over its skirts to the patio stones. This fate is what combcrawlers and hoisterjacks refer to as the "glory of splatterdom." Incongruous as it is, this phrase comes to Basenji's dreaming mind and offends by its slangy graphicness.

Not solely because it mocks death, though that has its part.

Shaking and damp on the topmost shelf of his patio, the arduous climb at last done, Basenji turns and surveys his holdings. How meager they are, even for a man the stature of his dream self. Now his robes seem even more ridiculous, sweat-soaked as they are, and he tries again to tear them off. They won't come, they bind him in.

He succeeds, however, in tearing away from his garment the golden sash about his waist. This he wraps evral times about his hands. The sash has tassels at regular intervals along its bottom edge: an overpretty belt. Basenji, perhaps summoning energy from his sleeping body, tries to rend it to pieces.

Thwarted, he ceases and begins walking back and forth along the shelf, looking at the miniature trees.

Finally he settles upon the older of the two willows, the one with the more artfully sculpted form, and expends his last reserves of strength and will getting into the Chinese pot and knotting the sash in a way he thinks appropriate to his purpose.

After which, using the sash, he hangs himself from the willow: A little man dangling unnoticed beneath foliage so delicate and veil-like that a picture of impact-upon-concrete rises before his backward-rolling eyeballs as if in reproach. What warrior has ever killed himself in so womanish a way? It is too painful, this thought. He is a Judas to himself.

But then the limb of the bonsai snaps: Basenji falls on his kimono-clad backside into the pot he sweated so hard to clamber over, just to get to a place where he could hang himself. Now this. Lying there bruised, the broken willow branch attached to him by a golden umbilical, he finds himself shamelessly weeping, whether out of frustration or out of remorse at having disfigured the bonsai he cannot tell. He hopes that a robin or a cardinal (species officially sheltered inside the Dome) will come along to sever his bond to the willow and to devour him, piece by grateful piece.

High overhead, through cascading leaves, the little orange moon blanks out: an extinguished jack-o-lantern.

After this, Basenji invariably woke up, sweating his inevitable sweat. It happened less often now that he had hit bottom, but it still happened. What he needed was a Joseph or a Sigmund Freud to unravel the symbolism. Not really. He could do it himself, he was fairly sure, if he genuinely wanted to. But he didn't. He genuinely didn't want to. It frightened him too much, the image-ridden virus of his nightmare.

Nevertheless, two or three pages in his battered notebook were devoted to an account very much like the one given here.

6. *Ty Kosturko*

Outside the Kudzu Shop, she thought: Two hundred UrNus, that baa-ad news. And Basenji, he crazy.

Well, she wasn't going to go back down to their cubicle to wait until he came dragging in with the next shift-change (which he could observe or not observe as he liked, anyway). If she didn't have two hundred earnies to squander on a potted fancy-pants bush, she at least had pay-credits to go shopping with, and she was sure enough going to prom a few of them for some kind of brightener; a compensatory purchase, something to make up for Basenji's nastiness. Then, afterwards, there was eurythmics for all the glissadors in the Level 9 Coenotorium. She just might go. It was pretty good sometimes, though about an hour of it was enough for her.

Georgia/Queequeg got back to New Peachtree as quickly as she could. Lizardly fellows, more evil-mean than the hoisterjacks in the hive, hung out in the city's crumble-down corners, and she didn't like the looks of some of the stoopsitters she was seeing sidelong. Basenji, in a rare moment, had told her once that he had been beaten up one evening leaving the Kudzu Shop; but since he never carried any money or kept any in his greenhouse building, the stoopjockeys and thugboys didn't bother him anymore. That anecdote, related offhandedly, had impressed Queequeg: no bite maybe, but ballsy enough to go in and out of a neighborhood worse than Bondville. In fact, she'd never been scared in Bondville, not the twitchy, uneasy way she was here.

Even so, she'd come to see Basenji twice, hadn't she? Right through the brick dust, and the potholes, and the unemployable street lizards (both black and white) "sunning" themselves on old porches. But no more. No, sir, not never again.

Back on New Peachtree, Queequeg slowed down. Her long stride turned into a kind of graceful baby-stepping as she turned this way and that in front of the store windows, looking at the merchandise on display behind the tinted glass, looking at her own tall body superimposed on the merchandise, a beautiful gaudy phantom about to strut sensually through the glass. Yoo-rythmics, she thought bitterly. Well, hell, she'd probably go anyhow. She was just getting used to it. Shopping first, though.

Queequeg went into the colossal, perfume-scented escalator lobby of the Consolidated Rich's building, the city's biggest department store and one of the few still in operation from pre-Evacuation times. The Urban Nucleus owned it now, though, and the building didn't look very much like the original one, a huge picture of which hung in a revolving metal frame over the shoppers crowded into the escalator lobby. Queequeg glanced at it perfunctorily, then picked her escalator and rode up to a mezzanine level high enough over the lobby to give her a good view of two of the adjacent pedestrian courts outside.

People preening and strutting like pigeons, which, once, the city had almost got rid of.

Standing at the mezzanine rail, Queequeg noted the tingling in her feet: high, high up. And she lived down, down, down, almost forty meters under the concrete. Not forever, though; one day she was going to ride an escalator right out of there. . .

When she turned around, she saw a willowy white boy leaning back on a doodad counter and grinning at her like a jack-o-lantern.

"Ty!"

"Hey, Queequeg," Ty Kosturko said. He had called her that, too, ever since explaining about Herman Melville and white whales. He was wearing a matching trousers and shirt, with cross-over-color arms and legs: pink and white: apple blossoms. Loose and gangly, he was as tall and as athletic as she, but less visibly muscular.

They had been glissadors for about the same period of time, seven or eight months, though he was one of the few whites in their ranks and had got his appointment by badgering his father, an influential ward representative, to exercise his influence. The boy had bragged of, or elaborated on, his threatening his old man with going hoisterjack if he, Ty, couldn't put on glierboots: it was all he wanted. And so the old man had capitulated; better his son a menial than a maniac.

"What you doin' here, Ty?"

"Same as you, I'd imagine."

"Yeah? What you think I up to, then?"

"Down-chuting your pay-credits, since you're so much like me. That's what I'm doing, getting out from under my money."

She showed her wide teeth. "Oh, I tryin', I tryin'. But I ain' got so much I can prom for anythin' I want." She told him of attempting to buy Basenji, her cubiclemate's, miniature willow. "No way I gonna down-chute two hundred earnies, Ty. I savin' for to say goodbye to 9."

Ty was one of the only three or four glissadors to live sur-faceside, an amenity owing to the fact that he rented from his parents. Therefore, the boy commiserated. "I know what you need, then. Come with me."

He took her hand and led her through the many counters on the mezzanine, moving so gracefully that she had to look at his feet to convince herself that he wasn't wearing glierboots even now. They climbed a stairway hidden behind the men's and women's lounges, and she tried to strangle her mirth as Ty Kos-turko, leading her through the tie-dyed ceiling drapes and batik wall banners, affected the sleazy nonchalance of a dick on shoplif-ter lookout. Finally, Queequeg giggling, Ty nonchalantly rub-bernecking, they got to a room with a rounded portal over which were these words: *Paintings & Prints.* Into this make-believe king-dom he led her, a gallery of white wallboards and simulated mahogany parquetry.

"If you can't get a tree for your cubicle," Ty said. "Try a print. One of the Old Masters. Nothing better for flinging off a funk. Every two or three months I buy or trade one in."

And Georgia/Queequeg, who had never before been in the *Paintings & Prints* gallery of Consolidated Rich's, walked in awe among the wallboards. Here since abstract expressionism had fallen into disrepute, were all the Old Masters of pre-Evacuation representational art: Whistler, Homer, Cassat, Albert Ryder, Remington, Thomas Hart Benton, Grant Wood, Edward Hop-per, the three Wyeths, and others whom even Ty had no know-ledge of. Even so, he dropped all the names he could and im-pressed Queequeg by telling her who had painted what, even when she covered with her hand the title plates on the frames. Only two or three times did he miss, and each miss he accom-panied with gargoylesque grimaces.

"Damn," Queequeg said. "You good, Tyger."

Ty Kosturko bowed. Then he took her hand again and led her to another of the partitionlike wallboards. "Now this," he said, a sweep of the hand indicating the prints on display here, "is what you're looking for, Queequeg, this is what you can take downstairs to homey up your humble abiding place."

Queequeg, she didn't say him nay.

7. *Appreciating Norman Rockwell.*

About four hours after Queequeg visited him, Simon/Basenji left the Kudzu Shop, locked its doors, and made his way to the central lift terminal on New Peachtree. It was the weekend, Friday evening, and he carried with him his battered notebook. A false twilight was descending, by design, on the towers of the Urban Nucleus, towers looming over Basenji like shafts of frozen air. People were crowding toward the transport terminal, and he added himself to the flow of pedestrians, virtually riding the current they made into the vault of the terminal.

In the hall fifteen crystal lift tubes went up and down the levels of Atlanta. The air was smoky here, wine-colored. Every up-turned face shone with nightmarish radiance. Pandemonium, Basenji thought. He half expected Beelzebub and a few of his cohorts to start pitchforking people into the lift tubes, whose gliding capsules glowed with red emergency lights. Up and down the capsules went, packed with shadows instead of human beings.

Basenji found his way into a cordoned lane to a descent capsule and at last got aboard, with nearly a dozen others. "Sardine time," two teen-agers sang, "sardine time." Then Basenji felt the catacombs rise up around him like a hungry mouth. "Sardine time," the boys sang. They were all being swallowed. Like little fish. . .

Once down, it took Basenji threading his way among disembarked passengers from other lift tubes, almost ten minutes to reach his own cubicle. Standing outside it, he heard Queequeg laughing and an adolescent male voice saying, "That's right, you know. Absolutely on-target. I'm the foremost expert on pre-Evacuation magazine art in the whole cruisin' glissador corps, Atlanta or anywhere else."

Ty Kosturko. Friday night, and he had to share it with Ty Kosturko, the twenty-first-century's Kenneth Clark of popular culture. A boy who, when he wasn't wearing glierboots and uniform, dressed like a department-store mannequin; who *oohed* and *ahed* over his, Basenji's, Japanese figurines like a gourmet over well-simulated lobster Newburg. And his voice was so self-assuredly pontifical you could hear him right through the walls. Goodbye, Friday night.

Basenji put his thumb to the electric eye beside his entrance panel, which promptly slid back, admitting him. He stopped in the middle of the spartanly furnished central room. He placed his notebook on the back of the upholstered chair beside the door.

"Hey Basenji," Queequeg said, turning from the opposite wall. She grinned at him.

"Hello, Mr. Fowler," Ty Kosturko said. He called Georgia Queequeg but he didn't call Mr. Fowler Basenji. Self-proclaimed expert or no, son of a ward rep or no, he at least had that much sense. But look at his clothes: pink and white: a lanky harlequin in drag.

"Look what I prommed for at Rich's today, Basenji. Ty, he holp me pick 'em out. Not too spensive, either." *Holp.* Plantation English, which was enjoying an unaccountable renascence among the city's blacks. "Come on now," Queequeg insisted. "Come look at 'em."

So Basenji crossed to the formerly naked wall and looked at the three prints they had affixed there, matted but unframed, with transparent wall tape. The prints were Norman Rockwells. They filled the cubicle with children, and loving parents, and the Apollo 11 Space team.

"Jes' ten earnies each," Queequeg said. "Which mean I don' have to auction off my brothers' ole socks. It all be paid for in two months, and you, you stingy Basenji, you gonna get to look at 'em too."

With Queequeg and Ty Kosturko on either side of him, Basenji felt like a matchbook between two tall, carven bookends. The lanky boy said, "The print on the left is called *New Kids in the Neighborhood*. It was commissioned by *Look* magazine in the late 1960s. The interesting thing about it is the way the composition's balanced, the moving van in the back kind of tying together the three white kids over here," pointing them out, "and the black boy and his little sister over here," sweeping his hand over to the black children. "Look at the way Rockwell's given the little girl a *white* cat, while the white kids have this *black* puppy sitting in front of them. That way, the confrontation's mirrored and at the same time turned around by the pets the children have."

"And what's the point of that?" Basenji asked.

"To show that the *color* on the two sides shouldn't make any difference. The painting has sociological significance for that period, you know. Rockwell was making a statement."

Basenji stared up at the print. "Cats and dogs," he said, "are completely different kinds of animals. Was the artist trying to suggest an innate . . . antipathy . . . between the children, as between cats and dogs?"

"Antipathy?" Queequeg said.

"No, Mr. Fowler, you're trying to read too much into it now. The animals are just animals, a cat and a dog. An interpretation like yours would probably lead you to misconstrue Rockwell's intentions."

Basenji was silent. Then: "Well, go ahead. Tell me about the others."

"The one in the middle is from the Four Freedoms series: *Freedom from Fear*. The one on the right shows you the first men to land on the moon, with the NASA engineers and the American people behind them."

"But no cats or dogs," Basenji said. "Those men walked on it, and we can't even see it."

"Let's sit down so we can look at 'em easy," Queequeg said. "Forget 'bout the moon." She and Ty Kosturko sat down on throwrugs while her cubiclemate lowered himself into the wingback. The notebook balanced on top slid down the chair's cushion. Basenji retrieved it and held it in his lap. Then the three of them stared, without speaking, at the prints.

Goodbye, Friday night. He hadn't been planning to do much with it, though. Go to his visicom console and read. Or try to make sense, in his notebook, of how he had come to a place where his privacy could be so effortlessly violated. Or maybe just sit and stare at a wall, a blank one.

Then Ty Kosturko said, "Come to the eurythmics with us, Mr. Fowler. It's for glissadors, but you'll be our guest."

"Yeah," said Queequeg, touching his leg. "Otherwise, you jes' sit here all night thinkin' gloominess."

"No," Basenji said, earnestly shaking his head.

"Well, if you don't go," Ty Kosturko said, "we're not going to go either. We aren't going to let you sit here in solitary on Friday night. That's inhuman, Mr. Fowler."

"No, it's all right."

"Inhyooman," Queequeg echoed her companion. "You ain' gonna sit here doin' nothin' on a Friday night. We won' let you."

So Simon/Basenji, not understanding why he had allowed himself to be so bullied, went with them to the Friday night eurythymics in the Level 9 Coenotorium.

8. *Eurythmics.*

In the Level 9 Coenotorium, which lay (it seemed) an infinity of concourses away from their cubicle, a hundred or so people moved about under shoddy Japanese lanterns: little orange moons, like decorations for a high-school dance. Most of the people were black since most of the glissadors were black, and the lanterns filled the hall with a dismal orange smoke similar to the quality of light in the New Peachtree lift terminal.

At the far end of the hall Simon/Basenji saw an elevated platform on which a man in white leotards demonstrated the proper eurythmic responses to the music of his accompanists, a flute player and a man sawing on a highly lacquered bull fiddle. The music had just enough melody to prevent its being censured as neo-avant-garde (a term even more ludicrous, Basenji thought, than the activities it was supposed to squelch). Ripples from the flute, reverberations from the bass. . .

Ty Kosturko led Queequeg and Basenji into the middle of the floor, where variously attired dancers surrounded them. Arms, legs, hips, bellies, and buttocks moved past Basenji in a stylized and regimented choreography. In fact, everything about these languidly swaying body parts was too damn deliberate. Planned. Everyone kept an eye cocked on the white ghost on the far platform, aping his well-tutored spasms.

"Is this eurythmics?" he asked Queequeg.

"Yeah. It ain' much, but it better than sittin' home. Some of 'em here even *likes* it. Come on now, you do it too." She began snaking her arms around her body, bending and then lengthening out her smooth naked legs. Ty, without touching or looking at her, did the same, his harlequin's body assuming and relinquishing so many odd postures that he, Basenji, was intimidated by its mechanicalness. "Come on," Queequeg insisted.

"I don't know—"

Ty Kosturko revolved toward him, very nearly brushing one of the ubiquitous paper lanterns. "Anybody can do this, Mr. Fowler, it's all just mental, you know, and almost anyone can think." He did a premeditated butterflying movement with his arms and swam back to the little florist. "My father remembers the days of fission opera, renaissance swing, even terror-rock, when you could let the beast out and explode all over yourself without worrying about where the pieces'd land."

"Shoot, my brothers and me were *livin'* that a few months back. We'd jes' go out in the street and close if off and splode to somebody's ole records till the slum trolls and spoil-it squad come along and tell us to silent down." Without ceasing to gyrate, Queequeg chuckled. That was a human memory; you could almost feel homesick for old Bondville. Almost. "Us and the neighbors. Too many for the ole spoil-it squad to junk up in their jails."

"Yeah," Ty said. "Raggy music, abstract art, and free verse. Gone with the wind, my queen McQueequeg."

"I don't like that, that McQueequeg bidness, Ty. Anyhow, yo' own daddy, who say he 'member what it used to be, he one of them what voted it all out the door. He one good reason we got yoo-rythmics instead of music."

"I know that. And that's one good reason I'm a glissador instead of an accountant or an aspiring ad executive."

Basenji, forgotten in this exchange, walked over to a folding table in front of the hall's concessions booth and sat down. Bodies continued to hitch and snake and revolve past him, without any real expenditure of energy. No one threw back his head, no one pumped his knees, no one shimmied as if possessed. It was like watching a ballet performed by graceful wind-up toys, if that were possible. And Ty Kosturko looked like a sure choice to dance the part of Oberon, even though his competition was not inconsiderable.

Rock music, and atonal music as well. Abstract art. Free verse. And free-form video-feedback compositions. All gone with the wind.

Basenji didn't miss too many of these; his tastes ran in other directions. Nevertheless, he remembered when you couldn't walk down a surfaceside concourse without going by a row of imitation Mondrians and Pollocks. The Mondrians were there for their symmetry, the Pollocks for their vigor. Outside, in the parks and pedestrian courts, you could listen to people reciting Baraka, or Ishmael Reed, or maybe even their own unstructured verses; whereas today, if you dialed for the works of such people on your visicom console, the word "proscribed" rolled into place, and you could be sure that your key number had gone into the belly of a surfaceside computer. As for music, the Urban Nucleus itself had once sponsored, in the Omni, free retrospectives of artists like Schönberg and the virtually deified Allman Brothers. Though never crushingly attended, these performances had always summoned genuine enthusiasts, and Basenji himself, on two different occasions, had gone to the atonal and dodecaphonic concerts. He remembered, too, a time when the dome's citizens had access to the works of such early video experimenters as Campus and Emshwiller; programmed tapes to feed into your own visicom console. No more.

About eleven years ago—five years after the assassination of Carlo Bitler, a charismatic demagogue, and just one year after the disappearance of Bitler's wife—the Urban Council and the Conclave of Ward Representatives had together voted to remove the abstract paintings from public concourses, halt the outdoor poetry readings, and cease the funding of free concerts, except for those of designated classical works and contemporary popular music. There were simultaneous crackdowns on hand-operated duplicating machines, distributors of underground comix, wielders of portable video equipment, and unchartered, "fringe-riding" religious groups. Only the Hari-Krishna sect and the Orthodox Muslims, with histories of influence in the city going back to pre-Evacuation times, secured legal exemptions from this last stricture of the Council/Conclave's sweeping decree.

The year of these "Retrenchment Edicts" had been 2035, the same year that Simon Hadaka Fowler committed his mother to an UrNu geriatrics program. Three years later she had died. . .

Since then, he had worked himself down from tower housing, surfaceside, to his cubicle on Level 9 under: it averaged out to a little better than a level a year. And now he was sitting at a folding table in the hive-people's Coenotorium watching the glissadors move about eurythmically under Japanese lanterns. Amazing, this turn in his life.

Although the bull fiddle continued to throb in a subsonic hinterland that he was dimly aware of, the flute abruptly stopped. Queequeg found him, and Ty (all fluttering apple blossoms) came trailing along behind her.

"You lef' us, Basenji," Queequeg said.

"I didn't know how to do that."

"Do you want to learn, Mr. Fowler?"

"No," he said, looking up into the stratosphere where their heads always seemed to reside. "There are too many important things that I haven't learned yet." Implacably young, they stared down at him. "I'm more than twice as old as you two are," he added: a kind of apology.

Queequeg leaned down and pecked him on the cheek. "You right, Basenji," she said. "Anyhow, you done seen it. And I tired of it. Let's go on home. I fix us a drink."

Ty Kosturko tried to persuade them to remain, but, much to Basenji's quiet pleasure, Queequeg refused to be persuaded. "OK," Ty said. "Call me *mañana,* Miz Cawthorn."

Out in the murky corridors they walked side by side, she striding smooth and silent, he newly self-conscious about his lack of stature, in a more acute way than he had been when all three of them had walked *to* the Coenotorium. Then the boy had balanced things a little.

But Queequeg, the lady harpoonist! Didn't the terrible fragrance of her, the smell of sweat-touched cologne and untrammeled woman, break over him like a *tsunami?* A tidal power set in motion not by the moon, but by the passions of vulcanism and earthquake! Anyhow, Queequeg's presence, her aura, diminished him to a cipher; he could not speak, even though their mutual silence, as much as her size and smell, was disarming. In the bleak corridors of Level 9, he was a samurai without a sword.

9. *Soulplaning.*

Georgia/Queequeg, she was damn glad to get away from that flute and fiddle, from the posturing zombie on the grandstand. It was OK for a while, but she didn't have Tyger-boy's knack of making what was "just mental" into a kinetic showplace for her instincts. She kept looking at what she was doing and wishing she could shake off her skin and emerge into an unclad rioting of the blood. To let the beast out, like even Ty said. Because he understood the other even if he could almost manage to bury his brain with the Friday night eurythmics. Shoot, they *all* understood the other, they were glissadors. And Ty, he could be sweet, he certainly could.

"You ain' sayin' much, Basenji," she said, after they had turned into a concourse perpendicular to the one to the Coenotorium.

"You aren't either, Queequeg."

"No, *I* was thinkin'. What you been up to, down there?" She grinned at him; he appeared to wince, just in the muscles of his face. So sensitive-crawly he couldn't take a bit of juicing, which was what he accused her of when she didn't whicker her nose off at one of his infrequent intellectual puns. Shoot, he only made them so she wouldn't get them, that was the point of his doing it. Whereas she wasn't trying to be nasty a bit. "I mean you been thinkin' too. What 'bout, Basenji?"

"About being a basenji, a little dog."

"No you ain'. I bet you wonderin' why I asked you to come to somepin I don't like mysef."

"All right," he said agreeably.

"Well, I didn' ask you. Ty did. I jes' say Yeah to what he already asked. But I know why *he* done it."

"Why?" Now Basenji was just being polite, saying Why? because it was easier than jumping down on her with some rudeness. Well, she was going to tell him anyhow, he needing telling.

"Ty worried 'bout you, Basenji. He say you workin' nigger-hard to get as far down as you can, and you done got as far unner as this city gonna let you. Nex' step: the waste converters over on Concourse 13. But how and when you get there, that up to you, Ty say."

Basenji laughed; a sort of snort.

"So he asked you along. When we home, you make me splain why we keep goin' to them sickly yoo-rythmics. You hear?"

They walked the rest of the way to their cubicle without saying a word to each other, although Queequeg softly scatsang a bit and, once, wished out loud for her glierboots. Since a few of the apartments along the way had their panels slid back, she waved at the people she knew. Solidarity against hoisterjacks and down-from-up spoil-it squads.

Home, she fixed toddies (the air conditioning made it cool enough) and made Basenji sit down in his chair. A throwrug for her, her legs straight out before her like pillars of polished oak. Basenji was letting her determine his evening as he had never let her manipulate his time before. It was all guiltiness about the bonsai, she decided, that and maybe a little dose of the big head. After four months she had finally got him curious about something—even if, to be specific, it was only himself.

With the mug of hot liquor between his hands, he said, "You told me to make you explain why you and young Kosturko go to the eurythmics even though you're not enamored of it." He had a tic in one moist, narrow eye.

"You wanna hear that, Basenji?" If he did, maybe he wasn't so dragged out on himself after all.

And he said, "Please": a surprise.

"OK, then. Because we glizadors. They only twelve or fourteen of us on each level, you know that? Yeah. The city pick us 'cause we good—even Ty, whose daddy holp him get set up in the corps. They wouldn't've took him *only* because of who his daddy was. He can fly, Ty can. He belong on glierboots.

"Anyhow, we keep the unnercity, the down-beneath part of it, together. We the Pony Express and the 707 airmail combined, we the fleet elite of New Toombsboro.

"In four months, jes' since I come down here, I been to the boondocks of this level and out again. I done run letters and packages 'tween ever' concourse. I been in on the dumpin' of twenny or so deaders down the waste converters, includin' one ole woman dressed like all in tinfoil and holdin' a baton so it wouldn' come loose. I skated through at least four gangs of them sock-headed hoisterjacks, and I gone up to substitute on other levels, too. We all do that, Basenji, and we fine at doin' it." Look at that Basenji, she thought; he listenin' to me, eye tic and all.

"Then one day the councilmen and ward reps, even the house niggers sittin' upstairs with 'em, say *No more tomtoms down there, no more axes and ivories,* and give us a yoo-rythmics program to chew on. Shoot, that don' kill us, we glizadors. We keep our heads on.

"Now, by *we* I really mean them who were glizadors in 2035 when them 'Trenchment E-dicts' was passed. But that don' make no difference: A glizador's a glizador, even 'leven years later. So we—all of us, then and now—we went to what they gave us to go to. And some of us wooleye those council fellows by learnin' to like the bullshit they sen' down here for music."

Basenji said, "Are you sure they didn't 'wooleye' you, inducing you people to like the eurythmics? Wasn't that what the council-men and ward reps wanted?"

"Nah. It may seem like it, but it ain'. They never wanted us to like it at all, they jes' wanted us to *do* it. But we knew what they was up to, we all the time knew—so we done beat their plan by likin' that stuff when we s'posed to jes' do it."

"But you *don't* like it, Queequeg." Damn, he was listening almost closer than she wanted him to. A starved little slant-eye drinking his toddy and eating up her words: *smack, smack.*

"No. But it's tol'able. I can stan' it 'cause I know I a glizador. That make up for the music they done stole from us in '35."

"You were seven then," Basenji said. They were quiet. A moment later he leaned forward, and she could see the gray in his otherwise jet-black sideburns. "Don't you ever get tired?" he said. "Don't you ever get sick of going up and down the same ugly hallways? As if you were a rink-refugee forever?" He was asking about himself, really. About himself and her, too.

"No," she said. "No, I don'. You know what *volplane* mean?"

He shook his head.

"Use to, it mean what a airplane do when its motor quit. Down here, we *volplanin'* after a good run down a concourse, when the balls in our boots get rollin' like rounded-off dice. Yeah. That's real volplanin'. Jes' yo' whole body slippin' through air like a rocket or a arrow, goin' head up and flat out, gamblin' on the brains in yo' muscles to keep you from headin' over inna heap. Soulplanin', we call it when ever'thin's smooth and feathery, and it make livin' sweet, Basenji. It beat liquor and new peaches and a lovin' tongue, it beat mos' anything I can think of. Doin' it, you forget 'bout concrete and levels and how no one see the moon no more. That the truth. That real soulplanin'. And Ty, he'd tell you the same thin', Basenji. That why we glizadors."

Queequeg stopped talking and examined her cubiclemate's face. He was blushing a little, red seeping into his pale brown cheeks. Shoot, she'd embarrass him again, then. The air conditioning had leached away at her toddy's warmth, had put a chill on her legs. She drew them up under her, without a great deal of attention to the arrangement of her skirt. Another surprise: he didn't hurry to look away.

Good for him, he was usually prim as a prufrock, whatever that meant. Ty always used that expression, and somehow it was just right for Basenji. In a three-room cubicle, with the bath booth between two sleepers, you couldn't practice or pretend any body-shame, ritualistic or real, unless you were an expert. Which Basenji was. He was never anything but dressed, and if she dropped a towel in front of him or strolled nighty-clad out of her sleeper, *zup!* he was right out the door: prim as a prufrock.

But tonight, his cheeks looking like somebody brutish had pinched them over, he didn't let the drawing up of her Zulu's legs at all befuddle him. His eyes swept across her whole body, they flashed with a toddy-fed humor. He said, "And what will you do when you're too old to volplane?"

"I gonna las' till I forty at leas'. We got glizadors been lacin' on glierboots since ten years fo' I was born."

"Then what? After forty? You could live sixty more years."

"I gonna do it, too. Die in the wunnerful year 2128, when they won' be no more dome and the earth will have done took us back."

"But before that happens? And after you're through with the glissadors?"

"Babies. I have my babies to raise up. Then when I feeble, I got 'em to talk at and to baby me. If I need it. Which I won'."

"How do you know you won't, Queequeg?"

"I jes' like my mamma, and she don' need nobody but my daddy and not him all that much. She love us all, I mean, but she ain' gonna fall over if somepin happen to us. A quittin' streak don' run in her. Or me neither."

"Maybe." He said that cocky-like and lifted his eyes from her. Whispering, he breathed out the word, "Babies," as if he didn't believe it.

Queequeg fixed Basenji another drink, which he accepted and slowly sipped off. But he wouldn't talk anymore, even though she plopped herself immodestly down in front of him. He went to sleep in the wingback. Thank you, thank you nor a stimulating evening. Well, it had been: stimulating, that is. Moreso than any evening she had ever shared with him in the cubicle. He was sweet too, Basenji was. . .

Queequeg took the heavy mug out of his lap and removed his shoes. Then, mug in hand, she stood in front of her Rockwell print . git hit her that she was almost like the parents in the *Freedom from Fear* painting, tucking in the children while thugboys beat up the citizens surfaceside and hoisterjacks terrorized pedestrians in the understrata. In their cubicle, though, it was cozy: air-conditioned cozy. A sad-making peacefulness suffused Queequeg, and shuddering with the ache of it, she put the mug on the kitchen board, dialed down the lights, shed her clothes, and lay in her sleeper cove gazing into the impenetrable darkness. Her hands rested on the planes of her lower abdomen, the tips of her fingers pressing into the wiry margin of her pubic hair. How still and big the world was. She felt connected to everyone in it, a deliverer of universal amity. And she was a long time going to sleep. . .

10. *In the descent capsule.*

Simon Hadaka Fowler, alias Basenji, woke up and lifted himself out of the chair where Queequeg had left him. He had slept dreamlessly: no visions of a tiny incarnation of himself climbing the shelves on his patio. Ordinarily, he did not go into the Kudzu Shop on Saturdays, at least not to open it; if he did go, it was to secure the plants for the Sabbath. Then he would retire back into the hive and his own private cell. This morning, though, he quietly changed his clothes and prepared to leave for surfaceside, two hours before the city's meteorological technicians would dial up daylight.

Outside her sleeper he paused. "Queequeg," he said.

No movement, and the glowing clock on the kitchen board didn't give him enough light to see into her room. Very well.

Off Basenji went. Out of the cubicle, through the Level 9 concourses, up the lift-tube shaft (in a capsule by himself), across the pedestrian courts, and into that faintly inimical district where the Kudzu Shop tried to bind a collapsing empire together with flower chains.

On his door he put a sign reading OPEN. Then by the fluorescents in the greenhouse, he worked until the artificial dawn gave him enough light to move out to the patio.

The morning went by. He even had a few customers. Queequeg

stayed on his mind. Occasionally he shook his head and said, "Babies." Was that what she thought you relied on when your own strength ran out: your grown-up babies? Not altogether, apparently. She trusted her own resources too; she was just like her mamma. So she said.

At the noon shift-change Basenji looked at the newly layered willow in its covered stand; in two warm, sealed-over wombs of sphagnum moss it was beginning to generate new life. He hoped. A year it would take. . .

He watered the other plants on the patio shelves, then picked up the bonsai willow he had not altered and carried it straight out the shop door. The locking up was made clumsy by his holding the miniature tree in its shallow oriental pot while he struggled with his key.

Then he walked all the way to the New Peachtree lift terminal with the willow swooning in his arms, half concealing his face. Aboard a descent capsule, seven or eight black men and women surrounding him, Basenji tried to pretend that he wasn't clutching a pot to his stomach, a willow to his chest. Not really. Grins on every side. The Big Bad Basement was swallowing them all, rising like irresistible water around them.

"What you got there, man?"

Basenji started to answer.

"A bush. He carryin' that bush home."

"That ain't no bush. That a tree, Julie-boy."

"Well, it don't got a proper growth, anybody tell you that."

A woman asked him, "What do you wanna take a pretty tree like that into the basement for? It doesn't belong down here, not that one."

Basenji started to answer.

"He takin' that bush to his dog," Julie-boy said. "He mos' likely got a dog hid out in his cyoob'cle."

"A dog?"

"Yah. A little one that don' make much noise. So he don' get junked by the concourse trolls."

"It's for decoration," the woman said, answering her own previous question.

"He takin' it to his dog."

Speculation went on around him, entertaining, speculation. He couldn't get a word in. Then they were down: all the way down, without having stopped at any of the other floors; the Level 9 Express. Everyone disembarked.

"Take it on home to yo' dog," Julie-boy insisted. "See to it he don' has to hike his leg on the wall."

"Fuckin' fine tree," someone else said. "You got a fuckin' fine tree."

Laughter as they dispersed, although the inquisitive woman had already taken herself out of earshot of Basenji's jovial assailants. Huffy, huffy. As the others tapped off toward various corridor mouths, a wiry man with big luminous eyes turned back to him.

"You take care of it," he said. "It could die in a place like this. You tend it now." Then those eyes, too, revolved away from him.

Basenji, balancing the plant, at last turned from the lift-tube passageway, walked down a poorly lit auxiliary hall, entered a wide concourse, and reached his own cubicle. After he shifted the willow so that he could hold his right thumb to the electric eye, the panel slid back.

11. *Declaiming a poem.*

Queequeg, when she woke up, was surprised and disappointed to find that Basenji had gone off somewhere. Standing in her *penwah* at the kitchen board, she ate a bowl of cereal (fingernail-colored flakes that dissolved into a paste when she moved her spoon around and drank some instant orange juice. She scatsang to herself and mashed a few imaginary muscadines with her bare feet: muscadines and scuppernongs. Her daddy always called the latter *scup'nins.* Sometimes you could find both varieties of grapes in the city's supermarkets, especially in the Dixie-Apple Comestibulary on the Level 4 mall. The checkout boys and stockers didn't seem to know where they came from: they were probably growing all over the dome, right over everybody's heads, out there where nobody poked his old noggin anymore.

I bet Basenji could raise 'em up in the Kudzu Shop, Queequeg thought, if he had 'nuf room. Which he prolly ain'.

She got dressed, a body stocking. What was she going to do?

Not shopping. She'd already prommed away enough pay-credits for a while. The Rockwells. She sat down in Basenji's chair to look at them. A sharp nub cut into the small of her back. "Umpf." It was the corner of a beat-up old notebook, a notebook wedged between the back of the chair and the seat cushion. Queequeg pulled it out and began thumbing through it.

Lord, look at all the soot-smudged pages. Basenji wrote as teeny-tiny as anyone she'd ever seen, as if this was all the paper there was in the world and he wasn't going to waste none of it. As she flipped along, the notebook opened out flat, of its own accord, to two pages where his little handwriting was even tighter than elsewhere. She read:

> *Bushido is the way of the warrior. But our own instinctive bushido has been bred out of us. Most of us have forgotten what horror exists outside the dome to keep us inside. Whatever. . .*

That was enough for her. Bushido. Boo-SHEE-doe. Whatever that was. Some of the other words on the page looked mighty funny, too. Back she flipped, leisurely thumbing. It was a journal, though not a very well-kept one. The entries went all the way back to 2039, seven years ago. A year or two in between didn't seem to be represented at all. She stopped thumbing when she saw this:

> *you gave me the willow*
> > *with the loving remonstrance*
> *that the tree become*
> > *something other than a decoration,*
> *the diffident point of an effeminate*
> > *motif;*

Whew! Queequeg was reading this out loud. It wasn't any better than the other, but it looked pretty on the page. It had that to speak for it. And her. She spoke some more:

> *and though I still go*
> > *through gardens looking askance*
> *at the total sum*
> > *of your commands and my hesitation,*
> *the willow itself has become animate:*
> > *a thief.*

> > *what it has taken*
> > > *from the days I wear like leaves*

A line into the second stanza, Queequeg had levered herself out of the chair and begun pacing. She was declaiming nicely by the time she got to "leaves." Then it stopped. She had to stop too, which was too bad because she'd almost reached the volplaning stage. Actually, there was more, but Basenji had very effectively crossed out the final two stanzas: violent red slashes. He had done it so well that she couldn't read any of the words in the obliterated lines, not a one.

So she started again from the beginning, gesturing with one arm and walking back and forth in front of the Rockwells. L-O-Q-shun. Maybe it wasn't so bad, after all. Bad enough, though. Anyhow, reading it again, she knew that it was about the bonsai she had tried to buy the day before. Or the other bonsai just like it.

At the bottom of the page Basenji had written the date, Winter 2041, and two more words: "Oedipal claptrap."

Queequeg put the notebook back in the chair, exactly as she had found it. For a few minutes she scatsang variations on the phrase *you gave me the willow,* still pacing. What had he gone off for? Maybe just to close up for Sunday. Anyhow, if he hadn't gone off, he'd probably be scrunched over his visicom console tapping into the *Journal/Constitution* newstapes. Last night was a fluke, one big fluke.

The clock on the kitchen board said 11:10. Queequeg went into her own sleeper cove and dialed Ty Kosturko surfaceside, up in the towers.

His mother answered: very, very politely. Finally Ty was on.

Queequeg said, "Meet you for lunch, Level 4 mall."

"Sleepy." He sounded it, too.

"How long you stay?"

"Till it was over. It got good then. Everybody talked."

"Well, I hungry, Tyger."

"Where on the mall?"

"The Dixie-Apple."

"OK. Thirty minutes."

" 'Bye."

Quick, quick: a spray shower, which she should have taken last night. Then, a summer dress, orange and yellow.

Maybe they'd have scup'nins in the produce department, shipped in from the Orient or Madagascar (ha, ha) or the kudzu forests where no one supposedly ventured anymore. If they did, she'd buy her daddy some. Besides, it had been a couple of weeks since she'd been over to Bondville. She'd take Ty with her, turn him loose on her mamma. . .

Out of the cubicle she went, fifteen minutes ahead of the Saturday shift change. And up to Level 4 before the crowds came waterfalling down.

12. *Simon Hadaka Fowler*

The cubicle was empty. But he found a cereal bowl and a juice glass on the kitchen board, both wearing the lacy residue of their contents. Staring through the branches of the willow, he saw that the clock behind the breakfast dishes said 12:40. Which had to be right: it was linked to a strataencompassing system tying it into The Clock, a computerized timekeeper housed in a tower on New Peachtree. So what? He was disappointed that Queequeg wasn't in (an unusual response, he knew), but mildly gratified that the time it didn't make any difference to him. The disappointment and the gratification canceled each other out: quasi'srenity.

Put the bonsai down, Simon.

Holding it, he turned around. Where? In a place where it would be displayed to advantage. Fine. But the central room of their cubicle didn't offer that many possibilities. Beside his chair? Under the Rockwells? Either side of the kitchen board? Not good, any of them.

Well, it was evident to him why he had brought the willow down to Level 9, it would be evident to Queequeg as well. Why not let its placement say unequivocally what, just by exchanging a glance, they would both know?

Very good. Therefore, Simon Hadaka Fowler carried the pot into Queequeg's sleeper cove (the first time he had been through that door) and set it at the foot of her bed. She had thrown her nightgown, he noticed, over her pillow. Meanwhile, her presence, her aura, hung in the room like a piquant incense, not yet completely burned off. That was all right, too.

But an unmade bed didn't do much for the miniature tree, and he wasn't going to touch her nightgown so that he could remedy the bed's rumpledness. He moved the tree to the back wall of the cove. Then he went into his own room and came back with a rolled bamboo mat and a small scroll of rice paper, also rolled. He put the bamboo mat under the glazed vessel containing the tree and affixed the scroll to the wall with the same sort of tape Ty and Queequeg had used for the Rockwells. He went out and came back again. This time he stood a bronze ornament on the mat next to the bonsai: an Oriental warrior, sword upraised.

Scroll, tree, figurine: the display formed a triangle. Good. That's what it was supposed to do. The scroll bore a poem that he had written as a boy:

> *The moon and the mountain*
> *Mailed themselves letters:*
> *These were the flying clouds.*

His father had criticized him for messing up the syllable count and for writing about inaccessible phenomena: moon, mountain, clouds. His mother had said it was OK, very nice. He had never tried to straighten it out.

Simon Fowler went again to his own sleeper cove, shed his trousers and tunic, and performed his daily regimen of exercises, which he had forgotten to do that morning. Afterwards, he took a spray shower, conscious of the cool droplets clinging to the cabinet from its previous use. A smell of scrubbed flesh trembled in these droplets.

Fowler fixed himself lunch at the kitchen board. He decided, knowing Queequeg, that he would have the entire afternoon ahead of him. Maybe the evening, too. All right. His soul was at rest. Heaven would accept Simon Hadaka Fowler: moon, mountain, and clouds. For the first time in eleven years it seemed certain to him, inevitable. Only the demands of conscience and honor remained. After lunch, he sat down at the visicom console and tapped into the *Jour/Con* newstapes.

13. *Wedding bells.*

Ty Kosturko and Queequeg came in a little after eight, laughing and punchy-hysterical. They had been at each other in Georgia's old bedroom in the surfaceside Bondville tenement and hadn't really pulled either themselves or their clothes together even yet. The boy's long, neo-Edwardian shirt, embroidered flowers going up and down the sleeves, might have been on backwards: its design made it difficult to tell. And Queequeg's flaming scarf of a dress looked like an old facial tissue, everywhere crumpled.

Fowler, when he came out of his room to greet them, took all of this in at once, even the sexual compact between them. Especially the sexual compact. It had shone in their gestures and lineaments before, but then he had been either pre-emptively indifferent or unbelieving. Now he was neither: he smiled.

"Basenji," Queequeg said, putting an arm over his shoulder, "we gonna get married, Ty and me."

"That's right," the boy said, and dropped, grinning, into Fowler's wingback. He shifted uncomfortably, pulled a smudged notebook from behind him, and lowered it to the floor as if it were an incunabulum.

Fowler said, "Very good. Congratulations. Congratulations, both of you."

"After Quee—" Ty broke off and nodded deferentially to the girl. "After *Miz Georgia Cawthorn* called me this morning, my mother gave me the mail. The UrNu Housing Authority says I can have a cubicle of my own. They said—"

"His daddy done holp him again, that what it was. How long *we* have to wait, Basenji, how long it take *us* to find a place?"

"Well, my daddy, Miz Cawthorn, wanted me out of the house. As far as that goes, I think my mother did too. But I digress. The Housing Authority said the cubicle was two-person only, Mr. Fowler, up on Level 3, but that the double-occupancy requirement could be waived since the requisitioner's father was T. L. Kosturko. I didn't want that, but I didn't want to roost forever with Mommy and Daddy either.

"So when I met Queequeg at the Dixie-Apple—Miz Cawthorn, I mean—, I said, 'Move up with me.' She said, 'I got a cubiclemate.' I said, 'You haven't got a bonafide, signed-and-delivered body-burner.' 'No,' she said, 'jes' a bodyburner.' So I said, 'Well, let's sign and bind, with options, durations, and special clauses to get worked out between now and the wedding.' "

"Which gonna be nex' Sattidy."

"She said OK. Which'll leave you without a cubiclemate, Mr.

Fowler, but the Housing Authority won't toss you out because of a wedding. You'll have a grace period and a chance to screen the first five people on the relocation list for the one you most want to move in with you. Which neither you or Queequeg got to do when you were thrown together from the top of the lists. So I hope you aren't upset with me for stealing your cubiclemate."

The boy had never seemed so earnest, not even while explaining the Rockwell prints or instructing him in the theory and practice of eurythmics. Maybe his shirt *was* on frontwards.

"No, that's fine," he told them. "But I want a clause permitting me visiting privileges."

"Yeah," Queequeg said. "You 'member that one, Ty."

The boy nodded and wrote a make-believe message to himself on the palm of his hand. "Anyway, Mr. Fowler, we've already told Georgia's parents and you. But I've got to break the news to Ward Rep Kosturko and his lady, who'll be—" rippling his wrist in demonstration, "—determinedly delighted." He laughed, that incongruous falsetto. Then, looking at Queequeg, "Tomorrow's Sunday. I've met yours, you gotta meet mine. Come up in the afternoon, three or so. All right?"

"OK. You tell 'em who I am: a glizador, jes' like you." She reached down and pulled Ty out of Fowler's chair. "Only better." They kissed, decorously, though he didn't believe the decorousness was for his benefit; they were simply expressing the calm their affection had come to.

"Goodnight, Mr. Fowler," Ty Kosturko said. And he went out into the concourse, where he was at once absorbed by the red fog hanging there.

14. *Georgia Cawthorn*

She was high, high, high. Like yesterday at the mezzanine rail in the Consolidated Rich's before meeting Ty. Like looking down on the pedestrian courts, out through the tinted glass. The world spread out like a map, the flat kind like they used in geography: Africa on one side, America on the other. So that you could fall off either end, right into the chalk tray. Well, she was volplaning back and forth across the whole landscape.

"Hey, Basenji," she said, walking toward her sleeper cove, "what you think? You 'prove?"

"I approve," he said, right behind her. In fact, he was following at her heels, which never happened: he didn't do that. But when she turned toward him from the darkened cove, he was right there. Like a little dog that's been left shut up all day, eyes begging, tail ticktocking. Except Basenji had his arms folded self-composedly and was standing straight and still at the edge of the shadow just inside her door.

Facing him, she dialed up her light. "Hey," she said again, smiling. Prim as a prufrock he looked, out devilish too, a little bit of witchman in his Japanese eyes. Last night had not been a fluke; he was somehow turned around, wrinkles fallen out of his soul as if he'd hung it up overnight to drip dry. Neat on the outside, neat in: that was Basenji now.

He unfolded his arms and pointed at the wall behind her.

Georgia turned to look. She saw the willow, its blue ceramic pot glinting with highlights. Saying, "Oh, Basenji," she crossed the room and knelt beside the tree. "You givin' it to me?"

"No," he said.

Her head jerked up, her mouth turned down, before she could stop either of these involuntary responses. Damn.

"I can't. If it isn't outdoors most of the time, it will die. As I said yesterday, it needs weather. But we can keep it down here for the weekend. *You* can keep it."

"It won' die?"

"It shouldn't. Not because of two days downstairs." Straight and still he stood; a trifle stiff, too.

"Take you a seat, Basenji." She pointed him to the bed. He was going to protest, she could see it coming. "Go on now. Ty, he plonk down in yo' chair, you plonk down right there. An res'."

"Oh, I've had plenty of rest." But he did what she'd told him to. And he watched her as she picked up the bronze samurai. "The bonsai display is very formal," he said, "if you bother to do it right. There are always three points of focus, and the tree isn't necessarily the main one, although it always represents the corner of the triangle standing for Earth."

"Well, that seem natch'l enough. What this one?" She waved the sword-wielding warrior at him, then set it down in its place.

"A figurine representing Man." He pointed at the wall over her head. "The scroll stands for Heaven. Those are the three principal aspects of the universe: Heaven, Earth, Man. In the Shinto formulation, I think. I can't really remember anymore."

Georgia stood up to examine the rice-paper scroll. She read: "The moon and the mountain/Mailed themselves letters:/These were the flying clouds." That was OK. Nice. It beat the poem in his notebook all up and down. She looked at him sitting on the bed. His shirt was open at the collar, dark hair curled below his throat. (Ty's chest was as bald as a baby's.) Too, he smelled like soap.

"Each point of the triangle," Basenji said, "also represents a vital human attribute. Heaven is soul, Earth is conscience, Man is honor. You have to fulfill the requisites of all three." His eyes were merry, like the eyes of a preacher who didn't mind taking a nip now and again. A nip for a Nip. She grinned at him as he finished talking. "And that's not Shinto, or Muslim, or Ortho-Urbanism. That's my own formulation."

She sat down beside him. They looked at the display together. No nervousness in him at all, not even the teeniest blush under the almost translucent planes of his high cheeks. Serenity was riding him like a monkey. It was about damn time. For four months he'd been shooting up a jillion cc's of crotchetiness a day and staying together by making sure his clothes were straight. Then, last night. Now, today. Sitting in *her* sleeper cove, on *her* bed, with his collar open. OK.

Georgia Cawthorn took Basenji's left hand, which was calloused from his work in the Kudzu Shop, and bit it gently in the webbing between thumb and forefinger. Then she lowered the unresisting hand to her thigh and helped it push the hem of her crumpled yellow dress upward to her hip. His hand seemed to know what to do. Leaving it there, she began to unbutton his shirt.

"You ain' tired, are you?"

"No," he said. "Are you?" It was a sweet question, not sarcastic. She could tell by the way his eyebrows went up to a little *v* when he asked her.

"Well, I ain' gonna think 'bout it right now." She moved a kiss across his mouth and let her hands come down to his waist. He, in turn, pressed her backward, slowly, like a gentleman, so that her cast-aside nightgown lay under her head.

Everything else happened just like it was supposed to, although she had to wait until the first round was over to get her dress all the way off. Then she got up, dialed down the light, and quickly came back to the hard muscular, curly-chested Basenji. They lay together in her bed, her head on that chest. She could certainly feel her tiredness now, weights in her arms and legs.

After a while she said, "You invited to the wedding, Basenji."

"Next Saturday?"

"If Ty and me get the papers set up."

"Well, I hope you do." He did, too. He was thinking of something else, though, just like she was thinking of going up to the tower tomorrow and sitting down with Ty to figure out options and whatnots. Maybe they could finagle authorization to go glissadoring on the same level, so long as it didn't take Ty's daddy to finagle it.

After a while she said, "The way you dress, you been hidin' all them muscles you got." She touched one.

"I do push-ups," he said. Then, like a naughty boy: "And yoga."

She laughed. "Bet you could glizador. Bet you could ven nine out how to soulplane, jes' you get started."

15. *The Geriatrics Hostel.*

Putting his arm over the girl's bare shoulder, Simon Fowler said, "I want to tell you a story, Queequeg, something that happened eleven years ago." All his life since then, he had been looking for someone to tell it to; the notebook had been the only listener he'd found. "It's a confession, I suppose."

"Well, if it happen 'leven years ago, it ain' gonna have to do with me."

He was silent. Did she want to hear it?

She recognized his hesitation. "No, that *good*. I don' *wan'* it to. You go ahead, Basenji."

And so he confessed, doing for his conscience what Queequeg

and Ty Kosturko and the bonsai had somehow managed to do for his soul. "Eleven years ago I gave my mother to the UrNu Geriatrics Hostel. Do you know what that is?"

"I think so."

"Well, it's a place for old people, a hospital and nursing home. Some of the old people there aren't sick at all and live in a separate wing, almost a hotel. Most who go there, though, are waiting to die. Geriatrics Hostel. The name itself is a contradiction, meant to inspire hope when you know you shouldn't have any."

"I don' know what's hope-inspirin' 'bout a buildin' full of hostile ole people," the girl said. She waited for him to laugh. Which he didn't. "That's a joke, Basenji. One of yo' snooty *puns.* You ain' the only one smart enough to make 'em, whatever you think." She chuckled. "Good one, too."

"Touché." It had stopped him, he had to admit. To save face, he pinched her nipple. "May I finish?"

"Ouch. Yeah. Don' do that."

Georgia Cawthorn listened while he told her about taking his mother, Kazuko, who had been born in reconstructed Hiroshima in 1970, to the UrNu Geriatrics Hostel. His mother was only sixty-five, but he had been taking care of her as if she were a child for six or seven years, since Zachary Fowler's death in 2028 (the year she, Georgia, was born) of "insult to the brain."

Kazuko had taught him everything he knew about horticulture, bonsai, and miniature landscaping; and he, after he was old enough to run it himself, had taken her with him every day to the Kudzu Shop, even though this had entailed pushing a wheelchair through the corridors of the tower complex, into and out of lift tubes, and across spotless pedestrian courts and pitted, unrepaired asphalt. The medicaid physicians told him that they could find no measurable deterioration in her legs; perhaps her condition derived from an irresistible and ongoing loss of neurons, nerve cells, in the brain, a failure owing to oxygen deprivation. "Premature senescence," they said. Perhaps. In any case, they didn't know what to do about it since they had no long-range methodology for reversing vein constriction in the brain or for increasing her blood's oxygen payloads.

"One of them said *payloads*," Simon Fowler said. "Aerospace jargon. The men in the descent craft *Eagle* were part of its payload."

"They talk like they has to, Basenji." She could see him nosediving into bitterness. But he pulled out.

"Finally, I went and talked to the people at the Geriatrics Hostel. They were soliciting tenants, patients for the hospital section, residents for their quasi-hotel. Part of a study, all of it. The director told me that my mother's apparent 'premature senescence' might in reality be a response to alterations in her life over which she had no control.

" 'Look,' he said. 'Your mother was born in Hiroshima. She came to this country with your father before the turn of the century. She watched the Dome go up over Atlanta, actually saw the steel gridwork—over a ten-year period—blot out the sky. The United States turned into the world's only Urban Federation before she was even granted American citizenship. So instead she had to apply for enfranchisement under the new Urban Charter. You were born only after she and your father had obtained that enfranchisement. That made her what?—thirty-seven years old?— when you were born, Mr. Fowler, no small adjustment in its own right. Twenty years devoted to raising you, then, while the Urban Nuclei cut themselves off from all contact with their own countrysides, not to speak of foreign nations, your father degenerated into alcoholism. Then your father, the one person she knew who had seen her homeland, who could talk about it with her, was cruel enough to desert her. By dying. Mr. Fowler, your mother's time sense has been upended, her cultural and her emotional attachments pulled out from under her. Her psychological metabolism has sped up to keep pace with the alterations she sees occurring in the external world. She is aging because she feels intuitively that she must, that it would be a chronometric impossibility for her *not* to be aging. Physiologically she is neither older nor younger than any reasonably healthy woman of sixty-five. We have other victims of the same malaise here, some barely into their fifties. The roots of this syndrome, in fact, are a century old. Older. Leave your mother with us, Mr. Fowler, and we'll try to help her. That's all I can promise.'

"I said, 'All of her emotional attachments haven't been pulled out from under her. She has a son, you know.'

" 'Yes,' the director said [I can't even remember his name], 'and from what you've told me, you've been castigating yourself for not being your father. Or an improved version of your father: all the strengths, none of the weaknesses. Your own sense of guilt runs very deep in this matter, Mr. Fowler, as if you blame yourself for being both a late *and* an only child, neither of which conditions you had any control over. And you've done well to seek help here.' "

"You don' still feel that guilt, do you?" Georgia asked.

"I don't think so. If I ever felt it. But I'm not through confessing. The greater guilt is ahead.

"I gave—*sold*—my mother to the Geriatrics Hostel. They had been soliciting tenants, as I said, as subjects for a gerontological study, and they offered me a considerable sum to submit my mother to them. I did. They promised that she, along with the others, would be a recipient of intensive care and treatment, not simply a guinea pig for their researches. And in that, I think, the director told me the truth.

"During the first year I visited the Geriatrics Hostel every week, usually twice a week. Wednesday evenings and Sundays. They were working to alter my mother's time sense, to bring it in line with that of a normal woman in her sixties, maybe even to slow it down below the so-called normal threshold. The director did not believe in the biochemical approach, though, and that seemed good to me. No untested repressants or hallucinogens. Instead, they placed my mother in a controlled environment, a room in which everything took place at leisurely, but prescribed, intervals. They encouraged the reintroduction of Japanese motifs into her life, in the decorations of her room and in the material available for her to read. I brought a different bonsai with me each time I came; when it had been indoors for two or three days, an attendant carried it to the balcony outside my mother's window— which, on the director's orders, they kept curtained. But she still had scenery. A false window in the room opposite the curtained balcony, ran hologramic movies of the Japanese gardens in San Francisco; my mother could watch the people come and go, come and go. Or she could wheel herself over to the wall and let a curtain drop into place here, too. More, they permitted her company from among the Hostel's other 'guests,' and they didn't shut her off from news of the city and the other Urban Nuclei; they just monitored and restricted its content.

"The first month, no progress. Not much the second one, either—though by the third month she had begun trying to walk, supporting herself on a movable aluminum frame they had kept in her room since the beginning. This didn't last. The director went by tunnel to a conference on aging research in the Washington Nucleus. While he was gone, someone proposed a room adjustment; patients were shuffled around. That did it. We *think* that's what did it; the results of this bungling didn't begin to show for a while. In fact, the new room my mother was given was exactly like the other, down to the false window and the holog-ramic movies of the San Francisco botanical gardens, except that the floor plan was a mirror-image of the other. Even the adjust-ment's having been made in its entirety during my mother's sleep couldn't compensate for this; the director later said it may have even complicated matters, since if my mother had witnessed the shuffling, her sense of disorientation would not have been so great."

"Thoughtlessness, Basenji. The program don' soun' bad, the director don' soun' bad."

"No, they weren't. But that's not the point. This is a confession, not an indictment. May I finish?"

"Go on. But let's pull up that sheet." The air conditioning, the interminable, almost imperceptible droning of the air con-ditioner. They adjusted themselves against each other under the rumpled drifts of linen.

"From that point on, my mother failed. When I came to visit her, we sat opposite each other and, more often than not, stared. She had sores on her legs and arms from lying so long in bed. She scratched the sores and the skin came away. The attendants left the sores undressed so that they'd be open to the air and the prospect of healing. I found myself fixing obsessively on these raw wounds; it was as if I expected on one visit to see her shin bone or elbow joint peeping through the worn flesh. And her eyes, the skin around them was sagging and red, falling into pouches. Queequeg, I expected—I was afraid—that one Sunday afternoon her eyes would roll out of her sockets into the little bags on her cheeks."

"Hey now!" She drew away from him, a reprimand.

"Come back," he said, and she did. "I wouldn't admit to myself the horror I felt, I still don't completely admit it. Later when I went to visit her I had to introduce myself; I had to tell Kuzuko Hadaka Fowler, my mother, who I was. It was just her eyesight, the director told me, not her memory. But then she would ask questions about my father, who she seemed to think was still living in the tower complex with me. Or she would speak in Japanese, which I had never learned. In English she would reminisce about what it had been like to survive the A-bomb blast of August 6, 1945, although not even her own parents had been alive when that first bomb was dropped. Even so, after the reversal in her progress, it was the key to almost everything she talked about. She once described for me the photographic images of human shadows burned into the sides of Hiroshima's buildings by the blast. Maybe she saw a few of them when she was a little girl, three or four years old, I don't know. One or two such images may still have existed then.

"At the end of the first year in the hostel she wasn't even talking about that, just sitting in her wheelchair and nodding, or asking me every ten minutes or so what time it was. Which I wasn't supposed to tell her. I had been seeing a woman quite frequently during this time, but I finally stopped. The visits to my mother had started to tell on me: a depression I couldn't exorcise.

"I went three weeks without going to see her, my very first break in a year-long routine. Then, on a Wednesday evening, I rode a lift tube from street level to the floor of her ward in the Geriatrics Hostel. When I came out into the hall, I heard an old woman's voice saying over and over, 'Please, please help me.' I saw her, my mother, in her wheelchair at the end of the corridor:

nothing terrible seemed amiss. She looked all right. But she kept begging for someone to come to her aid.

"They were mopping out the rooms along the corridor, and several other 'guests' shared the hallway with her, all of them deaf, maybe even literally, to her pleas. I threaded my way through the wheelchairs, and when she heard me coming, knowing that I was neither a patient nor one of those who ordinarily tended to her, she stopped begging. She held her head up and started nodding and smiling.

" 'How do you do,' she said. 'How do you do.'

"I said, 'Mother, it's Simon, it's your son.'

" 'How do you do,' she said. 'How do you do.' In the past my introducing myself had gained me at least a slow-coming acceptance. This time, only her grin and those terrible nods of the head. I waited. That was all I got. 'How do you do, how do you do.'

"Then I saw that the skirts of her robe—a hideous robe I had never seen before, kimonolike, with Mount Fujiyama embroidered over her left breast and the name of the mountain stitched across the right—well, the drape of this hideous robe was drenched. A pool of urine lay under my mother's wheelchair, droplets hung from the frame on which her feet rested. 'How do you do,' she said. She wasn't going to let a stranger, even if he had just introduced himself as her son, help her with something as personal as a bladder she could no longer control.

"Courtesy, dignity, self-reliance."

" 'I'm your son,' I said. 'Mother, let me—'

" 'How do you do.'

" 'Someone help this woman!' I shouted. 'Someone help her!' Four or five time-savaged faces revolved toward me. An attendant came out of one of the rooms.

"I backed away from my mother, I turned and walked up the hall. Waiting for the lift tube, I heard my mother saying again, 'Please, please help me.' The attendant took care of her, I think: I didn't look back to see. Then I left the Geriatrics Hostel and never went back again until almost two years later when they notified me that my mother had died."

Beneath drifts of linen Simon Fowler and Georgia Cawthorn lay against each other. He was thinking, Heaven is soul, Earth is conscience. These I have salved. . .

16. *The samurai and the willows.*

It was the Saturday of the wedding. The clock on the kitchen board said 1:20. She kissed him. "You come on up now, the Ortho-Urban chapel. You hear? We both gonna be late, Ty gonna kill me."

"Go on, then."

"You comin', Basenji? You better come." He was smiling, the way a quiet little dog smiles. And you never find out what it's thinking.

"In time," he said.

"*On* time," she said, "you be *on* time." Enough. She went out the door into the concourse, her shoulder capes, intense burgundy, twirling with the power of her stride. No need for glierboots, he thought.

Simon Hadaka Fowler went to his sleeper. He took his notebook out of the drawer in the cabinet compartment of the visicom console. He tore out two blank pages toward the back. Then, pulling a metal waste can toward his chair, he dropped the notebook in and set it afire with a pipe lighter from the console. He pushed the waste can away from him with his foot.

This done, he began to write on the first of the two pages he had saved back from the miniature holocaust in the waste can:

"Ty, Queequeg: I am leaving the Kudzu Shop to you. Here is the name of a man who may offer you a good price for it, should you not wish to keep it." He wrote the name and level station of the man. "The bonsai on the patio I hope you will keep, especially the willows. Under the counter in the main shop I have left instructions for completing the layering and transplanting processes of the willow now putting forth new roots. It should not be too difficult if you follow them to the letter. They are good instructions."

He leaned back in his chair and thought. Then he wrote:

"My mother once told me a story of two young Japanese men who recklessly stormed the home of a great lord who they believed had impugned the good name of their father. Perhaps the lord had been responsible for their father's death. (My memory fails me here.) In any case, the two young men—neither of them yet twenty—were captured.

"The lord whom they had tried to kill, however, was impressed by the young men's courage and refused to condemn them to death. Instead, he commuted their sentence to the mercy of committing seppuku, ritual suicide.

"To a Japanese, my mother tried to explain, the distinction between execution and seppuku is by no means a fine one. On the one hand, disgrace. On the other, the satisfaction of one's honor. An Occidental mind struggles with this distinction, attempts to refute it with reasoning altogether outside the context of its origin. It is only in the last two or three weeks that I have recognized this myself.

"To return to my story, which I am almost done with: The gracious lord whose home the young men had attacked even went so far as to include in this commuted sentence the six-year-old brother of the attackers, even though the boy had been left at home during their mission. Nevertheless, on the appointed day he sat between the two brothers and watched carefully as each one of them performed the exacting ceremony. Then, with no hesitation at all, he took up his knife and did likewise."

Fowler set this page aside.

On the second sheet he wrote:

"Queequeg, I go in joy. This is no execution. You have commuted my sentence."

The equation in his mind he did not write down. Heaven, Earth, Man: soul, conscience, honor. Shortly, he thought, I will have salved all three.

Much later, when Georgia Kosturko-Cawthorn could weigh with some degree of objectivity what had happened, she told Ty:

"He changed a lot. The blessed part is, he started asking himself questions 'bout who he was. He got a long way. But he jes' never asked the last question, Ty, he jes' never asked it." In the spring of the year that followed, working from Basenji's directions, Georgia and Ty began two new trees from the layered bonsai willow. Both trees took.

Honorable Mentions—1976

Aldiss, Brian W., "Appearance of Life," *Andromeda*.
———, "Journey to the Heartland," *Universe 6*.
Asimov, Isaac, "The Bicentennial Man," *Stellar 2*.
Benford, Gregory and Eklund, Gordon, "The Anvil of Jove," *F&SF*, July.
Bourne, J. R., "The System," *F&SF*, December.
Broxon, Mildred Downey, "The Antrim Hills," *Aurora: Beyond Equality*.
Campbell, Ramsey, "The Tugging," *Disciples of Cthulhu*.
Cochrane, William E., "Weather War," *Analog*, September.
Cohn, Gary, "Rules of Moopsball," *Orbit 18*.
Cowper, Richard, "Piper at the Gates of Dawn," *F&SF*, March.
Dann, Jack, "The Dream Lions," *Amazing*, September.
———, "Starhiker," *Amazing*, July.
——— and Zebrowski, George, "Yellowhead," *New Constellations*.
Darnay, Arsen, "Aspic's Mystery," *Analog*, September.
Davidson, Avram, "Bloody Man," *Fantastic*, August.
———, "The King's Shadow Has No Limit," *Whispers 8*.
Davis, Grania, "New-Way-Groover's Stew," *Fantastic*, August.
Drake, David, "Firefight," *Frights*.
Effinger, George Alec, "Contentment, Satisfaction, Cheer, Well-Being, Gladness, Joy, Comfort, and Not Having to Get Up Early Anymore," *Future Power*.
———, "Target: Berlin!" *New Dimensions 6*.
Ellison, Harlan, "Seeing," *The Ides of Tomorrow*.
Girard, James P., "The Alternates," *New Dimensions 6*.
Gotschalk, Felix C., "Charisma Leak," *New Dimensions 6*.
———, "The Day of the Big Test," *Future Power*.
———, "The Family Winter of 1986," *Orbit 18*.
Grant, C. L., "A Crowd of Shadows," *F&SF*, June.
Haas, Charlie, "Shifting Parameters in Disappearance and Memory," *Universe 6*.
Haldeman, Joe, "Tricentennial," *Analog*, July.
Knight, Damon, "I See You," *F&SF*, November.

Lafferty, R. A., "Oh Tell Me Will It Freeze Tonight?" *Frights.*
———, "Smoe and the Implicit Clay," *Future Power.*
Lanier, Sterling, "Ghost of a Crown," *F&SF,* December.
Le Guin, Ursula, K., "The Barrow," *F&SF,* October.
Leiber, Fritz, "The Death of Princes," *Amazing,* June.
———, "The Eeriest Ruined Dawn World," *The Ides of Tomorrow.*
Maddern, Pip, "Broken Pit," *The Altered I.*
Malzberg, Barry N., "On the Air," *New Dimensions 6.*
Martin, George R. R., "Or the Many-Colored Fires of a Star Ring," *Faster Than Light.*
———, "Starlady," *Science Fiction Discoveries.*
McIntyre, Vonda N., "Screwtop," *The Crystal Ship.*
———, "Thanatos," *Future Power.*
Monteleone, Thomas F., "Breath's a Ware That Will Not Keep," *Dystopian Visions.*
Mundis, J. J., "Christmas in Watson Hollow," *New Constellations.*
Plauger, P. J., "The Con Artist," *Analog,* December.
Pohl, Frederik, "The Prisoner of New York Island," *Odyssey,* Spring.
Priest, Christopher, "An Infinite Summer," *Andromeda.*
Randall, Marta, "Megan's World," *The Crystal Ship.*
Reamy, Tom, "Dinosaurs," *New Dimensions 6.*
Robinson, Kim Stanley, "Coming Back to Dixieland," *Orbit 18.*
Robinson, Spider, "By Any Other Name," *Analog,* November.
Russ, Joanna, "My Boat," *F&SF,* January.
Scholz, Carter, "The Eve of the Last Apollo," *Orbit 18.*
Sellers, Sally A., "Perchance to Dream," *IASF,* Spring 1977.
Scheckley, Robert, "The Never-Ending Western Movie," *Science Fiction Discoveries.*
Sheldon, Raccoona, "Beaver Tears," *Galaxy,* May.
———, "Your Faces, O My Sisters!" *Aurora: Beyond Equality.*
Sterling, Bruce, "Man-Made Self," *Lone Star Universe.*
Thurston, Robert, "Aliens," *F&SF,* December.
Tiptree, James Jr., "Houston, Houston, Do You Read?" *Aurora: Beyond Equality.*
———, "The Psychologist Who Wouldn't Do Awful Things to Rats," *New Dimensions 6.*
———, "She Waits for All Men Born," *Future Power.*
Tuttle, Lisa, "Stone Circle," *Amazing,* March.
———, "Woman Waiting," *Lone Star Universe.*

Utley, Steven, "Ghost Seas," *Lone Star Universe.*

————, "The Man at the Bottom of the Sea," *Galaxy,* October.

Varley, John, "Bagatelle," *Galaxy,* October.

————, "Goodbye, Robinson Crusoe," *IASF,* Spring 1977.

————, "Gotta Sing, Gotta Dance," *Galaxy,* July.

————, "The M&M, Seen As a Low-Yield Thermonuclear Device," *Orbit 18.*

————, "Overdrawn at the Memory Bank," *Galaxy,* May.

————, "The Phantom of Kansas," *Galaxy,* February.

Vinge, Joan, "The Crystal Ship," *The Crystal Ship.*

————, "Media Man," *Analog,* October.

Waldrop, Howard, "Save a Place in the Lifeboat for Me," *Nickelodeon 2.*

Watkins, William Jon, "Coming of Age in Henson's Tube," *IASF,* Spring 1977.

Watson, Ian, "The Event Horizon," *Faster Than Light.*

White, James, "Custom Fitting," *Stellar 2.*

Wilder, Cherry, "The Remittance Man," *The Ides of Tomorrow.*

Wolfe, Gene, "The Eyeflash Miracles," *Future Power.*

————, "Three-Fingers," *New Constellations.*

————, "When I Was Ming the Merciless," *The Ides of Tomorrow.*

Yarbro, Chelsea Quinn, "Dead in Irons," *Faster Than Light.*

About the Editor

Gardner Dozois was born and raised in Salem, Massachusetts. He sold his first science fiction story in 1966 and entered the Army almost immediately thereafter, spending the next three years overseas as a military journalist. He has been a full-time writer since his discharge from the service in 1969. His short fiction has appeared in *Orbit, New Dimensions, Analog, Quark, Generation, Amazing, Worlds of If, Chains of the Sea,* and other magazines and anthologies. He has been a Nebula Award finalist five times, a Hugo Award finalist four times, and a Jupiter Award finalist twice. He is the editor of a number of anthologies, among them *A Day in the Life, Future Power* (with Jack Dann), *Another World,* and *Beyond the Golden Age.* He is also associate editor of *Isaac Asimov's Science Fiction Magazine.* He is co-author, with George Alec Effinger, of the novel *Nightmare Blue* and is currently at work on another novel. A collection of his short fiction, *The Visible Man and Other Stories,* is forthcoming. He is a member of the Science Fiction Writers of America, the SFWA Speakers' Bureau, and the Professional Advisory Committee to the Special Collections Department of the Paley Library at Temple University. Mr. Dozois lives in Philadelphia.